Power of the U'tanse

Henry Melton

Power of the U'tanse

Henry Melton

Wire Rim Books
Hutto, Texas

WRB

Printing History
First Edition: December 2017
ISBN 978-1-935236-69-6

ePub ISBN 978-1-935236-70-2
Kindle ISBN 978-1-935236-71-9

Website of Henry Melton
www.HenryMelton.com

Printed in the United States of America

Wire Rim Books
www.wirerimbooks.com

Acknowledgements

I'd like to give special thanks to someone who has helped me with this entire series, **Jonathan Andrews**, from modeling for Abe on the covers of books to regular input on my text, he has helped a lot in forming this story. For this volume in particular, he has helped develop plot and characters beyond the call of duty.

For all of the people who have saved me from embarrassing mistakes in the text; thank you.

This book was marked up by: **Jonathan Andrews, Jim Dunn, Mike Lynch,** and **Tom Stock.**

Contents

Western Ko

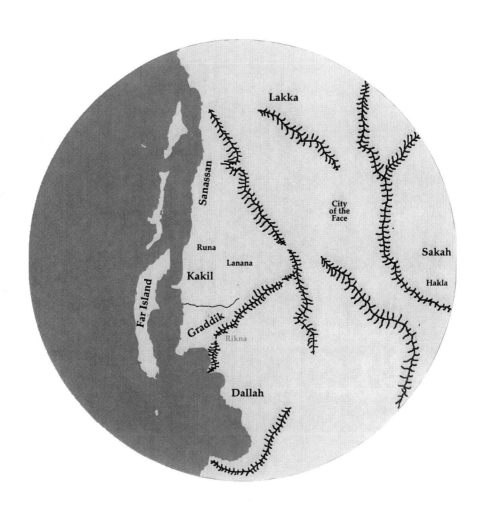

Eastern Ko

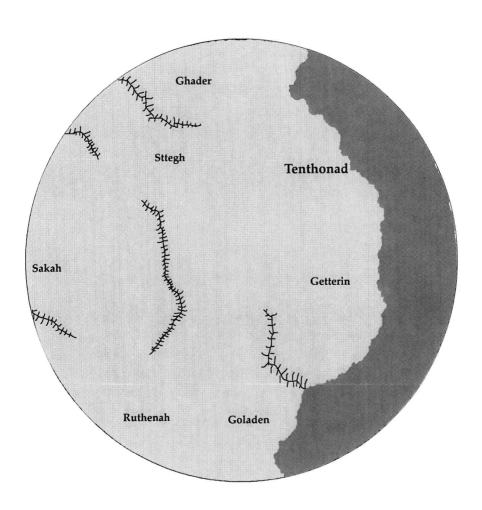

The Wait is Over

It's been generations since we arrived at Ko, humans captured by the Cerik and made slaves in exchange for our lives. Our masters couldn't even pronounce 'humans' and called us U'tanse instead, and we accepted it. On a world where we couldn't even breathe the air without burning out our lungs, we had no choice but to live in enclosed burrows, keeping the planet's technology running so that our Names would buy us the power needed to keep our air clean.

Workers abandoned by their masters and left for dead, over time, became the Free U'tanse, hidden in secret and building their own culture, thriving on the remnants of technology left by the previous slave race.

Those Delense had rebelled once, and had been exterminated for it. Resolving to avoid that mistake, Free U'tanse blocked every thought from reaching other telepaths, Cerik and U'tanse alike. Struggling with limited hydroelectric power and hiding their every action from the flying boats that might discover that they existed, the Free U'tanse waited, just like those U'tanse in Homes who lived under the claw of the Cerik Names.

And then, an explosion damaged their only independent power source. With no power to filter the air or grow crops in their underground base, the Free U'tanse had no future. They could no longer wait. They had to look beyond their ancient water power and find a way to tap the energy from space that drove the whole civilization of the Cerik.

Joshua, the son of Cyclops, the first free born U'tanse, faced great dangers to rescue a man who perhaps had the needed clues to that space power. It was time to act.

The Tale of James

Joshua nodded to the group collected in Ford's workroom—there were barely enough chairs and some were sitting on the tables. They'd all come—the group leaders and those in charge, but many, like Factory's leader, Ford were looking at papers, anxious to get back to their posts. For now, the major decisions for the Free U'tanse were going to be coming from these people at Factory, rather than from his father's room at Base across the bay. Cyclops was too injured, out of the control position for the foreseeable future—maybe forever. Not even the healers expected his recovery.

Familiar faces stared at Joshua as he stood. "The rescue was successful, although not without losses. Ophelia of Kakil was killed, but her infant son is now one of the newest of the Free U'tanse.

"A few days ago, I urged us to rescue three people in immediate danger. Two of them are now among us. Clark the fisherman is at Base. Today, I would like to introduce you to the other, who has chosen the name Prometheus."

There were a few frowns as he spoke the strange name. Anra, Factory's lead healer, always striking in her albino-white hair, was silently mouthing the name. They all knew he was talking about George bar Ted of Kakil, because the *tenner's* rescue was the highest priority. But, taking a new name after being rescued was an established practice among the Free U'tanse, especially if the old name was well known. For some of them, any hint of a rescue could be a big problem for their families, still under Cerik control.

George was certainly well known. Elehadi, the Name of Kakil, had arranged for George to be assigned to a construction job alone in *haeka* territory, specifically so that he'd be killed by the fierce beasts.

3

In an ideal world, everyone of the Free U'tanse would always have a solid block so their minds couldn't be read by the few Cerik that were telepaths. The unfortunate reality was that blocking skill, *ineda*, had to be learned, and there was always a risk that a stray thought could be caught and reported to the top predators that ruled this planet.

Prometheus chuckled at people's reaction to his choice. "I'm already having second thoughts about this name. Call me Prom for short."

Joshua asked, "Well then, Prom, could you tell us what you know? Specifically, how does the Tenthonad Clan acquire all the power they sell to the other clans?"

He looked a little timid. "Um. Do you want the short version?"

The lights flickered, as they had all day long. Half of them glanced over at the lamps with a grim expression. Betty, the reclusive expert in Delense technology, was adjusting the power settings on the new reverse-pump she and Ace had installed in the turbine's bypass channel. With the main turbine blades damaged, their primary power system had failed and everyone knew they were just one more glitch away from a quick slide into darkness from which they might never recover. Without power, the Free U'tanse were doomed.

Ford sighed, then said, "We *need* to understand how to tap into this alternate power source. Tell us everything you know."

Prom nodded, "Okay. Cut me short if I get off track. I tend to ramble."

He shifted in his seat and nodded to himself.

"My mother was born at Tenthonad Home. She was an early reader and spent her younger years in the library they keep there. She read as many books as she could manage, including some of the originals that came from old Earth. She read the Book, and assisted in one of Tenthonad Home's projects: making careful copies of the original text.

"When she came of age, she was chosen for Festival and was traded to Kakil Home in the All-Ko Festival of that year. At Kakil, she was successful in getting a job helping with the Kakil library. From what she told me, the Kakil library was much smaller than the one she knew before. When she asked about the missing books she knew existed, the Kakil elders weren't interested in trading for them."

Prom was getting into the spirit of the tale. He waved his hands, and his eyes twinkled. Joshua noticed Ford already regretting asking for full details.

But Prom leaned forward and tapped the table for emphasis. "Now if you'd known my mother, you'd know that a 'no' wouldn't stop her when she wanted something. She made a telepathic contact with people working at libraries in other Homes. She explained her problem and managed to collect lists of the books at the other libraries. She compiled a master list and made some deals, copying some of Kakil's books by hand and privately trading them through Festivals when she had the chance. The thing is, *none* of the Western Homes had all the books Tenthonad Home had in its collection. She began to suspect that Tenthonad had deliberately kept some of the older books private. Certainly her requests for book lists from her friends back at Tenthonad were ignored."

There were frowns around the table. It was common for the U'tanse Homes to trade among themselves, and to keep some secrets that helped them maintain a trading advantage, but it didn't sit well with anyone that the *original* books, maybe even from the first generation after humans had been captured and brought to Ko, would be kept secret from other U'tanse.

Prom continued, tapping on the table, a nervous habit Joshua remembered from the days when he'd spied on him clairvoyantly, "By the time I was learning to read—being a *tenner* and a bit of an outsider because of that, she told me about some of the books that she suspected were being kept secret by Tenthonad Home.

"One in particular was the fascinating story of a *tenner*—the first *tenner* in fact. He was the first experiment in preserving that part of our genetic heritage that had no psychic skills. He had been chosen to go into space, to take an *attached* girl to the planet of the Ferreer."

Prom held up his hand. "Now, I know what you think. A story that fantastic has to be fiction. No U'tanse have ever been taken into space once we arrived at Ko. For years, I thought my mother made it up, giving me a *tenner* hero when I was feeling picked on for being bred without telepathy.

"But when I was older, after she died in an accident, I did a little research. The writer of the story, James bar Bill, was indeed listed in the family tree as the first *tenner*. The girl he supposedly left on another planet was listed as having died at an early age of an illness, which was not described.

"My mother just told me the story as an adventure tale, but she said it was written as James bar Bill's report, ordered by Father himself, and included details about how to fly a boat out of the atmosphere and how the starship managed to charge itself and its boats by sending a beam out into space."

Everyone in the room listened intently.

Carson, the pilot of Boat B, suggested, "Tenthonad restricted the book to protect their monopoly."

Ford asked, "Can you tell us how it's done?"

Prom spread his hands. "My mother told it to me as an adventure story because that's what interested her. Only later, once I convinced myself it was real, did I realize how important it was. I've spent years trying to fill in the blanks."

The lights flickered again. He looked up. "Power is the most important issue, right?"

Joshua said, "Right."

Prom nodded, "Okay, here's what I've worked out.

"James bar Bill reported that the Cerik pilot shot a beam into space from the starship. Shortly thereafter, minutes later, power arrived and they had to shut the beam down quickly to avoid overloading their power cells.

"I assume the beam is the same kind boats use to push or pull the air. If so, when he was in space, he aimed the beam at something so far away that it took minutes for the beam to reach it."

Ace, their *tenner* physics expert, spoke up, "We already know that the tractor-pressor beams travel at the speed of light. Minutes would make it an enormous distance. Another planet maybe?"

Prom nodded. "That was what I suspected. According to the Book, it takes years for light to travel to other suns, the stars in the night sky. It takes only a second to travel to Ha, Ko's moon.

"The Cerik never developed the science of astronomy as described by Father, but they do have a mythology that includes the demons in the sky. Some of them are stars, but if there are visible planets, I thought that perhaps clues could be found in the Cerik Tales.

"I was already following those clues when Samson acquired the tale-speaker from Elehadi. It was the perfect opportunity for me to index a great number of Ko's historical tales, all at once. I was excited to discover that the demon *Katranel* was in a different part of the sky when its tale was written. If so, if it is, indeed, another planet under the same sun that lights Ko, then a powerful beam aimed at it might reach it in minutes. The Book by Abe-the-Father, in chapters on astronomy, states that planets travel in elliptical paths around their sun, and that the closer a planet is to its sun, the faster it travels. Ko and this other planet would have to have different speeds."

Ace shouted out, "Of course! It's just like the reverse water pump. If the other planet was moving away from us and if a tractor beam failed to pull it closer, then the beam would feed power back to the power cell! If it was a powerful beam, then it would collect power in great quantities, since nothing on a human scale could possibly change the motion of a whole planet. That's it! That's where all the power comes from."

Ford asked, "So, can we do it? Can we put a beam on the other planet and get the power we need?"

Prom said, "Yes and no. Yes, in theory, we can do it. But in practice, there are many problems. We'd have to be above the atmosphere, because driving a beam like that through the air for minutes at a time would drain any power cell we have and likely cause a storm from the disturbance.

"We'd also have to know exactly where this planet is. I've looked and tried to draw maps. There are, indeed, a dozen or more lights in the night sky, but which are stars and which are planets is still a mystery. The Tenthonad clan knows, but we don't."

Ace added, "I have no idea how much power it would even take to lift a boat all the way out of the atmosphere. And how does that even work? Doesn't a boat fly by throwing air around? How does that work when you're so high that there's no more air?"

Ford grumbled, "That hidden book would be helpful, but getting it may be impossible. We'll have to discover much of this on our own, or watch what the Tenthonad are doing much more closely. But any way you look at it, we'll need a lot more power just to make the attempt."

Bernard, Factory's semaphore communicator, said, "Before you start spending power on test flights, remember that Base is still hurting for enough power to light their fields to grow our food."

Larson, the dockmaster, raised his hand. "All the boats and the submarines need to be charged as well, just for necessary transport."

The meeting quickly shifted over into a debate about where their limited power should be allocated. The corn crop had already failed, and the wheat was looking poor. Getting power to charge the submarines was necessary to move people and food between Factory and Base. There were still two of the flying boats stranded at New Home; and Angel, the last one boat remaining at Factory, was being drained for power to keep them going. Each person there had their own idea of what was most important. But Prom's dream had spread. There was a lot to do, and a lot to learn. They just had to figure out how to accomplish it.

Factory Work

Ford was buried in work, still new to the position of leader, so he assigned Simon and Grellin, two of the metalsmiths to help with the minisub repairs.

"What happened to this thing?" The sub was hauled out of the water and up on wooden blocks. Simon was horrified to see bare metal exposed. Grellin, the older of the two shook his head and fingered the marks, too. They had an audience. Only a dozen feet away, the fire pit they used for a makeshift kitchen during the power outage had a half-dozen people eating grilled fish with their fingers.

Joshua ran his finger over the streaks on the hull. "These are teeth marks. We ran up against a *jandaka* in the open sea." He shuddered. "It was enormous, and Prom's blood in the water made us too tempting. It tried to swallow us whole, sub included, but it couldn't hold on when I hit the pumps. I got a couple of huge teeth out of it. I'll bring one the next time I make a run to Base."

Simon nodded. "Scary looking, but we've got to get sealant over this metal quickly. Seawater or unfiltered air will start corroding it away in no time."

Grellin nodded, "I'll get on it." He hurried out.

Simon leaned down and put his face next to the hull. "There's a slight warp. I'd just give you a new hull if I could, but that'll have to wait until we have power for the tank fabricator."

Joshua tried to see the bend in the hull, but couldn't. "I didn't notice much of a drift on the ride over from Base, but I guess I need to keep an eye out for it."

Simon shrugged. "If you're navigating by *sight*, then it shouldn't be a problem, but a *tenner* following a map would be in trouble."

The only *tenners* among the Free U'tanse were Prom and Ace. Joshua made a note. It might affect others as well as the non-psychic *tenners*. A sizable fraction of the U'tanse population didn't have the right kind of clairvoyance suitable to navigate the sub. His wife Sally needed visible landmarks when she piloted the minisub across the bay.

"The sub is only half built, I know," Joshua said, "but it's been valuable. Whatever you can do to extend its life, or improve its range or capabilities would be greatly appreciated. In fact, I want more of them. New Home needs its own sub, maybe more than one."

Simon was leaning over, checking the ballast tanks. "It's a fascinating gadget. How well does it work, with no seat to secure you in place?"

"Not bad at all, when I'm with my wife. It's a little uncomfortable with another guy."

Simon chuckled. "I can imagine. I can fit a couple of low seats in here, if you want."

"Okay. As long as we don't have to crawl up into the hull to escape another *jandaka*."

. . .

Joshua was amused to see Prom standing in the hallway, holding hands with Anra. Then, he got closer and realized the healer was examining his arm.

She smiled, "It looks like it's nearly mended. Stay on your diet and you should be okay, Prometheus."

Prom nodded. "Thank you."

Joshua went up to him. Prom was still watching her retreat.

The historian sighed. "She's strikingly beautiful, isn't she?"

Joshua nodded. "She has the First Mother's hair. People are always comparing Anra to her."

"The Book talked about many different hair colors in the original humans of Old Earth. Black and yellow, even. All we've got is various shades of brown and that rare white-haired individual like her."

"Our limited gene pool. Yes, I'm aware. We only started with one couple. It's surprising we have as much diversity as we do."

Prom sighed. "It was all her doing, Sharon the First Mother. She had seventeen children, and used her *sight* and skills to select the most diverse sperm. Mother and Father knew from the very beginning that the U'tanse were doomed unless they made very hard choices, no matter what suffering their children had to endure because of it."

Joshua looked closer at his downcast face. "Are you talking about yourself?"

Prom looked up and smiled. "Don't mind me. I've long gotten over being a *tenner*. It's a bit lonely at times," he looked down the hallway, "but Ted bar Carl, my father, is still content managing his herds, and I don't think I would have been happy following in his footsteps. I'm glad my life has turned out differently."

"Ace is our only other *tenner*. He's the guy I go to for mechanical and scientific problems."

Prom nodded. "He's the guy who was guessing the answers early in my tale of James bar Bill, wasn't he?"

"Right. His place is near here. Let's drop by and see if he's in."

...

Betty was even more reclusive than when he'd first met her at New Home. After the introductions, Ace and Prom had hit it off immediately. Joshua was only staying because Betty seemed so distressed, finding a place behind the table, alternately looking at Ace and averting her gaze from Prom.

The two *tenners* were laughing.

"... and it's like those times when everyone in the room stops talking— their eyes stop tracking, and then everyone laughs."

Prom nodded, "And then when you ask what happened ..."

Ace shook his head, "They say, 'Oh, nothing. Ignore us.'"

Joshua could understand the tenners bonding like that. He looked over the papers that Betty and Ace had been working on. Most of it was indecipherable to him, but there was a sketch of the reverse-pump that was now generating power for them.

He asked Betty quietly, "Are you finished with your adjustments?"

Betty looked at him with that quiet fear he always saw in her except when she was with Ace.

Ace turned his way, "No, it's almost done. Betty is just at the stage where her adjustments will be more infrequent. Power should be stable except for minor glitches when we make tweaks to the settings in the middle of the night."

Betty managed a nod of agreement.

Joshua smiled. "That's good."

He had many more questions, but Ace and Prom needed to talk, and he'd never been able to have a real conversation with Betty. Back at New Home where he'd first met her, it had taken a while before he heard a single word from her. Joshua wondered why she'd become so walled off from everyone—except from Ace, of course.

Joshua let out a sigh. "It's nice, you two being here together." He shook his head. "Sally is stuck at Base for a while. I miss her."

Betty didn't respond, but at least she didn't appear panicked as he talked. That was the best he could hope for.

He just settled back and with his *sight* took the time to check up on the signal flags and the semaphore operators at Base and New Home.

The conversation intruded, but only a little.

Prom was saying, "There were four *tenners* at Kakil, including me, but I never interacted with them. The two older guys were more like you, working on machines, fixing Delense things and keeping the products coming. They didn't really have anything in common with a historian, and they were stationed at the Delense facilities, anyway. There was a teenager as well, but he was cautioned to stay away from me. I suppose I was a bad role model for new *tenners*."

Ace chuckled, "I can see that!" They both laughed.

Ace told about his rescue, when he was twenty and just starting his first permanent assignment at a copper mine in Dallah. His job was to manage the machines that collected placer copper from the river deposits. The metal was smelted into ingots heated by the constant flow of a lava stream from a building volcano. During one Large Moon, the lava overflowed its dikes and spilled into the river. Ace had to make a run for it when the acid steam cloud overwhelmed the facility. He had been checking on one of the dredger platforms at the time, and couldn't get back to the safety of the burrow.

The winds were from the southeast, and he barely had the chance to paddle south out of the path of the cloud. But that left him stranded and alone at sea.

He had shouted for help in his mind, hoping the telepaths would come rescue him, but after three days in the water, with his breather filter exhausted, he had given up. They weren't coming. He was just another U'tanse abandoned to the hostile planet. He dozed off, rasping from lesions in his lungs from breathing the bad air, and then woke in Robert's submarine with a beautiful healer leaning over him, signaling him to close down his *ineda*.

"Anra?" Prom asked.

"No, she was Comfort. I had a crush on her for a bit." Then he turned and smiled at Betty. "But that's all over."

Betty had been listening intently at Ace's tale. To Joshua, it was a very familiar story, but Betty and Prom hadn't grown up with dozens of similar rescue stories like he had.

...

It was two days later when Joshua stopped at the entrance to Ford's new office. Taking over the leadership role meant he needed different work space. "Are you busy?"

Ford looked up from the table holding seven stacks of papers. He glared. "Is your father showing signs of improvement?"

Joshua moved in and sat at the table. "I think I can see progress. Maybe he's just better at hiding his pain, but he seems more stable and happy. He's still insistent that he can't be trusted with status updates, but his *ineda* slips are fewer."

Ford picked up another document. "I hate this new place. Nothing but paper and shelves." His previous workshop was a place where he could take things apart and repair them. There were plenty of shelves there, but they usually contained parts lists and diagrams.

Joshua bit back his instinct to advise Ford to delegate some of his paperwork tasks. Let someone else make that mistake. One wrong word and he'd end up with his own stack of paperwork to deal with.

Instead, he came to the point. "I've been monitoring Elehadi, and he's very suspicious about what we did."

"What do you mean?"

"Prom vanished, but they didn't find his body. The same with Clark and Sterling. This and the death of Omelia, all at roughly the same time."

Joshua sighed, "Not to mention the strange girl reported with Omelia who was never seen again. The Name isn't stupid. He has to consider that all these are related."

Ford frowned deeper. "But does he have enough clues to point to us? I don't see it."

"Elehadi is likely to blame his misfortunes either on another clan or on the U'tanse. He hates our entire race, so of course he'll consider us the cause of his troubles. We really need more people monitoring his movements."

Ford sighed. "I've just assigned several of our best people with good long-distance *sight* to locate and track the Tenthonad clan's delivery boats. It's important to find and track boats that go up into space. We need to fill in all the gaps in our knowledge about the process."

"Aren't there more people out of work because the foundries are shut down?"

Ford grumbled, "That won't last forever. We barely have enough power to keep the lights on, but at least we're not draining the boats anymore. If we shut down Factory's ability to manufacture our replacement parts, we're doomed."

"But if we don't have the power to do metalworking—"

"I've approved the plan to raid the clans for power." The older man cut him off, staring intensely at the paper in his hand.

For an instant, Joshua didn't understand. The room was still. Not even the distant echoes of Factory life made any impact. But then his eyes widened, and his mouth opened as his gut churned. He took in a breath.

The chair scooted under him as Joshua leaned forward. "But that's—" He hit the table with his fist. "Any mistake, any miscalculation, and the Names will come down on us like the Delense massacre! They'd treat it as a direct challenge. They wouldn't stop until we're wiped out."

Ford laid his paper down on the table. He glared at Joshua.

"You think I'm stupid. You think you're the only one who can see how dangerous it is. Well, you're not in charge! Patrick and Hugo have been working on this since the day boat C was stranded at New Home. I've been getting reports *every day*. I've rejected the plan five times before! But each time, they come back with more issues addressed. We need the power, more than we can generate with our makeshift repairs. Experienced people have given me a solution, so I'm taking it."

Joshua's heart was beating fast. He'd realized other people were in favor of stealing power cells from the clans, but he'd expected older and wiser heads to keep that from happening.

"Can I see the plan?"

"No! And I *expect* you to keep quiet about this. No internal leaks."

Joshua nodded, at a loss. He'd been advocating secrecy all this time—limiting information to the people who needed it directly. Ford was in charge. It was past time for objections.

He could only mumble, "Call me in if you need me."

Ford picked up another paper. "It will take a while to make the preparations."

Joshua forced himself to remember why he came there in the first place.

"I still need more clairvoyants to monitor Elehadi. I guess I need to recruit them at Base. Do you mind if I head back there?"

Ford sighed. "You'll have to swim. We have no power for the sub just yet; scheduled supply runs only."

And Joshua was well aware that his minisub was still in Simon's hands getting modifications. He nodded. "Okay. I'll pass the word. I can probably tow a small load; messages and tools."

Ford dug into one of the stacks of documents. "Here's the latest requests from Base. Can you take them a load of air-filtration powder? They're running low."

Family Time

The long swim across the bay from Factory to the hidden chambers of Base deep within its granite dome gave Joshua some time to clear his head. The Free U'tanse were too big now for one person to handle everything. In spite of his desire to keep his fingers on the pulse of every action, it just wasn't possible.

I go where the trouble is. I'm linked to everyone through the semaphore operators and through the seers *that report to me, I have the best grasp of what many of the Cerik are doing. I know more people than most, because I've traveled back and forth among all the Free U'tanse locations. I have to do my job the best that I can and trust the specialists to handle their own areas of expertise.*

As the tall, steep granite wall appeared when he looked ahead, he checked with his *sight*, looking for Sally.

She was already down at the dock, talking to some people. Did she know he was coming? He hadn't bothered to send a semaphore. He put a little more effort into his strokes, dragging his tow bag even harder.

Sally was waiting for him at the dock when he arrived, but when he reached the top of the ladder, the others she'd been talking with were gone. She had a towel and a tunic.

She tugged him over to a bench. "Sit. You're not going anywhere until I check you out."

He smiled. "Do I look that bad?" He put his arm around her.

She looked stern. "I have my own spies. You haven't had a good night's sleep the whole time you were gone."

He muttered, "You're just lucky I'm exhausted from the swim."

She put her arms around him as well, but he suspected she was using the skin contact to check on his condition with her healing skills, but when he kissed, she kissed back stronger.

He wondered who had been reporting on him, but she had a bowl of warm fish stew for him, and the aroma overpowered the salt air and the decades of machine oil and drying fishing nets.

As he sat and ate, he realized that he wasn't the only one eating. Ever since the blackouts, the docks had become a backup meal room of sorts. Base was a maze of small chambers, spread out over several floors, and the docks was the largest open area available. When all the lights went out, the only practical place to illuminate with an open fire was here. And since electricity was scarce, this was the most logical place to cook over a flame.

Docks that had been kept open, or else stacked with crates and tanks to be shipped out with the submarine, were now littered with tables and chairs. When things got back to normal, all of those would have to be moved back to the rooms from which they came. He just didn't know how long that would take.

A tall, broad-shouldered man walked by. Joshua called out, "Hoop!"

The dockmaster came closer. "What's up?"

Joshua pointed at his tow bag. "There's a canister of filter-powder in there. Could you see it gets up to the fifth floor?"

Hoop nodded. "None too soon. The air in here makes me a little light-headed. I'll take care of it." He opened the bag and pulled out the long tank and hefted it onto his shoulder.

Joshua mumbled, "Showoff. He could have used a cart."

Sally poked him in the ribs. "Are you jealous?"

He nodded. "I didn't have any trouble towing it, but it took two of us at Factory to get it down to the water."

She squeezed his bicep. "You're plenty strong enough for me."

He smiled, scraped the last dregs of the stew from the bowl, and then asked. "So, you've been spying on me?"

She opened her eyes wide. "Well, I have to do something to keep track of my new husband—always running off to some other part of the world."

He took her hand. "How have you been? I admit I took a peek back here from time to time. What was that when you spent several hours outside the nursery, lingering in the hallway?"

18

Her eyes were a little shiny. She hesitated, then sighed. "I'm having trouble with Sterling."

"Oh?"

She looked away and shook her head. "No, it's not a problem with him. It's me."

He ran his thumb over the back of her hand, just listening.

She took a deep breath. "Maybe it would have been better if I were his birth mother. I'd have gotten used to the idea."

He said, "Come on, let's go for a walk."

She nodded, deliberately not looking to see how many other people on the dock were looking at them.

Hand in hand, they walked over to the ramp and started the slow climb.

She said, "I think I wouldn't have had any problem if Sterling had rejected me, or something like that. He's little. His real mother has vanished out of his life, and I could have dealt with that."

"He likes you?"

She nodded, with a twist of her head. "He likes everyone. I'm no one special to him. I'll hold him and he likes it. But then Sylvia or Veronica or Jinger will come by and he'll reach out for them as well, and be just as content with them."

Joshua gave her hand a squeeze. "Isn't that how it's supposed to be?"

Sally nodded, then shook her head. "I don't know. All my training says a mother isn't supposed to get too close to her child—the danger of attachment is particularly great for an infant. Words of wisdom directly from the Mother of us all: Don't get too possessive. Until their personalities get solidly formed, infants should be raised by the nursery. A birth-mother should just be one of many. Fight the instinct."

Sally shook her head, "But it's hit me so strongly. Sterling is mine! He's a tough little guy, but ever since Omelia put him into my hands, I feel so ... *attached* to him!"

She shot him a glance in the dim light of the ramp. "Deadly word, I know. And we're *not* sharing thoughts, really. It's just my instincts kicking in. My mothering instincts."

Joshua felt a little out of his depth. "I've always been proud of my parents, but I can remember, when I was little, being a little confused. I couldn't quite understand what made Debbie and Cyclops *my* parents. I mean, I was closer to Comfort and Abbie than I was to Debbie. I grew up thinking that living in the nursery with parents coming by occasionally was just the way it was always supposed to be."

Sally shook her head. "But it's not! At least at the instinctual level. Nurseries are a social construct Mother created to *weaken* the mother-child bond. For telepaths, it's a necessity. It's all part of woman's training. Parental *ineda* and mixing up the caregivers is drilled into us. No one wants a damaged baby who can't think for itself and just echoes the thoughts of its mother.

"Legend says Mother's birth-mother back on Old Earth discovered the benefits of telepathic isolation on her own, and Sharon had to refine and build on it to raise the first generation of the U'tanse."

Joshua said, "I remember something Father wrote in the Book. 'We've made bad choices as human beings, but necessary ones as U'tanse.' I've wondered what he meant by that. I guess deliberately fighting basic instincts is one."

They reached the second floor and tapped the lock code on the nursery.

Sterling was happy to be held. Joshua, having grown up in this very room, knew all the right things to do to keep a baby happy, but Sterling was just as happy to move on to Sally, and then Jinger.

Veronica showed up when she heard her brother was visiting.

He smiled. "Hello, Very."

She twisted her face. She came closer and whispered, "Don't call me that any more."

"What? Very?"

She said, "I've been meeting a lot more people lately, and when I said my name was 'Very', they kept saying, 'very what?'"

"So… Veronica now?"

She shrugged. "I guess. But I guess you should know… I haven't been sketching anything new lately."

He grinned. "*Very* good to know."

She shook her head and sighed. "I wish you'd never given me that nickname."

But Joshua was glad she hadn't made any new sketches in her book. His sister was unique among the U'tanse in that she had nightmares of events that hadn't happened yet. No news, no new sketches in her notebook, was good news.

"So you've been spending more time out of the nursery?"

"I started out helping Debbie in the gardens. Rachel has been showing me around."

Joshua asked, "I heard the corn crop failed?"

Veronica winced then whispered, "Mom was crying. The reduced lighting just made it a lost cause. She shut the whole patch down and I've been helping her salvage the stalks for mulch."

"That's sad. But knowing Debbie, she has seeds for next time, right?"

"Mom gave me a big lecture on preserving enough seed corn for times like this."

He chuckled. "I got the same lecture when I was first moving out of the nursery, but it probably has more impact when you're right in the middle of a crop failure. By the way, when did you start calling her 'Mom'?"

"Oh, she mentioned that you called her that once, so I started."

"Interesting. Does that mean she likes it?"

She spread her hands. "Maybe."

...

They had a family meeting in the rooms where Cyclops lived. There were chairs all around his bed for when visitors came by.

"It's good to see you all," he said. He was propped up into a sitting position, and no one gave a second thought about the blind man's wording. They were all comfortable being with the man who had no eyes. His clairvoyance was so good that he acted like he was really seeing them through the bandage he always wore across his face. Compared to his crushed spine and trauma from the accident, the blindness was nothing.

Sally said, "I'm going to have to sneak Sterling out of the nursery so that you can meet him properly."

Cyclops nodded. "While I approve of the sentiment—I'd really like to hold him myself—we can't take the chance. A telepath can look through the eyes of another. I've looked through a child's eyes myself, especially with older ones. Sterling is about a year old, isn't he?"

Joshua nodded. "Not quite, but close. He recognizes us, but I wonder what he'd think about your eye-mask."

Cyclops chuckled. "At that age, he'd probably pull it off. If I recall, you did that once when you were a baby."

"Really? I don't remember that."

Debbie laughed. "Yes, we were so scared that you'd be frightened by the sight, but you didn't seem to pay it any attention."

Cyclops shook his head. "No, I distinctly remember tiny little fingers reaching for my face."

Veronica cocked her head, looking at her brother. "I can't imagine Joshua as a baby. I think he was born serious."

Sally put her hand on his head and ruffled his hair. "Yes, I'm working on that. Give me time."

He took it with a sigh.

A few minutes later, when the conversation stalled, Joshua asked. "Um, could I have a moment or two with Cyclops alone?"

Veronica sighed. "More business, I bet. Running us out."

Debbie stood up. "Well, I expected as much. Girls, come over to my room and we can gossip to our hearts' content."

With the door was closed, Cyclops asked, "Is there a problem?"

Joshua scooted his chair a little closer. "Yes, but it's not something I can talk about now."

"Good. I really don't want to be dragged back into problems that I can't cope with."

"However, in spite of your desire to be left out of day to day operations, there is a task only you can do. I'm going to ask you to take on a project."

His father frowned. "I'm not the man I was before the accident. I may never be able to handle the tasks I did before."

Joshua spoke slowly, trying to phrase it carefully. "There is a task that can make the difference in our survival. No one else can do it. Only your clairvoyance has the detail to read text at great distances."

Cyclops gave a slow nod. "Tell me a little more."

"Tenthonad Home has secret books in their library. One was written by James bar Bill, great-grandson of Abe." After each sentence, Joshua paused to watch how his father reacted.

"This book describes his trip into space, where he observed, first-hand, a Cerik pilot tap energy from the planets."

That got a reaction. Cyclops opened his mouth, as if to speak, but then he closed it again, and nodded.

Joshua finished with, "I need you to locate and copy this book."

Cyclops took a deep breath. Joshua could see him considering the ramifications and the potential. After a moment, he asked, "How sure are you that this book, and the event it describes, are real?"

"The mother of the guy you told me to recue, Prometheus, read the book first-hand."

Cyclops took a moment to put all the pieces together. He looked tired.

"I'll make the effort, but I haven't tried things like this since ... the accident. I may no longer be capable."

Joshua nodded. "One way or another, the Free U'tanse need that book."

Cyclops sagged a little, back onto his pillow. "Give me time. I'll try."

The Watchers

The long bath with his new wife Sally and the long sleep together afterwards left Joshua as relaxed as he ever could be. Outside the granite dome, dawn was creeping across the landscape, but of course that made no difference inside.

Still, he was awake, and unwilling to move and wake Sally from her sleep. That didn't prevent him from making his regular rounds.

Through his *sight*, he confirmed that all of the status flags at each of the Free U'tanse habitats were okay. Base, Factory and New Home were green with black circles, proclaiming at all was well.

Many of the Cerik were up with the dawn, but Elehadi was still sleeping on his perch. Just as an exercise, Joshua stretched his clairvoyance across the single massive continent and located Tenthonad Home, far off on the East coast.

Like all of the U'tanse homes, this was a burrow originally constructed by the Delense, and created for their semi-aquatic life-style. But Tenthonad Home was the oldest of them all, the first place where U'tanse lived. It was there that Abe the Father and Sharon the Mother had lived out their lives.

He'd never really looked over the place before, and at first glance, it looked cluttered. Instead of a cluster of curved mud huts that was typical of all the Delense burrows, this one had been modified by human hands for generations. There were several airlock entrances around the perimeter, all built square to human needs.

One of the larger domes had been capped with glass segments, presumably to let in the daylight. Off to the west of the main living area, between large fields where herds of runners were kept, was a square-built structure that seemed to contain storerooms of machines. From this distance, Joshua's sight wasn't able to distinguish any useful details, but the stockpile was interesting. Next to it was one of many landing areas. There were five boats resting there, one of them on a large, wheeled cart. It was much later in the day over on the East coast, and people were out doing their jobs. All the Cerik he could see were resting by the boats. Even in Tenthonad Home, it seemed, the U'tanse had limited access to the boats.

Was this one of the places where Tenthonad stored their charged power cells before trading them with the other clans? Or, more likely, was it a place to repair damaged boats? Either way, it would be lovely if all the Cerik and their U'tanse turned their backs for a few days and let the Free U'tanse rummage through the place.

Sally shifted in her sleep, snapping Joshua's attention back. But his daydream of ransacking Tenthonad's storehouses would never happen. The Cerik were careful about certain things. The three boats owned by the Free U'tanse had all been abandoned as unrecoverable derelicts, and even then it had been good forune that the original clans that owned them had never noticed that they were missing.

Yet, one of those derelicts has to take us into space. Which is in the best shape? I need to talk to Patrick and his pilots about that.

And if the topic of conversation managed to drift over to the raid for power, that would be a lucky thing for me. I can't bring it up myself without breaking my pledge to Ford.

Next up in his seemingly endless list of places to monitor was to scan up and down the west coast line for any wandering Cerik. There were parties still looking for any rogue U'tanse to kill. Any severed head turned over to Elehadi was still a guaranteed visit to the breeding pits for a warrior that would normally never have a chance to sire cubs.

The hunters were difficult to find in a cold search, but Joshua had a list of groups. He knew where they had been the day before and how fast they were traveling. As long as he kept up his monitoring duties, he could find them quickly and note any changes in their route.

There were nomadic groups, as well. One of the more aggressive of the nomads was a special project for him. In his private thoughts, he'd started calling him Pet, although the very idea of a pet Cerik would send any sane Cerik into a murderous rage.

Pet had no name, although in his dreams he lusted for that day he could name himself and become the leader and sire of his own clan. He'd already started on that path, conquering a second nomad group. Joshua could read his frustration at having to wait to claim the leader role, but Pet knew there were at least two others who would immediately challenge such a claim. He felt strong enough to kill either of them, but not both at once. And his group was still too small to risk losing valuable hunters. He had to wait for the right moment.

This morning, Pet was scouting near the cliffs, fighting his natural aversion to water, and looking out into the surf.

Is he looking for me?

Twice they had met, and Joshua had talked himself out of being gutted by appealing to Pet's vanity and feeding him the information that had set the Cerik on this ambitious course. To Pet, he was the U'tanse-Who-Swims—not worth killing because all U'tanse were poisonous and couldn't be eaten, and yet this U'tanse was a prey who gave him interesting ideas.

Joshua had not planned either of the meetings, but the idea of a Cerik who could be trained kept nagging at him.

I'd better have more information for him the next time our paths cross.

Sally turned in the bed and draped her arm across his chest. The vision of the lone Cerik, five-days-hike distant, vanished from his mind.

She was asleep, her dreams a mesh of scattered memories. His face appearing in a splash of water came and went in a flash.

…

When the Base status meeting convened in the Map room, Joshua felt out of place sitting in the chair Cyclops used. He nodded to Lincy, and she started taking the notes.

"Let's do this. Debbie?"

They worked their way around the table, each person reporting on the tasks that they'd been given. Debbie brought them up to speed on the crops, detailing the reduced yields expected as the result of shutting down more than half of her fields. It had been a hard choice, but necessary, just to keep the lights bright enough for the rest of them to mature. Two thirds of the second floor of Base had, over the years, been converted to garden plots.

She was concentrating on producing enough basic foodstuffs to enable Base and Factory to survive.

"Expect the meals to be very bland. I've had to give up on strawberries, peppers, corn, and oh-so-many others. I'll be guarding my seed stores under lock and key until I can risk bringing more varieties back."

Joshua said, "We need to talk to the people who've arrived from New Home. They went through a restricted diet phase as well. Sally, you know many of them. Could you make the rounds?"

She nodded thoughtfully, "Yes, I've already met up with all the people who've moved here from New Home. But, the situation there was different. All of Base's crops are indoors. New Home had the luxury of growing a number of native crops outside. Obviously, we can't do that here."

Paul chuckled, "Not that there's any soil on this rock anyway."

The differences inherent in living on an island where there were no Cerik to wander by was on Joshua's mind a lot. It was great, as long as the Cerik never considered the possibility. To Joshua, it was just a matter of time until that changed. New Home would never be able to hide their presence if the Cerik ever flew that way.

Joshua said, "I'd like each of you who monitor the West Coast Cerik clans to report now. I need to get an overall picture."

As usual, there were a few border skirmishes, usually nothing more than a half-dozen or so warriors from one clan raiding the herds, or sometime the Delense product storehouses of their neighbors. It was then followed by chases or revenge attacks. The same cycle of events had probably been happening for thousands of years.

But it was different now. The Faces, a regular meeting of all the clans was coming up. Any serious land-grabs needed to be accomplished before all the Names came together under a pledge of temporary peace.

The hotspot for most of these border raids was the former lands of Rikna. Elehadi's forces had conquered it in one massive battle, and then had to abandon it when the other clans turned against him in the previous Faces.

Sylvia said, "The Name of Dallah is ordering more raids every day. He really wants to move that border line up to the southern foothills at least. He realizes Elehadi might get approval to buy more power from Tenthonad after the Faces, so he wants a wide buffer between Kakil's warriors and his biggest herds."

Lincy never looked up from her note-taking, but reported, "Keetac at the eastern border is the same—only since they're a minor clan, if Elehadi ever gets the power to move his troops around like he did before, Keetac is likely to get swallowed up in the conflict. Both Graddik and Dallah would love to have the northern border lands under their control, and there's no room for the little guy if the three big clans stage an all-out war."

Joshua revealed Elehadi's suspicions about rogue U'tanse. "He may not have any idea where the Free U'tanse are or how numerous we've become, but he has to suspect that we're capable of moving into his territory and rescuing people. The last operation was mostly successful, and I'd do it again, but multiple rescues on the same day at two widely different locations is just too coincidental."

After he assigned people to share the task of monitoring Elehadi's actions—at least the public ones—the reports were almost done.

He looked to his side. "Sally, do you have anything to report?"

She looked a little uncertain. "I've only been to these meetings a couple of times, so I'm not sure what to include. You've heard all the details about the rescue. Sterling is doing well." She frowned. "There's one other thing, but it was a New Home thing."

Joshua said, "Unless Otto told you to keep it quiet, just for New Home, I'm sure we'd be interested. The more information, the better."

She nodded. "Okay then. Um, you may know that I was part of an exploration party looking at a different Delense burrow on the island."

He chuckled, "I was told you were in charge. They said, 'Sally's girls.'"

Sally gave a little smile. "Sort of. Anyway when I had to leave, they promised to report what they found. Yesterday, I got a semaphore message from Doe, who's the new leader of the group."

Everyone was listening carefully. Lincy's pen stopped moving.

Sally continued, "The burrow is not a living area at all, strictly a work place for building something. There are fabricators much like the ones already in use at New Home. Only Doe suggests that perhaps they are making power cells."

Joshua shifted in his seat. "What?"

Sally looked his way. "That's what she said. The fabricators are the right capacity to be making two different sizes of power cells, and there's a storage area with nearly a hundred of the smaller units and eight of the large ones."

Joshua's heart was pounding. "Are they charged?"

Sally chuckled, "No. I'd have yelled out loud if they were. No, all are cold and show no sign of power. But empty ones could be useful, right?"

He laughed nervously. "You bet. Now I'm not technical, but I just bet Betty and Ace would love a chance to see that place. We've never known how power cells are made. As far as the Cerik are concerned, they're just magic bottles of power, and the U'tanse know little more.

"Sally, your expedition has made a major discovery. We have to get that information to Factory."

Coordination

Setting up a three-way meeting linked by semaphore operators was difficult. Ideally, there should have been two people skilled in the handwaving technique at each site; Base, Factory, and New Home. Unfortunately, while New Home had Holana and her apprentice, Stenny, the new girl was very slow. Base had Paul, Ash, and Joshua.

The worst off was Factory, who had Bernard but no backup. Bernard called in Robert to help him, but Robert's skills were basic, just what he needed to communicate while out in his submarine. A good semaphore operator needed the memory for the hand positions, the clairvoyance necessary to see the arms of the person, and the ability to encode and decode messages. It required inborn talents and lots of practice.

To make it easy for their remote partners, Paul, Ash and Joshua spread out across the room for room to wave their arms.

Joshua worked with Sally to report Doe's discovery of the power cells in an initial report, both to Ford at Factory and to New Home, although he suspected Doe had already given her people that information. Joshua wanted every one to start out with the basics before trying to manage a remote meeting.

A message from Hugo at New Home arrived. He and Jenta had hiked over to the new site and confirmed Doe's initial report. They had carried one of the smaller power cells back and, when connected to their equipment, the long-abandoned power cell had successfully held a charge.

The same report went to Factory. Ace sent a message back, asking a lot of questions that Hugo was unable to answer. Joshua was able to monitor the exchange, and Lincy was able to write it all down as he spoke.

"What's happening now?" asked Hoop. He had little to do with the explorations, but as dockmaster, he was there at the meeting.

With his *sight*, Joshua was watching the people at the other locations when he wasn't actively transcribing a message. He couldn't hear what they were saying, but body language told him a lot.

"Ford is arguing with Ace. I don't know what they're saying."

Sally chuckled, "I bet Ace is asking to fly over to New Home right now."

Joshua nodded. "That's my guess. Paul, as soon as Bernard looks this way, send a request to Ford: What is that charge status on the boats and the submarine?"

Paul nodded, faced Bernard, and put his hands over his head in the 'request to speak' position. A few seconds later he began moving his arms into the various positions, sending the text letter by letter.

Barely had that message been sent when Joshua saw Holana at New Home, send a message from Otto, the lead elder there. "Otto is sending a message."

Sally asked, "What did he say?"

Joshua shook his head. "I don't know. It was addressed to Ford, but was encoded—not one I know." There were various levels of encryption. He knew most of the ones used by Base and had access to a number of the other ones, but it was only reasonable that there was a special New Home-Factory code for restricted use.

Slowly, the conversation proceeded. Ace and Betty wanted to investigate the new facility. Ford was reluctant to let them go, since the bypass-channel power system was only just stabilized and the turbine was still limping along at a much reduced speed. Neither the sub nor the boats were charged enough for the expedition.

Otto officially invited them to come, and offered what basic food stuff they could since Base's gardens were crippled.

Sally whispered in Joshua's ear, "Just what we need, more bug stew."

He didn't comment. It was an important gesture on New Home's part. Base had sent supplies to them many times before. He replied for Debbie, welcoming the offer.

Then Joshua put his hands on his head again and sent an encrypted message addressed to Ford: "Time for show of unity. Get Simon to build minisub for NH wo pumps. Take days to charge main sub for round trip, towing msub."

He knew he was asking for a lot. If Ford could see this opportunity, it would be a powerful gesture. New Home, isolated on an island with no transportation of their own griped often about their second-class status. A sub of their own, even a small one, would do much to ease the remote community's feeling of being abandoned.

An hour later, after more message exchanges, it was decided. A submarine expedition would be attempted, but it would take days to get everything prepared and for the sub to be charged. Otto was pleased at the offer of a minisub. The pump-motor assembly would have to be fabricated by the machines at New Home and Hugo was ready to get started, but semaphore was a horrible way to exchange design details. It was decided they would wait until the minisub hull was delivered so that Hugo's team could make the critical measurements themselves.

Sally asked, "You're going, aren't you?"

Joshua nodded. "If possible. Are you able to leave Sterling long enough to come along?"

She tensed. "How many days until the sub leaves?"

"Maybe a week. It depends on how long it takes to charge the sub and to make the new mini."

"I'll have to think about it." But her eyes were bright with the anticipation.

…

When Joshua went to visit his father a couple of days later, one of the first things he noticed when he entered the room was a stack of clean paper beside Cyclops's bed. Cyclops wasn't in the bed. They were experimenting with seating him in a chair. It took two people to move him, but by this point, any change was an improvement.

"How are you doing?"

Cyclops looked at Debbie. "Could you get me something to nibble on? Something salty?"

She nodded, looking puzzled. "Okay. It'll take a couple of minutes." She glanced at her son as she walked out.

Cyclops waited until she was out of range, and then whispered, "I've located the library. It's large. I've sampled a few books and I can read them at this distance. It's just going to take a while to locate the right one."

"I looked at Tenthonad Home myself. I can barely tell one person from another at that range."

Cyclops snorted, "People are easy. Even under *ineda*, there's enough leakage to get a feel for identity. But don't expect results quickly. I can't work the long hours I did before."

"I'm sorry I had to ask."

He waved his hand. "It's okay. I can pace myself. I needed some task like this to help me exercise the brain."

Debbie brought in a tray with salted rice wafers. "I don't know if this is what you want. I made these a couple of months ago, so they're probably dry."

Joshua sampled one after Cyclops pronounced them just what he'd wanted. After talking about Veronica's trials in her new job working the garden, Joshua prepared to leave. Debbie walked out with him.

In the hallway, she put her hand on her son's shoulder and grumbled, "What are you asking him to do?"

He shook his head. "I can't say."

"He asked you to let him be! He needs time to recover. You promised to give him that."

He tensed. "Mom, it was necessary!"

She turned around to face him. "I've lived all my life with Cyclops asking people to do more than they were willing to do. I'd hoped *you* were willing to take a different path."

He whispered low, "He had his reasons. He was usually right."

Her eyes showed a glint. "And look at where it's gotten him! He'll never walk again. His mind is not as sharp as it was." The tears began dripping down her face.

Joshua sighed, staring at the floor, "That's my fault." He put his hand to his head, feeling the pressure build inside.

She wrapped him in a hug, something she hadn't done since he was toddling around the nursery. She sniffed. "I'm not talking about the fall. You just did what you had to."

He closed his eyes, wishing he could just let his mother hold him and everything would be all right. But times had changed, and that wasn't her job anymore.

Joshua said, "Cyclops will get better. I know it. I've seen it."

She straightened up, sniffing and wiping her face. Her face was grave, and Joshua knew that her mind was on her husband, watching him through the distance and the closed door. That's what she'd been doing the whole time since he came back to her broken.

She whispered harshly, "But he should never have been out there on that hillside in the first place. He was always pushing—himself and everyone around him. You can't tell me he didn't do it to himself!"

Joshua knew exactly why the two of them had been outside, and why their secret hike had been necessary. And he couldn't tell her the reason.

The survival of the Free U'tanse depended on secrets, and his mother knew that. She was just worried.

He hugged her back.

"Mom, I will take every precaution I can—for myself and others."

She looked at him sharply. "You'd better. You have family depending on you. You've dragged your sister out of the nursery before she was ready. And now you've got a wife and a son to take care of. You can't just sneak away and have your adventures any more."

"And I won't leave you. But I'm not going to give up, either. We've been successful living in this hole in the ground for all my life, but the dangers we face are just getting worse. We have to be ready for the next threat that comes our way."

I have to be more like Cyclops, not less. But I can't tell her that.

"Remember how it was when the lights went out?" he asked.

She shuddered.

He looked her straight in the eyes. "You were right on top of the situation. You knew what had to be done, even through the blackout was totally unexpected. You had a few options you'd never considered, like that firestarter trick to calm the cuties, and you used them.

"I have to be ready as well. Because I don't know what danger is coming our way next. I just know that we have to expand all our options.

"Mom, I can't do it all. If I have to ask you for help, I will. I'll ask Cyclops. I'll ask my sister. I'll ask Sally. I'll even ask Sterling to help when he can."

Debbie nodded. "I know. But I'll fight to protect you all, even if I have to fight against my own son to protect my husband."

"He's taking it easy, at his own pace. He said that. You have to trust him, too."

She turned away, looking back toward her husband's room. "Just don't ... take him away from me, please."

Cruiser

Joshua looked from the first minisub to the new one. They were both sitting up on blocks in one of the workbays just next to Factory's dock.

"It's bigger." It was maybe twenty percent longer than the first one, but the diameter was about the same. The new one looked more like a section of pipe with curved ends rather than the elongated egg shape of the original.

Simon nodded. "When Ford authorized the power to run the tank fabricator for one tank only, I tried to make the most of it."

Joshua looked at the new shape, and the familiar internal fittings. "You gutted these from the first minisub?"

Simon winced and waved his hand helplessly. "Only because of the time demands. I'll refit the first one once we finish this one."

Grellin said, "The air pumps are standard, but they were never designed to be installed inside a storage tube like this. We have to change all the flanges."

Stella, a new girl who'd arrived from New Home, was listening in. Joshua remembered her with a smile. She'd just delivered a cart full of pipe fittings. She said, "It's Cruiser; the new sub's name is Cruiser. I named it."

Joshua wasn't surprised. She'd pushed for names on all the flying boats as well. "I suppose you have suggestions for the others as well?"

She gave a slow nod. "I'm supposed to get them approved by Robert, since he's in charge of all the subs. He hasn't really done that yet."

"But you had ideas for them?"

She brightened. "Oh, yes. The big sub should be called Alpha, since it was the first. And the one with scratches over there, I'm calling it Bait."

"Bait?" He winced.

She nodded vigorously. "You know, like fishing bait. Since it got bit and all."

He knew it very well. He'd been between those teeth.

But Joshua tasted the words, "Alpha. Bait." He frowned. "Are you making a wordplay?"

She giggled, "I always do. But don't think too much about it."

He shook his head. "I'm just wondering how many pilots will be comfortable sailing out into the ocean in a craft named 'Bait'."

She chewed on her thumb. "Yeah, that might be a problem. But you used it, right?"

He nodded, then took a closer look at the insides of Cruiser. The breathable air tank and the ballast tanks were the same ones he'd used before. The power controls were missing, but there were two new levers.

"Are these to control the power?"

Grellin shook his head. "No. We haven't done anything with the power control, since New Home will add that part. The levers are to control the fin warp."

"Explain?"

Simon reached for one of the levers and pointed back to the fins at the rear end. There was a crossed set, a vertical pair and a much wider horizontal pair.

"Look." He pulled the lever and the vertical fins bent to the left.

"The fins are flexible, formed around a rigid spar on the leading edge. You push or pull the lever and that will make the sub turn in the water. This other lever will do the same to tilt the craft nose-up or nose-down."

Joshua nodded. He could have used that before. Steering Bait had been particularly difficult while towing a cargo tank behind it.

"And those brackets?"

"That's where New Home will attach the pump assemblies for thrust."

Joshua leaned down to see below the fin. "Four on the top and four on the bottom?"

Simon shrugged. "We just tried to make it flexible. From what you said about Bait's cluster of six, I thought keeping all the pumps below the water level made more sense. New Home could put four on the bottom, or a cluster of four, two high and two low, or whatever they thought best."

Joshua ran his hand over the canopy glass. "This is nice. It was always a struggle to fight the water when under full power."

"I'll be putting a canopy on Bait, as well, when I have the time. But I'm afraid that although Cruiser can run with air inside, Bait will still have to be flooded. There are too many places the water can get in and out."

"Cruiser can carry people dry?" Joshua could see that there were three seats, all in a row.

"Yes. But it will need those copper ballast bars to let it go below the surface."

Joshua had thought they were pipes, but looking closer, he could see that they were solid metal. "It looks heavy."

Simon nodded. "That's why it's on a wheeled cart. Getting it into the water will be difficult. Getting it back out will need a powered crane. That is, unless you dismount all the ballast bars first."

Joshua had enough details to absorb. "New Home will be happy to get this. I'm hoping they'll get some practice with it before we come back. Eventually, we'll need more."

Stella clapped her hands. "Oh, I'll need more names—a D name and an E name and—"

Joshua laughed. "Hold on. Don't you think the owners should get a say in the names?"

She pouted. "But we'll get to keep some of them, right?"

...

Ford took some convincing to let Sally come along on the trip, but Ace insisted. Betty needed all the help she could get to deal with the travel stress, and Sally had been there holding her hand when they had made the flight to Factory in the first place.

Joshua added, "And I just assumed she would be needed. She was the leader of the expedition that discovered the power cell factory. She is much more familiar with the layout than any of us."

Ford frowned. "Do *you* need to go?"

Joshua smiled. "Of course. I've developed a good working relationship with Otto, and he trusts me to speak for Base and Factory. But of course, we'll be sending messages back and forth to make sure you're kept in the loop."

As they left the meeting with Ford, Sally whispered, "That went well. I was worried I'd have to swim back to Base by myself."

"You did okay on the swim here."

She shook her head. "You towed my clothes in your bag, and you always know where you're going. My *sight* isn't that good. I'd be afraid I'd make it all the way to that granite cliff and then not be able to find the underwater tunnel into Base."

"I was exhausted when we got here. I'm amazed you used to make the trip towing even larger bags." She gave him a wink. "But I guess that's why you're so muscular."

As they walked, he said, "I've made longer swims, but I much prefer the sub."

He slowed, and his face showed a frown.

"Problem?" she asked.

"No, not really. It's just that I have so many things I'm trying to keep on track. Sometimes I just have to put one aside and trust that things won't fall apart while I'm gone."

She sighed. "Sterling will be okay. Growing up in a nursery is how it's supposed to be."

He nodded, although their newly adopted son hadn't been his worry.

Just two days past, Pet had discovered another three nomads and 'encouraged' them to join his growing nomadic clan. The day was coming when one of the warriors would claim a name and then there would be a battle for leadership. Pet had to be ready, or one of the others would take his eyes.

From Joshua's U'tanse perspective, Pet was the obvious choice for leadership, but in the Cerik world-view, it all came down to sharp claws, brute strength, and more than a little treachery. Joshua hoped he was up to it. There was nothing he could do to help. If Pet was taken, it wasn't likely he'd get any other chance to develop a Cerik ally.

...

Robert was all business, working his checklist, making sure the submarine had all its supplies loaded. He didn't want to be out in the middle of the ocean when he discovered that they were short on food, water, medicines or breathable air. The list was long, and it had grown over the years.

Ace helped him take precise readings of their power levels. This was the first trip to the island, and Robert wanted reliable measurements of how much power was consumed, both towing the minisub on the way there and without the extra drag on the way back.

Joshua sat on the dock and shouted through the hatchway, "Is Alpha all loaded?"

Robert stuck his head out. "I made fun of the boat pilots when that girl was all excited about naming their boats. I never thought I'd have to go through it myself. But yes, *Alpha* is loaded. We just have to secure the baby."

Joshua grinned, "Don't you mean Cruiser?"

Robert let out a long sigh and ducked back inside.

Simon directed the hoist that lowered the new sub into the water. He had three helpers, two of them in the water, so Joshua didn't feel the need to jump in and add his own hands. Grellin walked over to talk to Robert.

The biggest difference in the new sub's appearance from the preview he'd gotten was the addition of a single pump, strapped in place. Back when Betty and Ace had fabricated them at New Home, there had been seven in a cluster used as an underwater thruster used to move large rocks from the entrance to their tunnel. When the pumps were reused to form the engine for the original minisub, only six were used as a balanced cluster around the egg-shaped tube of its hull. There had been one left over.

They didn't really plan to use it, but this was the first submarine trip to the island, and they wanted every option in case there was unexpected trouble.

Simon watched it settle into the water. Leaning as far over the edge as he dared, he watched it sink lower and lower. Finally, he let out a sigh.

Joshua asked, "Any problem?"

Simon shook his head, not looking away from the craft he'd built. "Just worried I might have miscalculated something. I think I've got the ballast rods right, but I don't want to sink it the first time in the water."

When the hoist lines went slack, the sub was nearly submerged, but the canopy was still above the water line. Simon pointed down to the guys in the water. Joshua watched closely as they operated hand-squeeze pumps near the rear fins.

"It's easier to adjust the ballast from inside with the levers, but for towing you need to use the hand pumps on the outside."

Joshua asked, "So, if it starts to leak and drop, we can bring it back up that way?"

"If you act fast. If it leaks too much air, then you'd have to hoist it back up with cables. You can lose it permanently in deep water."

Robert came over to watch. "That's good enough. I'd rather have a little excess buoyancy than too little. The main sub will drag it lower. Let's get moving; the tide won't wait."

Grellin said, "I'm sorry this is last minute, but I'd like your permission to come along."

Robert said, "To monitor the minisub?"

He shook his head. "No, I want to move to New Home permanently. If they are going to have subs of their own there, it makes sense to have one of the people who built it."

Robert waved Simon over and they had a short private discussion. Grellin raced away to pack his possessions. It didn't take him long to return.

Betty was the last to arrive, nervous and shaking as she approached the sub. Sally helped her inside and then Robert waved to Larson, the Factory dockmaster. Workers pulled on long cables to spread the camouflage sheets hiding the dock opening to the outside bay, making a gap for the submarines to leave.

Like mamma and baby sea creatures, they slowly eased out into the bay, quickly submerging.

Seamount

Ace talked with Joshua as they both kept an eye on Betty.

Ace whispered, "I was afraid she'd panic when we went underwater. She was so nervous about the flight."

"I don't know. She seems to like it."

Betty and Sally were positioned near the front window. Occasionally Robert would point out a sea creature or one of his underwater landmarks.

"After here, the sea floor drops away and there's no more rocks. Fewer fish, too. The water gets very clear."

Joshua closed his eyes and stretched his *sight* out into the water ahead. When he opened his eyes, Ace was looking at him.

"What did you see?"

Joshua shook his head, with a little smile. "Nothing much. Just a little nervous after that encounter with that *jandaka*. We're too big for him anyway."

Ace asked, "Robert, have you been out this far before?"

The pilot nodded. "Yes, back when there was more power available for exploring, I ventured out this way a few hours, just to see what the deep water was like. It was boring, with nothing to see. I could just set the course and take a nap."

Joshua remembered flying over the area. "There's a seamount some distance ahead."

"Oh? How far?"

He shook his head. "I just noticed the sea changing color on a previous trip as we flew over. I'll see if I can locate it again."

Ace asked, "What's a seamount?"

"Just an underwater mountain that never got high enough to break the surface. If it did, then it'd be an island."

He shook his head, "I've never paid any attention to geology." He gave a short laugh. "If I had, then maybe I'd never have been caught off-guard by the lava flow that almost killed me."

...

About an hour out into the ocean, Ace asked, "Are we sure the minisub is trailing correctly?"

Robert replied, "It is. I check it regularly."

Joshua nodded. "I have, too."

Grellin spoke up. He was normally quiet. "There should be no problem. The weights are all symmetrical, and the tow ring is solidly connected to the hull."

Robert suggested, "We could surface, now that we're well out of sight of land. The waves look calm. We could open the hatch and you could look for yourself."

Ace frowned. "Is it safe?"

Robert chuckled. "I've done it before. Believe me, I won't try it if the weather is rough, but it's okay now."

Ace nodded, "Thanks. You guys with *sight* always have it so easy."

Grellin said, "Mine isn't very good at a distance, either."

Robert made the adjustments, and sunlight broke through as they surfaced. Betty squeaked as the ocean swells made her grab for a hand-hold.

"Hmm." Robert turned the sub to face into the swells. "Maybe we can't stay surfaced very long. The waves are bigger than I thought."

Joshua looked at where the water was riding on the hull. "I'll go with Ace. We'll just take a minute, okay?"

Robert nodded.

The hatch opened with just a few drips. Joshua pulled himself out. "Hang on to the railing." Ace followed.

Grellin watched from the hatchway. "Do you want a line?"

Joshua shook his head. "I'm not afraid of getting wet."

It was a balancing act, walking on the moving top deck. Ace grumbled, "Maybe it'd be better to crawl."

"Oh, it's not that bad. You can see the swells coming and time your steps."

At the stern of the sub, there was some splash as the propellers turned slowly. Thirty feet farther, the cable stretched to the minisub. It was riding lower, with only its top fin cutting a wake as they moved.

Ace grabbed Joshua's arm for stability. "It's *empty* out here."

Joshua looked up. The horizon was invisible, just a brown haze in the distance, not giving much of an indication when the ocean ended and the sky began.

Ace said, "I can't see the moon. I'm totally at a loss here. Which way is Factory and which way is the island?"

Joshua stretched out his *sight*. "Factory is off that way." He pointed. "New Home is off that way."

Ace shook his head. "Humans back on Old Earth were like me, like *tenners*, right? How could they possibly find their way across the ocean? It's impossible."

"I guess I never thought about it. It would be difficult. Supposedly the sky was clearer on Old Earth. They could see the stars at night. I don't know what they did when it was cloudy." He knew Robert and all the boat pilots had good clairvoyance—that was an obvious necessity for the job. Not that he'd mention that to Ace right now.

Instead, Joshua said, "Cerik of the Rear-Talon *tetca* who pilot the boats through the sky don't have *sight*. Instead, they use the navigation map in the boat. Probably the ancient humans did the same, once they developed the technology, but before that ... I have no idea."

Ace nodded. "That's reassuring."

"What is?"

"If the Cerik pilots are like me, then they'll be just as lost when they lose sight of land. Even their maps probably don't have any locations listed out here."

"Good point."

Just then a slightly larger swell caused them to shift their feet to maintain their balance.

"You done here?" Joshua asked.

"Yes."

They went back inside. Sally was holding Betty's hand and asked, "How was it?"

Ace spoke to Betty. "It's difficult to keep your balance up there. No handrails except near the hatch. But the minisub is in good shape."

Robert double-checked the hatch. "If you don't mind, I'm going to take us down so we don't have to fight the waves."

. . .

Later, Ace came up to where Robert was piloting. Joshua and Sally were sitting closely there as well.

"Betty has dozed off. What have you three been whispering about?"

Robert said, "We've been trying to decide whether to take a little time to explore the seamount or not. All three of us have an itch to see what it looks like, but it's not really fair to stretch this trip out any longer than it is."

Sally nodded. "I think Betty is trying to put up a brave front. She's not really comfortable."

Ace sighed. "I know. She does like the water better than the flights, but she's not really at ease unless she's sitting at a table solving a puzzle. But that said, she also understands how important exploration is. How long will it take?"

Robert glanced out the window. "I've already adjusted our path to take us within sight of it. How much we'll see will depend on how clear the water is. It isn't an island, so there's no river silt to cloud things up."

Joshua said, "As far as I can sense, the peak of the mount is probably twenty-five feet below the surface, but that's just a guess and it'll vary with the tide. We only have a couple of hours of sunlight left, so unless we get there soon, we couldn't see anything anyway."

Ace nodded. "Then push on. Get close and see what we can see. It ought to be interesting."

. . .

"I expected rocks," mused Sally, as they moved over the waving beds of seaweed. "Whenever I swam off the coast of the island, there were enormous piles of rocks."

Robert said, "I've seen areas like this, but they've always been deep enough so the tides don't uproot the plants. I think there's a magic zone where they're shallow enough to get sunlight and deep enough to be protected from the waves."

Joshua nodded at the window. "The fish like it here. Maybe they eat the plants."

Ace pointed at something in the distance, "What's that?"

Joshua frowned at the dark shadow. "It looks artificial. Delense maybe."

Robert shifted their course to bring them closer.

Ace leaned so close to the window that his forehead was against the glass. "No, it's covered with the plants. It's just a slab of rock or something."

"I've seen something like this before," Joshua said. "I think it is Delense."

Sally said, "It doesn't look like a machine to me."

Joshua pointed out the curve. "Okay, suppose the tub, or a water boat like it, sank here a long time ago and rusted out. The plants would take root on the metal as it corroded. Only the outline is left, a shell."

Grellin said, "It's a hull. Take a closer look. It's similar to the tub."

Ace asked, "So the Delense were here, a long time ago?"

Joshua squeezed closer to the glass. "Probably. Look for more clutter on the seabed."

Betty moved up to lean against Ace. He smiled. "We woke you?"

She pointed off to the left. "Artificial." Everyone looked. It was a squat cylinder about ten feet across. A crop of seaweed grew on its top, but as they got closer, it was clear that the top was level. The shape didn't show any irregularities. She was right.

Joshua said, "So the Delense were here and built things. It's just like around the bay, or off the coast of the island."

Sally asked, "Why would they bother building here?"

Joshua scratched at his cheek, thinking. "If I wanted a place the Cerik would never find and I had burrowing machines, a seamount might be perfect."

With that idea in mind, they began searching with *sight*. Thirty minutes later Robert eased them to a channel, probably formed by a lava outflow ages ago when the seamount formed.

Robert nodded. "That's an entrance tunnel."

Sally looked at the dark, circular opening. "Do we go in?"

The pilot shook his head. "Absolutely not. It's far too dangerous. We could get trapped."

Grellin suggested, "We could get closer. Doesn't this sub have lights?"

Robert reluctantly nodded. "Yes, but I never use them. The whole purpose of the sub is to hide our position, not give it away with an unnatural underwater light."

Ace pushed, "But there are no Cerik anywhere near here. We could come to a stop just outside the tunnel and shine the light in. It would tell us a lot."

Robert gave in and moved them closer. The lights switched on, causing a mass panic among the sea creatures who lived in the tunnel. The fish darted away instantly, but a creeper scuttled away slower, hunting for shadows.

Joshua said, "It *is* large enough for the submarine to go inside, but I agree with Robert. At this moment, we have more important tasks to complete, and we can't risk *this* sub on the unknown. But I should take the minisub inside."

Robert disagreed, "We should definitely explore the place, but on a later trip."

Joshua spread his hands. "Only Alpha has the range to reach this place. We can't do much from a boat, even one like Angel, which can land on the surface of the water. The first exploration has to be done either by a diver and I can't hold my breath that long—or a minisub. But we'll be leaving the minisub behind at New Home. Now is the perfect time to do that first, trial exploration. Cruiser is perfect for the job. It's small, and the chamber is certainly large enough so that I should be able to go in, look to see if there's anything interesting, turn around, and come back out."

Sally stated, "And I have to go with you to make sure you don't do anything stupid."

He frowned. "It's more reasonable for me to go alone."

"Not going to happen."

Grellin timidly raised his hand. "I'm familiar with the minisub." Sally glared at him and he backed away.

Robert sighed. "We only have an hour of daylight. I'm surfacing while we argue."

By the time they agreed to try it and suffered through the effort of hand-pumping more air into the minisub's ballast tanks, Robert frowned at the sun. "Daylight will be gone soon. Go in, look around, and come right back out, understand?"

Joshua nodded while helping Sally make the step from the upper deck of the submarine down into the tight confines of Cruiser. He quickly climbed in to the piloting position and they sealed the glass canopy.

"I'm liking this idea of a dry compartment," she said.

His clothes were dripping wet. Someone had to be in the water to unhook the sub and work the external ballast pump. "I'll reserve my opinion until we're done." Detached from the tow line and drifting free of Alpha, he pulled hard on the hand levers that were forcing water into the ballast tanks, causing them to sink.

He grumbled. "Cruiser is almost too big. It takes too long to adjust everything."

"Oh, quit pouting. You're enjoying this."

He watched the water level come up and finally cover the glass canopy. He realized he was gritting his teeth. There were no drips through the seal. There shouldn't have been, especially since they'd towed it all this distance with no leak. Maybe he was just worried about bringing Sally with him on when he didn't have enough experience with the craft.

"Okay, hang on. There's only one pump, and I've got to learn how to steer this thing."

He tapped the single button that turned on the pump for ten seconds. Gripping the levers that warped the fins, he tried to make the most of the thrust, turning them around and at the same time, taking them lower beneath the surface.

Visible a few yards away, Alpha's propellers slowly turned, and Robert attempted to move the big sub into position down by the tunnel to allow his lights to give more illumination.

"Watch out!" Sally called, as they almost bumped hulls.

"I'm trying!"

He added more water to the front ballast tank and they sank faster, getting below Alpha's hull. He stabbed the pump button again and they surged forward.

As they approached the black tunnel entrance, Joshua said, "I'm not going to slow down and wait for them. I can *see* well enough to avoid hitting anything."

"I need more hands." He raised the bow and leveled them off, taking a few seconds off the ballast levers to steer.

Sally said, "I wish I could help."

"All the controls are up here."

They slid into the blackness, and suddenly he couldn't even see the levers. "Joshua!"

"We're okay. I'm going to drift for a few seconds until ..."

Suddenly, the lights from Alpha illuminated the tunnel.

"Wow!" Sally was caught by the sight of the sparkling reflections off dozens of machines littering the floor of the chamber. Many were corroded, but there were some surfaces that looked like glass. Animal and plant life had moved in, finding their own habitats. Long-legged crawlers and long tubular swimmers were trying to avoid the lights.

Joshua carefully adjusted the ballast and drifted up. "There's air trapped in here."

"Breathable?"

"I have no idea. I'm not going to try. We're just here to look."

The canopy broke through the surface and Joshua pumped the ballast out to get better visibility.

"It's very dark. The light isn't making its way through the surface."

He nodded. "Not much of it, anyway. Look carefully. We've only got a couple of minutes before I have to turn around and get out of here."

Sally gasped. "Are you seeing what I'm seeing?"

He took a deep breath. "Yes." He pointed. "And over there."

"Oh, my."

The Island

Sally fetched Joshua a towel while Robert put the sub back on course for the island.

Ace asked, "Well? What did you find?"

"Bones. Eight perfectly intact Delense skeletons."

Joshua ran the towel over his head. "I counted nine, but she's right. Perfectly intact. They were in groups. A pair of couples. One group of five, all sitting together when they died. Although I can't imagine Cerik getting in there to kill them—that would have left the bodies mangled and bones broken. These Delense died peacefully."

Ace frowned. "Delense could swim, from all I've heard. Why didn't they escape out the tunnel?"

Robert had his eyes on the submarine's controls, but he was listening. "Maybe this was after the extermination. Maybe their rescue craft had been destroyed. This is still out in the middle of the ocean, too far for humans to swim, probably too far for the Delense. They were swamp-dwellers. They didn't migrate to the oceans. With no place to go, maybe they just starved to death."

Joshua shook his head. "Swamp dwellers would have been able to survive on all the fish in this area. No, they decided to die. Maybe they took poison, or just waited until the air went bad."

Ace nodded. "About that. Did you check the air?"

"No. I didn't trust it well enough to open the hatch. There was a huge bubble of trapped air, just like at Base, but the water was up above the level of the dock."

"Any other exits?"

Sally frowned. "A big round metal door."

Joshua added, "It was about the same size as the entrance tunnel. Large enough for big machinery. But it was sealed shut. It looked to me like the hinges had melted. I sensed long passageways on the other side, but it'll take skilled exploration teams to find out their extent."

Robert said, "Joshua, could you take the controls for an hour or so? I need to take a nap. It's been a long day."

"Yes. Let me change into something dry." He got up and rummaged in his bag.

Ace asked Sally, "How high was the water level?"

"A couple of feet above the edge of the dock. Some of the skeletons were half submerged. Others were on a platform near the metal door."

Ace nodded. "No telling what the gas composition is, then. There had to have been more air back at the beginning."

Betty said, "Oxygen."

"Right. Did the oxygen get used up when the metal door hinges melted? Or did gas molecules leak through the water itself? That's an experiment I'd like to try."

Joshua came back in dry clothes. "I want to know what's behind that door. The Delense had some kind of welding gear there. They closed the door and then melted it shut so that no Cerik could ever enter. Then they died, knowing there would be no rescue. What was so important that they had to seal it off?"

Robert gave Joshua a review of the submarine's controls. Ace watched as well.

Joshua tapped the controls. "Motor operated ballast pumps. So much easier than the minisub."

Grellin was listening. "Sorry, but adding powered controls meant a new power system, batteries, and an additional way it could fail when you were underwater."

Joshua shrugged. "I'm not an engineer. But believe me, the new one is easier to steer with that tail fin."

But he was also confident he could pilot Alpha toward New Home's island while Robert caught some rest.

Ace and Betty moved back to their seats, talking about pressure and diffusion and things Joshua didn't understand. Sally came up to sit beside him.

"You get to drive the big sub."

He smiled. "Just as long as Robert takes over when it's time to dock the thing. It's big and slow to maneuver. Do you want to try?"

She shook her head. "Only you and Robert have the *sight* to get us to the island. I'm fine with that." She closed her eyes and rested her head on his shoulder.

Joshua adjusted their course a fraction. With the seamount receding behind them, the sea life dwindled by the passing minute. Soon it would be just them in the empty ocean.

The Delense had extensive operations in the sea, much more than we ever suspected. The U'tanse were given the history that the Cerik knew, and their slaves were so much more clever than their masters suspected.

And that's good for us. The relics of the Delense have been a safety net for the Free U'tanse. And now we know a few things.

On the mainland, the island, and now this seamount, the Delense built underground bases with hidden tunnels to the sea. How many more are there?

It was going to take more exploration. Just like the trouble he had in locating Cerik out in the wild: even with *sight*, you have to know where to look. The world was a big place. Luckily, the Delense left their markers on the sea floor—old machinery, pipes, and other rusting relics. If you knew what to look for, any swimmer or submarine pilot should be able to notice the debris and mark the places that needed more extensive searches.

Robert should be right at the center of this. He's in charge of all the submarines. He will train the pilots. Searching for relics should be right along with ballast adjustments in his training.

Joshua opened his mind to the telepathic noise of all the U'tanse on Ko. The chaotic babble of all those minds was largely unintelligible, and none of his friends were included in the mix. The noise was always there, although he usually managed to ignore it. Everyone he knew, with the exception of a few in the nursery, had their thoughts smoothed over and protected.

What would it be like to live in a world where no one had to hide their thoughts? He'd never know. This was the the world of the Cerik, and they weren't going to go away.

But he feared for Kakil Home. Elehadi wanted them gone, and only the other Names were keeping him in check. What if he had to rescue them, like they had tried to rescue the remnants of Rikna Home? Would it be possible to move them to New Home?

I should really hunt for more locations, empty burrows where we could start a new New Home if necessary.

Islands would make the best homes. Cyclops found New Home's island. Does he know of any others? Will Debbie let me ask him?

. . .

Ace looked out the open hatch. "I'm glad the swells died down."

Betty raised her hand and nodded.

Joshua was looking over Robert's shoulder as the pilot slowly approached the island. "Are you sure that's not a star?"

"Stars are never that low on the horizon. And I can *see* a person."

Joshua could make her out as well. "I'm not sure who it is, but now that I've checked, I'm sure she's trying to identify the entry tunnel for us."

"So I can steer toward her light?"

Joshua checked again. "That's right. Position the sub several hundred feet straight out from her and then I'll transfer to Cruiser."

"You say it's a long tunnel?"

"Yes, much longer than the entrance to Base."

"And I can turn around once I get in?"

Joshua tried to remember the size of the pool under New Home's factory area. "I think so. At worst, I'll tow you out backward with Cruiser."

The pilot gave a sick smile. "That makes me feel so much better."

Joshua gave him a pat on the back. "Going outside."

Ace moved out of his way as he climbed through the hatch. "I counted four stars."

Joshua climbed on top of the sub and listened as the hatch was sealed and closed.

The ocean was much calmer. He stared up at the sky. There were nine, no ten stars that he could see. Perhaps if he let his eyes adapt to the darkness, he could see even more. He'd heard there were perhaps fifty stars that had been seen by various U'tanse over the years. The moon was riding low on the horizon, and that probably meant he wouldn't be able to see the fainter ones.

The light down on the horizon was larger. It flickered—perhaps a burning torch?

The submarine's propeller slowed, just a splash, splash, splash as the blade stirred the water. He took a running jump and dove in. He grabbed the cable and used it to guide him to Cruiser. He detached it from the minisub's nose, and then started working the hand pump to raise the hull higher out of the water.

Soon, he was inside, with the canopy sealed shut. It was too dark to see any of the controls, but he knew where they were. Shortly, he pulled up alongside Alpha and then moved ahead.

The big sub's lights came on, and suddenly he could see the tunnel entrance. He adjusted his ballast and steered his way in. Alpha's motors increased in pitch. Robert was coming in after him.

With the illumination, Joshua was happy to see that the rubble that had originally blocked the tunnel entrance had not gotten very far inside. He was cruising down a large pipe. He tapped the fin adjustments lightly, trying to stay dead center.

The light wobbled a little. Robert was doing the same thing, only with his size, the tolerances were tighter.

The distance wasn't bad—less than he had remembered. It was faster in a powered sub than it had been walking the corridors above.

Then, the inky blackness ahead became lighter, red like a dawn. It was the lighting of the dock area. When the tunnel opened up into the pool, he pumped the ballast water out, and broke the surface. People were there, waiting for them.

Well aware of Alpha on his tail, he punched the thrust button once more and drove toward the far end, steering nose into the ramp. There was a very light crunch as he nosed up to the incline.

Hurriedly, he unsealed the canopy. There were hands helping him, pulling Cruiser broadside against the ramp.

Hugo was there, grinning as he stepped out. Jenta and Lacruse had their hands on the fins. The whole engineering team had come to greet him.

"Thanks. Do you have a cable?"

Once he secured the minisub, they all raced over to help the others as Alpha eased up by inches, also broadside to the dock. Otto, the main elder of New Home, was there at the hatchway when it opened up, ready to welcome the first submarines to New Home.

Trek

"I just want to remind you all that the tunnel and underground chamber is secret." Otto rushed them all into a quick meeting. "More than half of the New Home residents have never used *ineda*, or else quickly forgot it. Should the Cerik discover us, this is a place of refuge and our possible escape, so I don't want it to be common knowledge."

Ace asked, "How do we explain our presence?"

Robert added, "Submarines are a secret as well, although everyone at Base and Factory know about it. We don't want the Names to be aware of our capabilities."

Joshua said, "If they see us, it's a secret that won't last long. We had to arrive somehow. If someone asks when we arrived, and you can't ignore their question, tell them to ask Otto."

The elder frowned, then nodded. "Yes, pass it on to me. I'll make the judgement."

Sally said, "Ace and Betty are very anxious to examine the new site. We'll leave as soon as we can."

Hugo said, "Jenta and I will be going with them. We've got to haul some test gear there to see if we can wake up the control systems."

Grellin said, "I'd be glad to help you with that."

Otto looked at Joshua and Robert. "And you two?"

Joshua said, "I'll be going. I observed the site from the air last time and there's some things I want to check out."

Robert shook his head. "No hikes for me. I figured you'd want me to stay and explain your new minisub. I'll be happy to stay down here."

Joshua smiled. "Remember Stella? She named it Cruiser, but I'm sure the name is up to you."

"So I didn't misread that. The little one is ours to keep?"

"All yours. It only has a single pump for propulsion right now, but Hugo can alter that to whatever you need. It can carry three people and tow cargo. It would be difficult to evacuate the whole Home with it, but if you were trapped, you could easy move supplies in through the tunnel and transfer people back and forth. Grellin helped with its construction and he applied to move here permanently."

Otto was absorbing the idea. "This is great. What's its range?"

Robert said, "That'll depend on how Hugo outfits it, but commuting to Base and Factory would be unreasonable. You could circle the island, I'm sure. You could even go far enough out to sea to be invisible from the land. One of our boats, Angel, can land on the sea, if the waves are calm."

Otto took in a deep breath. "Lots of things to think about. It gives us options, and we were short of them. Please relay my thanks to Ford."

. . .

Since Joshua's last visit, he was surprised how developed the underground hall had become. The huge vacant chamber now had rooms curtained off, stocks of food, and sleeping pallets. The others needed some sleep, so the hike was scheduled for noon.

Joshua got some sleep, but woke early. He got up without waking Sally. Hugo was down at the ramp with Grellin, looking over the minisub.

He joined them. "Good morning. Want to take a quick ride?"

Hugo smiled, but shook his head. "It's tempting, but I'm an engineer this morning. Just tell me what I need to know."

Joshua told him of his two trips in the craft and Grellin commented on how the control systems worked. Joshua made polite suggestions for improvements, trying not to offend Grellin. Hugo took notes.

. . .

It was strange, sneaking out of New Home, trying not to be noticed by the workers. From what Joshua could read from people's thoughts as they passed through the rows of cropland, the newly discovered facility was already old news. People taking the trail carrying backpacks wasn't worth a second look.

Sally led the way, with Ace and Betty lagging behind. Both of them were geniuses at the workbench, but neither spent much time hiking. But the only way out to the new mystery was to walk. They started off in good spirits, but after a couple of hours on the trail, Sally had to heal some early blisters and wrap Betty's foot. Hugo, Jenta and Grellin, all carrying packs of tools and equipment, went on ahead.

Six hours into the four-hour hike, Sally asked, "Did you bring lights? We're going to be losing the sun, and the trail doesn't get any smoother."

"No, and I just realized how stupid that is. We're going to be exploring underground."

"Well, I have a wind-up light, but sharing it will be difficult. We're already creeping along, what with all the breaks we have to take. We left supplies at our camp, but probably there's only a couple of lights."

Joshua had scouted out the rest of the route with his *sight*. "I could go ahead, get the lights, and return." Sally nodded solemnly.

He called over to Ace. "I'm going ahead. Let me carry Betty's pack."

Ace was sweating, having taken Betty's load as well as his own. Joshua knew he was the stronger, but he hadn't been willing to cut into Ace's gesture of help. Betty was his partner.

As Ace and Betty caught up. Joshua said, "We're running out of daylight and I'm going to try to bring back hand lights."

Ace looked around. The trail wound through the rugged landscape. It had been a lava flow originally, and now carried a brook deep enough to wet your feet. They had to push aside branches from the low vegetation as they walked. "You said there's no predators on the island."

"That's right. They have to make leather goods from sea creatures." He didn't mention that the island had its own set of poisonous bugs. Betty was already stressed enough as it was.

Ace handed over the backpack, and Joshua instantly regretted his offer. Betty had packed heavy gear, not clothing. But he could handle it.

Double-loaded, but able to travel at his own pace, he made better time.

As the sun settled behind the ridge, he used his *sight* more.

Strange not to be worried about a Cerik appearing in front of me.

He could appreciate the advantages of living on the island, where the Cerik made no impact on daily living. *We need dozens of islands. Even if one is discovered and attacked, the others would be ready.*

The question was: How many islands were there? There was Far Island, of course. It was even in the Cerik tales. Supposedly it was large enough to support a clan of its own, if there were enough prey animals for them to feed on.

But in the Map Room at Base, there was a map that showed two other islands to the north of Far Island. Those were larger than this one, but smaller than Far Island and as far as he knew, never named. Perhaps the Cerik didn't even know that they existed.

What we need are hundreds of little ones, like this. Too small to support a clan of predators, but large enough for our needs. But do they exist?

Joshua moved through a small gap and looked down at the campsite. A fire pit lit the *shash*-thatched lean-to with yellow light. Two women looked up at his arrival.

"Hello, I'm Joshua. Sally and two others are coming behind me."

The taller of the two nodded, and pulled off her breather. "I'm Doe and this is Keann. How far behind are they?"

Joshua pulled his breather free as well, just to be polite. "Not too far, but Ace and Betty are hobbling with blisters. I was sent to look for hand lights to help them in the dark."

Keann frowned. "The others have them down in the tunnels."

Doe turned to her and said, "We have the torches." She explained to Joshua, "Outdoor torches—nobbly fat is inedible, but it burns with a yellow flame."

Keann dashed over to the lean-to and came out with three of the torches and a bottle of oil. She began topping up the little tank in each. "I hate using these things in the tunnels. The smoke is vile. It even makes my saliva bitter."

Joshua realized they were coming with him. "Do we need to protect the campfire?"

Doe shook her head. "It's okay. We can restart it if it goes out, and there's nothing out here to burn if the wind picks up."

He pulled his breather back in place. "Who's down in the tunnels?"

Keann looked at Doe. Doe sighed. "Hugo, Jenta and the new guy went straight on in when they arrived. Patrick showed up a few days ago, once I reported the fabricators we'd found. Patrick is probably deep in the tunnels working with Tunice. She's a gadget freak.

"Like Betty?"

The girls laughed. "Nobody is quite like Betty," Doe said.

Keann lowered her voice. "June went with them. She really latched onto that new guy."

Joshua was glad he had his breather mask on. It sounded like Grellin had met a new friend.

He made sure the packs were stowed safely, even if the campfire blew sparks.

Doe led the way, moving quickly over the trail. She'd been that way several times before. When they met up with Sally's group, they lit the torches and a wavering glow provided light for the whole party. Joshua took Sally's pack and Keann badgered Ace into letting her carry his. It wasn't more than thirty minutes to get everyone back to the campfire.

Keann said, "I'll make some pallets. You're just lucky it's a clear night."

Ace was rubbing his feet with a smelly ointment after having done the same for Betty. "You don't sleep inside?"

Doe looked at Sally, but when Sally kept her peace, she said, "There's no airlock and it's all unfiltered air anyway. There are no lights. And sometimes, there are *lulurs* and other critters that inhabit the chambers. We'll move inside if it rains, but otherwise it's nicer out here."

Joshua asked, "How common are the *lulurs*? I've always wanted to cook one."

Doe wrinkled her nose. "You eat them? All those legs creep me out."

"At Base, it's a delicacy, but not too common. They've all been hunted out in that area. You have to cut out the good meat carefully, but supposedly, it's a handy survival food. I had it once, when I was younger."

Sally patted him on the arm. "I'll let *you* try it first."

Patrick and Tunice surfaced an hour later, chatting with Hugo and Jenta. Joshua caught Doe frowning at the tunnel entrance from time to time. Reluctantly, he reached out with his *sight* and began remotely touring the passages. Not too far from the entrance, off in a side chamber, he located the pair. Perhaps June was healing Grellin with that massage, but Joshua didn't think it likely. He closed off his clairvoyant view.

Joshua stood up and walked over to where Doe sat. "I just checked. Grellin and June don't appear to be in any distress."

She looked him in the eyes. "No distress." She sighed, looking tired. "I just wish they'd warned me."

Joshua shrugged. "I just thought you should know."

Doe straightened up. "If they're not in danger, it's not my business."

When he went back to where Sally waited for him, she whispered, "What did you expect? Girls on their own with too few available men. Grellin talked to me on the trip over. He left Factory because he didn't feel needed, just another hand. He jumped at the chance to move here where there were unattached women. I'm surprised Patrick hasn't picked someone out."

"Maybe. But Patrick always has some project that takes up his full attention."

Joshua wished he could share what he knew about Patrick's secret project to raid the clans for power, but until he knew more, it would be just speculation anyway.

I hope I have the chance to talk to him about it while I'm here. I have to make sure he's aware of the dangers to us all if he tries it.

Down in the Crater

The walls of the crater surrounded the little valley, except for the notch that led to the trail. Joshua, looking at the tunnel entrance built into a central rise, said, "I wonder if the notch is artificial."

They were waiting a moment for the party to collect. Breakfast had been greasy finger foods and some of them wanted to clean up a bit.

Patrick asked, "What do you mean?"

"This is a bowl, and normally I'd assume the rains would fill it up, but that notch provides a convenient drain."

"There is a little pond on the other side of the rise."

Joshua walked around the edge of the rise until he could see the water. Patrick asked, "What are you looking for?"

"Something is keeping the water from getting deep enough to flood through the tunnel entrance. Do you think the Delense cut the notch to be a drain for the crater?"

Patrick looked back at the notch. "I see what you mean, but I wouldn't put it past them to have other drains as well. Base has a number of hidden passages for air flow, and no one has ever found where they come out."

Joshua picked up a flat slab of light green rock. Sally walked up and asked, "What's that?"

"It's glass. This place was *flicked*. Sand and soil was melted into glass by the heat of the explosion."

Patrick reached for it and broke off a chip from the edge.

Joshua looked around. "These stones, at least here on the surface, have been remelted."

Sally asked, "What's that mean?"

"If you went back to Rikna Home, or the crater where it used to be, you'd see the same sort of rock. The heat of the *flick* melted the surface— just a fraction of an inch, but it's distinctive. I've searched the area several times with my *sight*. I'm seeing the same things here."

She asked, "So this place was *flicked*, too?"

He nodded. "Only this was more severe. I noticed the crater shape of the surrounding hills when we flew over as I left on my last trip here."

Patrick said, "I wondered why you wanted me to fly over this place. I thought you just wanted to wave at Sally."

Grellin turned to June, who was walking with him. "Were you here then?"

She nodded, blushing.

The wayward lovers had only shown up after dawn, but other than a quiet scolding June received from Doe, no one had said anything.

They entered the tunnel, feeling the air cool down as they moved lower.

Patrick ran his hands against the tunnel wall. "There are layers. We're moving below the glassy stuff."

Sally asked, "Why would they *flick* this place?" Her voice echoed from the depths.

"And *who* did it?" Joshua sighed. "I suspect the Cerik didn't know about this place, but if only the Delense knew about it, then it might have been an accident."

Patrick said, "It gives you something to think about. If this place had been a manufacturing site for power cells from the beginning, perhaps they had a defective cell that ruptured. Several charged cells might have exploded all at once. That would explain your more destructive explosion."

Joshua took a moment to crank the light he held, brightening up the tunnel walls around them, but it was still pitch black ahead.

"Now if it were me, I'd be nervous making a new power cell factory right on the same site as the one that just blew up."

Ace shook his head. "Maybe the Delense weren't as superstitious as we are. Perhaps it's just the fact that since they already had this crater, that it formed a natural barrier against any future blast wave."

Sally patted the cool granite wall of the tunnel. "It explains why this isn't built like all the other burrows. Nobody was supposed to live here. It was too dangerous. Was the New Home burrow built after the explosion? I wonder."

Joshua sighed. "I wish the Delense had a written history. They've left so many mysteries behind."

The echo of his words changed from one sentence to the next as the tunnel opened up into a larger chamber.

Patrick waved to Joshua, "Come with me."

They went over to a low workbench, one suitable for the Delense who moved around on all fours. Patrick grumbled. "It's murder on your back to work at this table. Here, help me connect this."

Once the lighting strip was connected to a battery, there was enough light for everyone to look around. Ace and Betty zeroed in on the control system.

Patrick showed off the power cell warehouse. He patted one of the cells. "If we could get all these charged up, the Free U'tanse would be fixed for years."

Joshua chuckled. "It'd take a lifetime to get them all charged from the turbine."

Patrick frowned. Joshua tried not to notice. There were still too many other people around to discuss the raids.

Shortly, Ace and Betty were so busy, they tuned everyone else out.

Sally edged up to Joshua and whispered, "This is the only time I've ever heard Betty use more than one word at a time—not that I understand what she's saying."

Joshua felt the same way. Maybe one word in three meant anything to him.

"It's technical. I know that much."

But there was progress. Hugo had brought a small power cell and they drained its charge into the plant's systems. Then, the controls lit up.

Patrick said, "How did the Delense get power into this place? There was a landing pad near the New Home system, and power could be fed from my boat. We're maybe a hundred feet below ground here and nothing could push a beam through all that rock. The only way that I can see is to haul a charged cell down here by cart. They couldn't charge up the ones in storage down here."

Joshua nodded. "They make the empties here, then take them up into space to be charged. Maybe they did that on purpose, to keep from having too many charged cells all together in one place."

Patrick grumbled, "Nobody stores a lot of power cells together. I've been looking."

And I know why you've been looking, preparing for your raids.

Out loud, Joshua said, "That's the Cerik policy, I guess. Is there some inherent danger that exists when one charged cell gets close to a bunch of others? Or is it just practical? Cerik clans would certainly steal from each other if they had the chance to get away with it. A bundle of power cells would make a nice prize."

Patrick shook his head. "I know some Homes have a backup power cell stored right next to the active one. And in the middle of some battle, you'd have to carry a charged cell on your boat to *flick* the enemy. There can't be a hazard from putting two cells together. At least not much of one."

Joshua frowned. "You're right. Tenthonad delivers cells to their customers. Does anyone know if they deliver more than one at a time? I've never heard."

Ace raised his voice. "Hey guys, you're distracting Betty. One technical problem at a time, please."

Joshua waved them off out of range. There were aisles of machines, some obviously pipelines to feed materials into the fabricators.

"If we ever want to restart this, we'll need to locate the source of the raw materials. But that's another problem for the geniuses. I just hope there's a list somewhere, and that we know the translation for it all."

Patrick said, "I'm content with the warehouse of empty cells. It'll be ages before the Free U'tanse have the need for more than those."

Joshua shook his head. "But what if we managed to free more people, a lot more people. What if we had to make dozens more free communities like New Home? We'd need power for all of them, and for the transportation they'd need. Yes, it's one thing to take care of the cuties in our nurseries. It's another to get all the other U'tanse out from under the control of their Names."

The pilot chuckled nervously. "You're thinking big. Is that even possible?"

Joshua paused a moment. No one was in hearing range. It was just Patrick. He spoke quietly, "You've got your secret projects. I've got some, too. And my monitoring has revealed that several of the Names are talking about eliminating their U'tanse Homes altogether."

"Other than Elehadi?"

"Unfortunately, yes! Although, he *is* the instigator of a lot of this talk. They're trying very hard to keep the telepaths from knowing about it, for fear that they'd panic the U'tanse and trigger more widespread Attachment. The end-goal is to *flick* all the Homes at once, without warning."

Patrick fumed, "Are they crazy?"

It was a question that had bothered Joshua. How many times had the Cerik pursued self-destructive actions? Wiping out the Delense had been suicidal. The discovery of the human substitutes to maintain their technology had been a lucky break for the predators.

"I don't know. Since the beginning, since the Arrival, there have been factions that have wanted nothing to do with the U'tanse. Now that we've activated all their old Delense factories and restored the technology they were about to lose after they killed off their Builders, the cost of supporting us seems too expensive. Clans that have gotten rich off of their U'tanse slaves now toy with the idea of getting rid of them."

Patrick sat down on a workbench. "You'd think they would appreciate our value."

"Rikna turned into a Ferreer-style hive mind. It was the biggest outbreak in history, and it scared a lot of the Names. They feel trapped."

"Why?"

"If the Name chooses business as usual, then their U'tanse breed more and become more expensive to support. The only way to reduce the human population is to sell some off to other clans, which was disastrous for Elehadi, or to kill them off through neglect, which could also trigger Attachments.

"The Names are watching Elehadi carefully. He's doing the dangerous experiments for them. Rikna Home had to be *flicked*. Now he's trying something else with Kakil Home, and that looks bad, too. If he can change the U'tanse into something more compliant and easier to manage, he'll achieve greatness among the Faces and others will copy his methods. If he fails again and Kakil Home has to be *flicked*, then they can kill or penalize him without upsetting their own U'tanse.

"As I said, many of the Names are secretly hunting for a way out of the trap. They could lose everything if their own U'tanse turned into monsters."

He pointed over to the waving light. Someone was approaching, carrying one of the wind-up lanterns.

Patrick nodded. He saw, but asked, "Does Ford know all of this?"

"He knows the details, but he has other troubles, like the survival of Base and Factory, to deal with. We may be the refuge of last resort for the U'tanse, but we may not be able to do anything when the time comes."

"We need to be more capable. We need more power."

Joshua nodded. "Yes, but we have to be careful we don't startle the Names. One moment of panic and some are already primed to act. If Names move wholesale against the Homes, even the safe ones will panic. The only way out will be Attachment, and that's just a different kind of dead end."

Patrick's face was dark and thoughtful. "I'm going back out. I need to take a walk."

He walked toward the upward-sloping tunnel.

Grellin with his lantern moved closer. Joshua saw June chatting with Sally, also coming his way.

Grellin asked, "I caught a little of that. Do you regret turning things over to Ford? It sounds like you feel trapped yourself." He eased down on one of the workbenches.

Joshua sat down beside him. "It's frustrating, but I'd hate to be sitting at Factory, managing the day to day operations. It's better for me to move around and get my own feel for how things are working."

Grellin sighed. "You deal with people better than I do. How do you cope, here at New Home? Just off the sub, it was like a flood. So many of them don't block their thoughts. It's like they don't care if you hear them thinking about you. Jenta is focused on Hugo, but when I arrived at the campsite and all the girls realized I was new here, and unattached, suddenly I felt like a runner surrounded by Cerik."

"Hey, it's nice having girls admire you and all, but its not like the first couple of generations, when guys had to service any girl that came by."

Joshua grinned. "How did that work out?"

The mechanic sighed and rolled his eyes. "I moved here so I could find a job where I was really needed, something I was the best at. You may not remember me, but I used to work in metal alloy fabrication until there was an accident. My lungs were severely damaged, and I was evacuated to Base for healing.

"Since then, I've never gotten back to my original job. I've just been filling in wherever they needed another body. Yes, the idea that there were girls here was appealing, but I didn't intend to get involved, not immediately." He smiled, looking over at the others. "Then I got to talking with June." The way he said her name, low and reverently, said a lot. "Things just fell into place."

He almost got up, but then sat back down. "But that didn't cure my problems!" He moved his hands as he spoke. "Now I feel a wave of resentment, both from the girls here at the campsite and even from those back at New Home who have picked up the fact that there is a new guy. It's like I personally offended every girl on the island by not choosing them. June is catching some grief over it, too."

He looked at Joshua earnestly, and asked. "How did you deal with it, when you resolved your differences with Sally?"

Joshua shook his head, and gave a low sigh. "You can't make everyone love you. There will always be people who resent you, either because you chose someone else or because, like me, you have opportunities they don't. You can't solve everyone's problems. It's a fruitless quest.

"Just focus on the person who is most important to you, or the task that means the most. The best you can hope for is that those two goals won't be at odds. Ignore the rest, if you can."

Return Plans

Holana, New Home's lead semaphore operator, was waiting for Joshua to *look* her way. He signaled his readiness to copy.

"Message from Debbie at Base to Joshua: Your father said he found what you wanted. Your sister had bad dreams, so do I."

The message said a lot, and since it wasn't coded, he could tell his mother was still angry about Cyclops's project.

But the book of James bar Bill had been located. If Cyclops reported that, then it was just a matter of time before it was copied. That was great news.

Veronica's dreams, her nightmares, were often accurate predictions of the future. She drew them out in her sketchbook. Then it was up to others to decide what they meant. Too often, her nightmares predicted disaster.

Joshua searched Base with his *sight* until he found Ash. The boy was Paul's apprentice, rapidly developing his skill with semaphore, but he was also Veronica's closest friend, and her confidant. It was his job to report anything unusual in her sketches.

Ash was hurrying down a corridor, carrying a paper. Messenger duty was part of the semaphore job, and Paul was all too willing to pass that task on to Ash.

Joshua shifted his seat on the hard workbench. The others were ignoring him. Ace and Betty were focused on the control systems. Sally had stretched out for a nap, although her bench was likely as hard as his. Grellin and June had vanished off on their own again.

Semaphore was an annoyingly slow communication system, but it was the only secure system they had. Telepathy was faster, but Cerik Names had their own telepaths as well. Joshua had heard it suggested that they had developed their rudimentary telepathy when they acquired the Delense as their slaves, just as a way to keep track of them. Certainly there were more Cerik telepaths now, after the Arrival when telepathic humans became their slaves.

If your mind was open to be read, those thoughts could be picked up by any telepath that had noticed you. It wasn't a way to transfer secrets. Luckily, Sharon the Mother had other skills, like the ability to see across great distances. With suitable arm-waving, a human clairvoyant could pick up long distance communication system. And there were no Cerik clairvoyants.

Ash delivered his message to Comfort in the nursery. Not a minute later, out in the corridor, he paused and faced toward the island, a semaphore operator was always watching. At this distance, it was impossible to tell whether Ash was looking at Holana over in the New Home burrow, or at him. But Joshua put his hands on his head. Immediately, Ash signaled his readiness to copy.

"New sketch? Details?"

Ash moved his arms. He used Joshua's personal code.

"She was upset. Crowd of people threw a man outside airlock and barricaded the door. Passing Cerik ripped him apart."

Joshua winced. While the idea of expelling a troublemaker from a Home had been discussed, he'd never heard of it in practice. It was a death penalty, no matter how you looked at it.

He queried: *"Which Home?"*

"She didn't know. Hasn't gotten over the blood."

"Thanks for report."

He needed to be back at Base.

Joshua walked over to where Ace and Betty were working. "How is it going? How quickly will you be done?"

Ace looked at him with a sad shake of his head. "You don't know how these things work, do you? We are investigating how the facility operates. Betty has determined that there is a strong resemblance between the fabricators over at New Home and these. However, there are significant differences, too. There's very little change we can make in the design of the cells—that's locked up. Plus, there's a whole set of tests done on the completed cells once they're fabricated."

"Tests?"

"I gather that the Delense wanted to be sure that there were no defective power cells. They charge them a little, make an endless set of minor tests that I don't understand yet, and then charge it a little more before running additional tests.

"We don't really have the power necessary to actually fabricate a cell and do the testing sequence, so Betty is digging deep into the machine instructions, trying to understand what it's trying to do."

Ace spread his hands. "It could take a year, maybe, to map all of this out."

Joshua sighed, "But is it critical? You and Betty—I'd assume you're working as a team?"

Ace nodded seriously, "We really don't want to be separated. We work best together."

"Then you two need to know that you're needed elsewhere. You're not the only ones who can read Delense script and fix their machines, but you've proved you're the best.

"Factory needs that second power generator. Ford could really use your insight in repairing the turbine. Simon did a good job making the second minisub, but we need more of them, both for New Home and for routine runs between Base and Factory and your insight is needed. Then, there's the exploration of the seamount."

Betty didn't look his way, but her hands had stopped moving over the control panel. She was listening intently, as well.

Joshua tried to make Ace understand. "I know you'd love to dig into this place for a year, but we have to make the fastest progress we can, on multiple projects."

Ace gave a tight smile, "Yes, I understand that, but what we're discovering here is *new*. You know that a power cell can be set to *flick*? Well, a couple of hours ago, we found the machine controls that make that happen. It's a special condition actually unrelated to the external command. The power cells have to be instructed to allow the overload. Their very construction tries to prevent such a condition from ever happening. The Delense added the ability to *flick* as an afterthought in their code."

Joshua frowned, "Probably ordered by some long forgotten Name. Yes, I see." The research was important. He understood that. Knowing something that the Cerik didn't could be the key to their survival. But they were short on mechanical geniuses. The Free U'tanse were short on many important skills. They were the leftovers, the dregs that the Cerik threw out.

And yet we're the key to the survival of all the U'tanse.

"Ace, I need to get back to Base and Factory urgently. It would be best for other projects if you two could return with me. Given that we have very limited power, trips back and forth have to be rare. What do you suggest?"

Ace leaned back and stared at the dome of the chamber overhead. After a minute, he said, "You could go back in the sub, carrying several empty power cells. When Boat Angel and those power cells are charged, come back. We can then use that power to charge up Boat C that's been stranded here at New Home.

"By that time that's accomplished, Betty and I will have done more research and we will have finished fabricating the second power system to be installed in place of the turbine at Factory. Such a system will be too large to be moved by the submarine, since it's hatch is too small, or by Boat A, so it'll have to come in Boat C. Betty and I will return at that time and assist in installing it. Hopefully by then we will have learned more about this place."

Joshua nodded. "That's reasonable, but the only glitch is that power is so limited at Factory right now that charging those cells may take too long."

Patrick had returned from his walk. He moved closer. "Sorry, I've been listening in. But there is another option."

...

Joshua scanned the landscape. The three of them had gone outside the tunnel entrance a couple of hundred yards from the campsite. Patrick insisted they needed the privacy.

Ace looked around. "I need to get back soon."

Patrick said, "But I need your input as well. Hugo and I have been working on an idea since I was stranded here. There is plenty of power available at the various Delense factories. Most of them were designed to be left running unattended, so the plan is to sneak in and steal power cells."

Joshua said, "It would cause quite an uproar, and if U'tanse were suspected, it could be fatal to us all."

Patrick nodded. "I agree. That's why we've gone beyond the idea of just walking in, disconnecting a power cell, and walking out. With the discovery of this warehouse of empty power cells, we could swap in an empty power cell and leave with a charged one. It wouldn't look like a theft any more, just an unexplained power drain."

Joshua asked, "Can people tell if it was the same power cell or a substitution?"

Ace shrugged. "Well, I could. Betty could. But the information is hidden pretty far down. I wasn't aware of the unique identifying sequence until this morning. Certainly Cerik wouldn't know about it, even if they could read the codes.

"I'm not saying there aren't U'tanse specialists that might know of it, but it's not common knowledge."

Joshua said, "But specialists from Tenthonad Home just might be familiar with the idea, and if the Tenthonad were blamed for bad power cells and were called in to explain the power loss, it might be discovered."

Patrick turned to Ace. "Could we hook up a portable something—some gadget that could transfer power from the cells, just like we do with the boats? That would leave the same power cells in place. We'd be stealing just the power, leaving the power cells untouched."

Ace asked, "You're not flying in with one of the boats to steal the power?"

"Not at first. We don't have power to spare to fly in. What I'm suggesting is that on the submarine trip back to Factory, we take a side trip to the nearest unattended Delense factory, hike in, and return with power.

"We follow the same plan you outlined to Joshua, but instead of powering up the cells from Factory's turbine, we charge them from the Delense factory. We'd shave months off the needed time."

"I can't leave Betty here alone."

Joshua asked, "But is the scheme even possible?"

Ace nodded. "Certainly." He looked up to the sky. "You'd have to align the cells, and then you'd need a signaling harness to bypass the factory's commands ... It could be done remotely, but without a boat's control system, it would need its own actuator. And a manual keypad, so you could visualize the process. Better if you only tapped part of the power."

He was starting to mumble to himself.

Joshua said, "Ace? Can you make a gadget so a stupid person like me could do the transfer without *flicking* myself?"

Ace nodded. "Um, yes. Over at New Home." He smiled broadly, "We've learned so much at this place."

First Raid

"I have got to take a nap," said Joshua.

Robert nodded. "Okay. I'm good until we get to the Dallah coastline."

There were four of them on the trip: Robert, to stay with the sub; Patrick and Joshua, to make the raid into the automated pipe factory; and Sally, to handle any healing that might be required. It took Patrick a while to face the idea that he'd be leaving his baby, boat C alone on the island. But this was his project.

It had been an exhausting three days, preparing for the raid. Not only had Ace constructed the power tapper as requested, but they'd had to handle the power cells as well.

They were taking four standard power cells to Base and Factory, but to get them ashore in Dallah territory was going to be difficult. There was no dock, no work crew to help. They'd need a two-man carrier that would fit through the submarine's hatchway, one that would also protect the power cells from the ocean water as they towed them to shore.

There had also been the promised food supplies, the gift from New Home to Base and Factory. Loading the sub, and then hours worth of practice using the power tapper, had left Joshua short on sleep.

He'd been right beside Robert on the tense exit, piloting the submarine through the tunnel and out into the open sea, but now he had to rest.

He stretched out between two large bundles and closed his eyes.

I wish I had the knack for falling asleep instantly.

But old habits persisted. Before he slept, he had to check the status flags. Then he checked the semaphore operators for anyone looking in his direction. Then, there was a list; Cerik warriors searching the coastline, Pet and his party of nomads, Elehadi, and Kakil Home.

The image of a Kakil Home resident swinging a short pipe, and connecting with another man's head dashed all hope for sleep.

What's going on?

There were dozens of people there in the crowed corridor, some trying to help the Smileys, Aarison's enforcers, others wanting to help the angry man. Bits of the story leaked through the chaos. Joshua struggled to put all the rumors and scraps of memory together.

After the rescue, when Sterling and Clark had gone missing, and Omelia was killed, Aarison, Elehadi's chosen leader of the Kakil U'tanse was called to account for his failures. Sterling, the son of Samson, had been a pet project of Elehadi and his loss wasn't something he was about to forgive. The Name sliced Aarison's face with his claw.

Aarison had returned from his interview and immediately went into hiding. Only a few of the Smileys and Aarison's personal healer had seen him, but everyone knew of the huge scar down the side of Aarison's face. It was devastating to the lone elder of Kakil Home. His carefully groomed appearance and his attraction to the girls had been constant reinforcement to his ego. Now, the scar drove him to hide in his chambers. The healer had done an excellent job of repairing the damage, but the scar had gone deeper than skin.

His ego was scarred. He couldn't look anyone in the face without imagining how they must see him. Even as the scar faded in the mirror, he still saw it.

Without his personal touch, several people talked openly about appointing new elders to take over. And the Smileys began stepping in to keep any group from forming to take real action.

Roland, one the more prominent of the Smileys, tried to report to Aarison.

Aarison stepped up, out of his bed, facing Roland and forcing the big Smiley to look down at the floor. A feel of the elder's old charisma came echoing back as he yelled at his subordinate.

"Little man, you've let things slide too far! You will go back there and let the dissidents know that rebellion won't be tolerated in these halls. You *will* make everyone do as you say, because if you don't, there's no place for you in Kakil Home, and you'll have to hike to Graddik Home and see if they'll take you in!"

From that day, Roland had changed. From a bully that was timid in the face of his master, he became more like a Cerik Second, just waiting for the moment to take the Name's place. The other Smileys came to him for direction, leaving Aarison alone with his healer.

The angry herder, gazed down at the bloody face of Eric, the Smiley he'd struck with the pipe. Blood rushed in Kurt's ears. He wanted to find Roland and make him bleed, too.

"Jumbo!" he called out, hoping Roland would hear him. "I'm coming for you! Nobody rapes my little Darla and gets away with it. I'll smash your nuts to paste!"

But the other Smileys were the only organized group in the Home. They formed a barricade in the hallway, holding stools to fend off the man with the pipe.

Roland yelled, "Porter, Ned, force him to the right!"

Anybody that might've helped Kurt abandoned him then. It was plain to everyone but the angry herder where they were driving him.

Quickly, they forced him though the airlock and into the night air outside. The door sealed shut.

Kurt slammed his pipe against the thick wooden doorway. "Don't think you can hide behind there forever! I'm coming for you, Jumbo!"

So intent on denting the airlock's outer door, Kurt didn't notice the Cerik warrior landing behind him, attracted to the angry shouting and the clanging of the pipe. The first swing of the claws severed the man's spine. The fountain of blood incited the killing machine even more, as he carved the U'tanse into pieces.

...

Joshua stared, wide-eyed at the dark, reddish metal hull above him. Other than his own ragged breathing, there was no indication of the carnage across the waves.

Letting his own heartbeat settle down, Joshua decided that his own companions didn't need the distraction. They didn't need any more than a sanitized version later.

But Very saw this in her dreams. No wonder it upset her like that.

Joshua felt the leaden realization that his faint hope that he could stop it from happening had been impossible anyway. He'd never been able to change what his sister had dreamed.

It's interesting, though. Before, her dreams had always focused on family members—my burns, Cyclops's injury, things like that. What caused her to pick up on this event? I half expected to be present when it happened.

...

Raids are something new. Joshua reminded himself. *We may have to abandon everything and swim for safety.*

The two of them pushed the inflated crate through the chop of the waves. Joshua noticed a seam in one of the dirty-white bags bubbling air. He paused a moment to crank the air pump, refilling the left-side bag. He mumbled to Patrick, "If we're discovered, stick a knife through the bags on both sides and get out of here."

The pilot grunted. "This is my plan, remember."

Joshua shrugged. "Habit. Your plan." *Mistake. I can't afford to make him my enemy.*

They reached the dark, volcanic rubble-covered beach and pulled the crate on shore.

Patrick said, "High tide is in six hours. If we don't get back in time, the waves will wash everything out to sea."

They'd brought four power cells, but they could only carry two on land. They wouldn't know until they tried if they could make two trips. With the excess two cells and the deflated bags stowed behind a large rock, Patrick took the front two handles and Joshua took the rear. Carrying the load up through an eroded waterway, they reached the flatter terrain in half an hour.

Patrick was breathing heavily and there was a hissing noise when he huffed out. His breather wasn't sealing tight.

Joshua said, "Let me take a quick scouting run up to the building and I'll make sure the entrance is accessible."

Patrick nodded, leaning on a rock, looking grateful for the moment's rest.

Joshua had all senses alert as he scrambled up the rest of the way to the empty landing pad. The area, blown free of gravel down to bedrock, showed that boats came to service the machinery and to load the completed pipes there.

The facility was a long half-cylinder, like a huge pipe itself, laid sideways and half-buried in the ground. The roof peaked thirty feet above him, but the sides were corroded and covered in vegetation that climbed high, clinging tightly to the exposed metal.

When Joshua reached out his hand to the entrance, perhaps large enough to fit a boat through, a loud, metallic rattle came from inside. He froze, probing inside with his *sight*.

He let out his breath. There was a bin that contained freshly extruded pipes, and periodically the pile got too high and pipes tumbled down to a lower level.

The doorway was Delense, and not familiar to him. The half-circular entrance was sealed from the weather by a curtain, hinged at the center on the ground like a huge hand-fan. He lifted one side and slipped through. He didn't have the time to figure out how it was supposed to work.

He stood in the darkness, looking over the large open expanse with his clairvoyance. The hillside behind was the ore deposit. In times past, Delense scooping machines would have kept the ore hopper filled, but from the shovels and carts, it appeared a U'tanse crew was brought in periodically to keep it topped up. Right now, it was two-thirds filled.

In the darkness, there was a pale red glow as heat leaked from the furnaces. The air was thick with gasses that were vented from the process.

Without the curtains open, the air inside might be too contaminated to breathe for very long, even with my filters. I need to keep an eye on Patrick as well. I don't trust his breather.

But between the furnaces and the extruder, there was a familiar control panel. He hurried over. *Yes!* There were two of the large-sized power cells supplying the facility. It would take a bigger work crew to move these, should they try to steal them directly. But if the harness worked properly, they could easily charge the two they brought and leave plenty of power for the pipe-making machine.

...

Patrick argued for more.

"This is an opportunity we can't pass up! We can fill all four of our cells. We could get all of our boats back in the air."

Joshua was bent over the power tapper, adjusting the level. His fingers were sweaty under his gloves. He was even tempted to take them off, but with the heat of the furnace, every surface was likely hot to the touch.

"Patrick, if we do that, this place will go cold before the next servicing crew arrives. The Cerik will demand to know how it happened, and probably blame the Dallah Home workers for the disaster. The Name will be involved and maybe they'll investigate what happened. No one can know we were here!"

He pointed at the little dial on his control pad. "See, if we just fill these two power cells and get out of here, then the plant will keep working. The service crew will realize they need more power brought in, but hopefully they will just assume it's normal variability in the process. We could get away clean with no suspicion.

"Patrick, the longer we can keep these thefts below their level of pain, the more of them we can pull off. The sooner the cry goes out that someone is stealing power, the more quickly we'll be shut down."

The pilot grumbled, "But that might happen this time, and we'd only have two cells worth for our efforts. It's getting close to the Faces, and more boats are in the sky because of it. A really good load of power now is better than two raids, with twice the danger of being caught."

Joshua shook his head. "You have to realize this is just a temporary fix! Just like our boats, we can only steal what they won't notice. We were doing fine for years making our own power with the turbine. If we rely on stolen power, our days are numbered. You've seen how much effort the Names have put into tracking down the rogue U'tanse, which they see like the Matt bar Keith family—just a few people barely surviving, hiding in a cave. If they suspect what we really are, a thriving group with our own boats and our own technology, then we'll be just as frightening to them as the Ferreer. They'll annihilate us all, just like they did the Delense."

Joshua took his hands away from the controls, making sure the transfer had finished. "No! If they know us for what we are, they'll put every boat into the air. They'll stop fighting each other and concentrate on finding us all, and eliminating the threat forever."

Patrick didn't reply. He just looked at the two large power cells, coughed, and sighed.

Uneasy Sleep

Back on course for Base and Factory, with two full power cells as the prize, Sally worked to make sure Patrick's lungs were fully healed.

He coughed. "You're not going to fight us on the next raid, are you?"

Joshua shrugged. "Not as long as we're smart about it. We need to investigate our targets carefully. Keep the thefts as painless as possible. Personally, though, I think we need to solve the main problem, how to get power from space for ourselves."

Sally inhaled sharply.

Joshua asked, "Yes?"

She looked at him. "You've heard about Kakil?"

Robert asked, "What about it?"

She looked at the others. "There was a killing."

Joshua shook his head in regret. "There was a power struggle. One of the Smileys—Aarison's people—raped one of the younger girls. Her father went hunting for the man with a pipe in his hand, looking for blood. It quickly got out of hand. One of the Smileys was hurt, but then the others forced the father outside. A Cerik came and killed him."

Robert looked sick. "I didn't realize it had gotten so bad there."

"It's getting worse by the day. I honestly thought things might get better when Aarison got slapped down for his failures, but it just made things worse. Instead of being a leader, he's hiding in his room, and his enforcers are running things on their own."

Sally said, "From what I can feel, the mood there is horrible. It's like Rikna all over again."

Robert shook his head. "I hope not. We're in no shape to pull off another mass rescue."

. . .

The mood at Factory was sober as well, in spite of their arrival with power cells. Ford had signaled via semaphore that the raid was to be kept quiet before they even docked. There were a few people that knew what had been attempted, but they were all in Ford's circle of advisors, and he had made it plain how critical it was to limit the number of people who knew. A charged power cell looked no different from a drained one. The discovery of more cells from New Home was noteworthy, but none of the new power went into Factory's fabricators, nor was any sent over to Base.

When they conferred in his room, Ford said, "Our top priority is getting the boats and the submarines charged up. Sitting here waiting while you guys went galavanting all across the ocean made me realize that getting back on track means quick and regular transportation between here and New Home. Nothing demonstrates it better than the minisubs. Factory can build the hulls and controls, but only New Home can make the thrusters that drive them. They've got technology in those fabricators of theirs that we desperately need in order to dig ourselves out of this mess."

He nodded to Patrick. "You've proven that a power raid is possible. Do you think we should do more?"

"Yes. Absolutely. Maybe we can power up everything on our own, but one raid on the clans and we now have the power it'd take Factory's hydro-electric system months to produce. Joshua is right to remind us that we're at a critical point. We need to be able to act quickly, no matter what the Names throw at us. We can't afford to wait it out."

Ford turned to Joshua. "You're the biggest critic of the raids. What do you say?"

Joshua stared at the table a moment, then faced him. "Patrick is right that a raid is a quick charge, but every time a power cell is drained, a Name is going to ask questions. If it happens once, it could be a technical problem. Twice, and he'll know it's theft, by somebody. By the third time, there will be warriors hiding in the shadows, waiting for us—at every factory site."

Patrick said, "So we'll rotate our targets. We hit Dallah this time, so Graddik the next time, and then Kakil, and so on."

Joshua shook his head. "No. Never Kakil. And we shouldn't be as predictable as heading north along the coastline. We can't assume the Names won't find out about raids on other clans."

"Why not Kakil?"

"Because the Names are going to find out about the raids eventually. They have telepaths, and they do try to spy on each other. Elehadi didn't make his private meadow to hide from us. He made it so he could plan his attacks on his neighbors without them listening in.

"Plus, all the clans get their power from Tenthonad. When the Names request more power than they've done in the past, Tenthonad will ask questions. If there is a thief, a Name will always suspect his neighbors first. And who is most in need of power?"

Ford nodded. "Elehadi is the best scapegoat. But looking at it from this angle, the Cerik are already hunting for rogue U'tanse that live on the coast. We need to avoid the easy coastline targets as much as possible. We'll need to fly in."

Joshua agreed, "We have to think about it as if Elehadi were planning the raids to get around his power restrictions. Nothing should point to U'tanse. Not even our scent. I worried about it at the pipe factory, but there were human tools all over the place. It won't be obvious that we were there."

The debate continued for a while, but the only thing decided was that the next target should be an inland facility in either Lanana, Runa or Lakka.

Sally, who had been listening the whole time, finally spoke. "This is all fine, but are we going to do *anything* about Kakil Home? The depression there is thick. I know from experience what's going to happen next—attachment! And when that happens, Elehadi will have his excuse. He'll *flick* the place. Maybe other Names will do the same, just to be safe."

Ford didn't disagree with her, but he didn't meet her eyes. "We have to focus on the tasks we *can* accomplish. If we can power up our boats, then maybe we'll be ready when disaster finally strikes."

...

The meeting ran long because they didn't have much time. Everyone felt the urgency of the moment. Ciara at Factory and Debbie at Base had gone over the listing of food supplies sent by New Home. The sub would carry the portions reserved for Base in the morning, and Joshua needed to be on the sub when it left.

Sally gasped, startled out of her sleep in the early hours. "Joshua, what was that?"

He struggled out of dreams he didn't care to examine. There were men shouting. He scanned the dock and muttered, "There was a small quake. Some loose rubble from the cliffs nearby fell into the bay, and the waves sloshed up onto the dock. Not much, but Larson's crew are making sure there was nothing damaged."

She leaned back down, resting in the crook of his arm. "I just hope the food was out of range."

"Probably. Half of it is sealed up tight in the sub anyway. Go back to sleep."

He half-dozed in the comfort of her presence. Shortly, he noticed her breathing slow down.

Why didn't I live in a time when I could live with her every day, and spend my days worrying about something boring? Some nice little chore like building furniture or herding runners? Wouldn't it be great to worry about keeping a dumb beast out of harm's way, instead of trying to manage a pet Cerik?

But once the thought intruded, Joshua couldn't help reaching out to the north, searching the most recent place he'd seen Pet and his group of nomads.

It was always harder for Joshua to find places in the dark, although he knew that clairvoyance had nothing to do with the light. It was his own mental quirk, he was sure. But the moon was bright, perhaps two-thirds full and overhead.

He found Pet, hunched down, peering from a cliff face in the higher mountains in Graddik territory, closer to Base than he'd expected. The nomad looked like he was hunting.

Pet turned his head, listening. Joshua tried to share the sound through his thoughts.

That's the buzz of a boat.

Pet zeroed in on the direction, moving closer to the rocks to prevent his outline from being seen. A flurry of tactical considerations flashed through his thoughts. He was on a steep mountainside. No boat could land close to him.

The buzz shifted and Joshua located the vehicle in his *sight*. It was descending, coming from somewhere to the south.

This is Graddik land. Who is it? Graddik's Perch is to the east. A raid from Dallah, maybe?

The transport cruised slowly and settled down on a wide patch of vegetation barely larger than the craft. Instantly, the hatch opened and two dozen warriors spilled out. Within seconds, they appeared to vanish in the deep shadows of the rocks. Less than a minute later, the boat lifted off and headed south.

Pet had seen it all. He watched, motionless until he saw the party move off westward toward the shoreline. Hurriedly, he moved to the other side of the ridge and raced to where his nomads were camped. They all needed to move. No matter what the warriors intended to do, if the nomads were discovered, they would be killed or captured.

Joshua split his attention, tracking the boat back to its source, and alternately monitoring the progress of the large party of warriors.

After a few minutes, he carefully removed his arm from under Sally's head, dressed, and threaded his way through Factory's tunnels until he reached Ford's room.

The man's snores were an easy hint that he was solidly asleep. Joshua rapped the doorsill. It took a few tries, but Ford snorted and mumbled, "I told you to let me get a solid six hours this time."

"Excuse me, it's Joshua."

Ford sat up and shook his head. "Sorry. Ed from construction has been waking me early for a week now." He sighed. "No help for it. What gets you up so early?"

Joshua chuckled ruefully, "I don't get much sleep, either. I discovered a new party of warriors, about twenty-five in all. They're about two days north of us, heading this way."

"Twenty-five! What are they up to?"

"It's hard to tell. The transport that dropped them off just an hour ago returned to Elehadi's staging area near the former Rikna Perch. There were dozens more warriors up and about there, as well."

Ford pulled on a robe and walked over to a work table. "Show me."

He pulled out a map, unrolled it, and set weights at the corners.

Joshua picked up a tiny metal cylinder, one of many loose on the table, and marked the location where he'd seen the warriors unload. He added a marker at the Rikna staging area.

Ford fingered the stubble on his chin. "That's pretty deep in Graddik lands, and staged from Rikna, you say?"

"Yes, Graddik has been moving its border with Rikna bit by bit. You think this is an attack on their rear? The warriors are keeping their movements concealed as much as possible."

"Possibly. I don't really care who claims the Rikna lands, but if they're moving as you say, they'll be right on top of us. We have to prepare to shut down again, quickly."

Joshua nodded. "That's why I interrupted your beauty sleep. My pet Cerik noticed their arrival, too, and raced out of the area to move his nomads."

Ford looked at him with a hint of distaste. "You're still watching the nomads? Why?"

Joshua shrugged. "Any Cerik is a hazard, in a clan or not. This one is interesting. I've spoken to him twice and walked away. Maybe there's something I can do with him eventually."

Ford shook his head. "Don't chase trouble. You have enough to do already."

Joshua sniffed. "I'm not doing this for fun."

Base Preparations

Everyone was up early and the submarine eased out from Factory in the dawn light.

Sally elbowed Joshua. "You look sad. Problems?"

He shrugged. "No more than usual. I happened to mention my pet Cerik to Ford, and he didn't like the idea that I was paying special attention to him."

Robert didn't divert his eyes from the window, but muttered, "Pet Cerik—*that's* a first."

"It's the one who chased Cyclops and me into the ocean, and its the same one I met when rescuing Prom. I actually talked him out of attacking me. I think he would be interested in talking more."

Robert shook his head. "That's crazy. No Free U'tanse should talk to a Cerik. You shouldn't even be seen."

"I didn't choose it either time. My job puts me near Cerik more than most. I've also spent years now monitoring them. It's no wonder that I'm interested in the way they think."

Sally put her hand on his wrist. "I don't like you being close enough to talk to one of them either. They're erratic and dangerous. They like killing, just for the fun of it."

He didn't try to argue any more. What they said was true enough, but it didn't look like anyone else could see the possibilities for a careful engagement with the Cerik. At least Ford, who was in charge, didn't give him explicit orders to avoid Pet. *I'll have to keep my thoughts to myself or he just might.*

...

Debbie and a work crew met them at the dock to unload the food from New Home. She frowned and gestured Joshua to the side.

He tensed, wondering what she would say.

"Joshua, what's this alert I just received from Factory about a possible blackout?"

He relaxed a little. He whispered, "There's a party of warriors heading down the coast, and they might come by here. If there's any chance they're too close, we'll shut down everything, just like last time. This group is larger than the last one, but it looks like they're just passing by. I hope."

She her frown deepened, "I hoped we were past that."

"We may never be past that. Even if full power is restored, we'll still have to go quiet when Cerik are around."

"Couldn't we just turn off the air circulation like last time? We don't *need* to go dark, do we?"

He nodded. "I bet that's what he meant, and just misspoke. Factory has to blackout the dock area so light doesn't leak through the curtains. It's different here. I'll signal to Factory for clarification."

Joshua looked her in the eyes and took her hand. "But right now, I need to talk to Veronica and Cyclops."

She tensed, then nodded. "We heard about the death at Kakil Home. That's what she dreamed, right? Why did she ever have to inherit that gift! I should have been more careful."

He squeezed her hand. "Mom, Very's gift is unprecedented. There's no way you could have known how to filter it out."

Debbie took a deep sigh. "Just don't make it worse for her."

He nodded. "I just need to talk with her some more."

"Go on ahead. I'll be hours getting these food bags sorted."

Joshua walked toward the ramp.

When it's time for Sally and me to have a baby, will I worry about which genes I'll be passing on? But I guess it's much worse for the mother who has to pick and choose which sperm makes it to the egg.

Joshua took a moment catch Bernard's attention at Factory and to semaphore a message to Ford: *"Clarification on Base blackout. Gardener panicking."*

By the time he had walked up to the second floor, Bernard signaled him with a reply: *"Watch status flag for notice. Shut down all machinery on signal. No power blackout."*

Joshua caught Ash on the ramp and told him to notify Debbie. He was glad to be right. Coordinating operations like this via semaphore was clumsy. It was better than signal flags alone, but each word had the potential for disastrous misunderstandings.

When he entered the nursery, he wasn't surprised that Sally had beaten him there. She was playing with Sterling as he was hitting everything in sight with a short stick made of bundled shash stalks.

"Hey there, Sterling," Joshua said. "I remember beating up on things with a stick, too." He picked up another of the play toys and sparred with his son. Sterling giggled.

Veronica arrived and waved to the cuties that were just a few years younger than she was. Sterling took that moment to make a very suspicious noise. Joshua smiled at Sally and handed the wiggly bundle back. She sniffed and gave her husband a frown.

"Gotta go," he said, gesturing toward Veronica. Sally glared and shook her head.

Outside in the corridor, Joshua asked, "You've heard about the Kakil Home killing?"

She nodded. "From what I heard, that was it. I've been trying to avoid thoughts from there as much as I can."

"I've got some questions, if you don't mind."

"Okay, come over to my room."

His sister led him to her place in a quiet section of chambers on the third level. Joshua noted the decorations on the wall: woven scenes, made from shash, corn stalks, and other seeds and leaves she'd collected from the gardens.

"Nice," he said.

She blushed. "It makes the gardening go a little easier if I'm looking for just the right leaf for my picture."

But then she looked serious. "What questions did you have?"

Joshua said, "Could I get some idea of what you were thinking about during the day *before* that nightmare?"

She relaxed a little, but frowned. "If I can. Why do you want to know?"

He explained about the family connection that was common to all the previous predictions. "I was afraid it was going to be something that happened to me or that I had to be there when it occurred, but that obviously wasn't the case. What triggered that particular nightmare?"

She leaned back, thinking. "I don't know what causes my dreams. It's not as straightforward as pulling weeds, and then dreaming about weeds—although come to think of it, that's happened."

"That was … I spent the day before in the nursery, helping out since Sylvia was on another project. Just an ordinary day with the cuties."

Joshua shrugged. "It's okay. I'm just trying to understand, as much as possible, how your gift works. I realize it's probably a lost cause, thinking we could control it, but just understanding the rules would help."

She laughed, "Does it have any rules? It feels random to me."

"There has to be some. I know of several nightmare-worthy events that didn't seem to trigger any dreams, and the ones we know about, other than this one, seem to have a personal connection to you."

She nodded thoughtfully. "Okay, if I think of anything. But I don't really have any connection to Kakil Home, though." She smiled. "I'm like you. I was born here."

Joshua frowned. "You have a little nephew now that was born in Kakil Home."

"Sterling?" She frowned. "I hadn't thought of that. Is there some kind of connection between him and the guy who died?"

"I guess it depends on how direct the connection has to be."

"Yes, I guess. If it's a friend of a friend kind of …."

He looked at the wrinkle on her forehead. "You thought of something?"

"Maybe."

"Explain."

"Okay, I was chatting with Jinger—playing with the *chitchit*, you know—and she said she was worried about a guy. Well, I know every guy in this rock, and Jinger doesn't know any of them, so I asked who it was. It seems she reads the thoughts of guys in the other Homes. She's even introduced herself, telepathically, to this guy. Don't remember his name …. Anyway, Jinger was worried about him, because he was worried about his family. And I think Jinger said he was at Kakil Home.

"Do you think that's enough of a connection? Seems pretty slim to me."

Joshua's mind raced at the problems Jinger could have caused just by introducing herself to a boy at another Home. She and a couple of others in the nursery had been rescued from Rikna and were well aware that Base wasn't the only place in the world. He'd never had the opportunity to tele-pathically meet girls, growing up in the rock.

But he had to get back to the issue at hand. "When people dream, they sort the day's memories. That's what I've been told. Maybe when you sorted that conversation, there was enough of a link back to Kakil Home that you picked up on … whatever it is that your dreams connect to."

"Weird."

He laughed. "It's in *your* head."

…

"Come on in," Cyclops called, as Joshua paused at the doorway.

"How are you doing?"

"Here, help me with this."

Joshua moved closer to adjust the cushion on his chair.

There was a stack of papers covered in his father's lettering beside the bed.

"It looks like you've made some progress."

Cyclops nodded, then adjusted the cloth around his head. It had slipped and exposed an empty eye socket, grown over with blank skin.

Joshua grimaced. "It does look better with your eye bandage."

Cyclops nodded. "Nobody admits it, but a man with no eyes makes people queasy. It's better this way."

Joshua nodded toward the stack of papers. "It looks like you've been busy."

"That library is twice the size of ours, and that's not counting all the log books and day-to-day record-keeping. I'm talking about real books. Many of them are the originals that were scavenged from the food trucks stolen by the Cerik from Old Earth. We have copies of some of them, but others were never duplicated.

"Tenthonad Home has an index, a list of all the books, and where on the shelves they are stored. It's lucky for me. But that list! In addition to the original books, there are histories of the early Homes. It seems copies were filed and kept at Tenthonad for at least the first five or six generations. I couldn't help myself from dipping into those."

Joshua smiled. He'd never seen his father so excited and pleased about anything. The man had been calm and serious about everything.

"Did you find anything interesting?"

Cyclops beamed, "It's all interesting. But for us, I guess the most important thing is the fights between the Homes."

"Fights?"

Cyclops nodded. "Nobody punched anyone, but it was a battle for markets, and for influence. At first, it seems, everything was shared. If one Home discovered a new technique for herding runners or repairing Delense equipment, they quickly shared it with all the others.

"But after time, and after a few Names expressed their anger at losing a trading advantage to a more nimble clan, the Homes began hoarding their knowledge. It became more formalized. New techniques were traded during the Festivals."

"Like we do now."

"Right. It's important to realize that the early Homes were as open and generous with information as we are between Base, Factory and New Home. But that's not how it is now among the Homes. The *ineda* that is a protection against the Cerik, and a protection for our developing children, has become a method of insuring trading advantages among clans and among the Homes.

"I guess that's when Homes started restricting which books they shared. That's probably when the history books stopped being archived at Tenthonad."

Cyclops nodded to himself. "And that's about the time that Tenthonad Clan took over the starships."

Waiting it Out

Joshua mused, "I think I've heard that term before. What's a starship?"

Cyclops patted the papers beside him. "The Book of James bar Bill is a treasure, and I certainly see why Tenthonad hoarded it. I'm only half way through it and when I get it finished, I want you to read it for yourself. For now, imagine a boat that was so large that a whole Home could fit inside. A starship has its own dock inside and an airlock where a half-dozen boats could be loaded."

"It has an airlock?" Joshua frowned. "Why?"

Cyclops grinned. "We have airlocks to keep filtered air inside and raw air outside. Starships have airlocks to keep the air in, because there's *no* air outside."

"No air?"

"Yes. Above the planet, there is no air. None."

Joshua took a moment to absorb the idea, but he had gotten very familiar with air pressure during the development of the minisubs. The pressure got higher the deeper into the ocean you went—it wasn't too much of a stretch to look the other way and realize that the air got thinner the higher in the sky you traveled.

"I see. The air runs out as you climb higher."

"Right. It took me a little bit to understand that, but I see you're ahead of me.

"But these starships are so huge that they can't ever land on the ground. They have to stay up in space. The boats, certain boats, make the trip from the ground to the starship to ferry cargo and passengers. One of those starships went to Old Earth and captured Father and Mother."

Cyclops shook his head. "I have trouble grasping it all. Supposedly there are several starships, and different clans owned their own. That's when the Ba and the Uuaa were captured, as well. But things changed. The Cerik were content with what they had and the starships were abandoned. At some point, probably suggested by the elders of Tenthonad Home, the other clans were prohibited from going into space to collect power. Tenthonad alone would make the runs, and thus control the supply of power cells to the whole planet."

Joshua frowned, "Why would the other clans give that up?"

"I don't know. I haven't seen an explanation. Maybe it was just easier for the clans to trade runners for power cells than it was for them to make the effort to get the power themselves. You reported to me that Elehadi was considering the effort to go back into space, but gave up the idea in trade for a *talespeaker*."

Joshua nodded. "Right. The gadget was a status symbol to Elehadi, but considering how important power to fly his boats is, it does seem that he settled too easily. But perhaps he was just bluffing. Maybe he didn't really know how to do it."

Cyclops said, "Let's hope there's enough information in the book. Patrick and the other pilots will probably need to look at it, too."

Joshua wondered if Patrick was too focused on the raids to consider it. But they would need power to make the attempt, so perhaps the raids were necessary.

Cyclops asked, "I know you're worried about other things. I can't help but pick up thoughts from the other Homes."

Joshua sighed, sadly. "Debbie is angry at me for bringing you into this."

He laughed, "I know. She scolded me for doing it. But I think it's been good for me. It's given me a chance to exercise my brain, and yet, I don't have to think about ... secret things that must not be leaked."

"I haven't felt any *ineda* leaks as we've been talking. You seem sharper."

He sighed, "I hope. But I have to take one step at a time. And it's been a refreshing change. Rest is important. I'm sleeping far too much these days, but I've needed to tackle something like this. Thanks for trusting me with it."

Confidently, Joshua said, "You're the only person who could do this."

"Maybe. Then again, since Homes are keeping more secrets from each other than I realized, perhaps there are others like me, and I've just not noticed."

Joshua laughed, "There's no one else like my father."

…

Ash frowned when the air grew still. Veronica looked puzzled. "What's the matter?"

Joshua, seated across the table from the two of them said, "The status flag at Factory changed, and all the machinery has been shut down. That includes the ventilation."

Ash nodded, "And that means that shortly, people are going to be calling on me to run around the rock since they'll all feel short of breath."

She looked up at the ceiling. "So, there are Cerik outside?"

Joshua took another spoonful of his bug stew. "They're not really looking for us. It's a group of warriors moving to ambush others from Graddik; one of the little clan battles that have been going on forever. Don't worry, I've been monitoring them."

"How long will this go on?"

"A couple of hours. Longer if they decide to go hunting."

Ash sighed, "There it goes. Paul is flagging me." He hurriedly scooped up the last of his meal and pushed his chair back.

Veronica offered, "I'll clean up."

"Thanks." He walked for the ramp at a brisk pace.

She picked up the bowls. "I wonder if I should go to the nursery."

Joshua shook his head. "Sylvia was warned in advance that this was coming. She probably has everyone down for naps. If Debbie wants you in the garden, then keep at it. I'm going to stop by and see Sterling anyway. If they do need any help, I'll let them know you're willing."

"Okay."

Joshua checked on the Cerik again as he walked to the nursery. They were spreading out, and the whole party was moving inland. They should be gone from the area within a couple of hours. He'd monitor their battle, but hopefully they'd return by some other route. Either that, or they'd be killed by the more entrenched Graddik warriors.

Joshua shook his head, dismissing the thought that must have come to many of the U'tanse. Life would be a lot better if the Cerik just managed to kill each other off.

The nursery was very quiet. Sally and Sylvia were sitting in rocking chairs, holding infants. Sterling was in his crib, sleeping along with many of the other cuties.

Jinger was rocking in a chair by herself, positioned so she could hop up and change diapers if the need arose. She looked looked up as he entered, but then nodded to him.

Joshua waved to Sally and silently picked up a stool and positioned it next to Jinger.

He whispered, "How are things going with you?"

Jinger knew him, of course, but they hadn't really talked much. She eyed him suspiciously. "Everyone's been down for a nap for nearly an hour now. Sylvia insisted."

"But what about you? How are you doing?"

He hadn't paid much attention to her in some time. Now, considering how she'd started hunting the planet for boys, he realized she had matured quite a bit.

He knew her story. She'd been one of the first ones they'd rescued from Rikna Home, during an early effort when a few cuties and infants were removed. That's when he'd met Sally, given the task to help him carry the infants.

Jinger had later suffered a case of attachment, strongly linked back to the minds of her friends back there. She'd never quite become part of the hive mind, and when the place was *flicked*, vaporizing all who were left, she seemed to return to normal. She was still a bit moodier than others her age.

Joshua had attempted to make her more sociable by putting her in charge of the pet *chitchit*. He wasn't sure that had helped. Now, she was near the age when she should be learning her *ineda* and considering moving out of the nursery.

She had no idea where she lived, other than that it was nursery in some other community. What she didn't know, she couldn't leak via incautious telepathy, like when making friends with boys in other Homes.

Jinger frowned, not sure what he wanted from her. "I'm okay, I guess. Sometimes it's a little boring. Your sister used to be here all the time, but she only comes by once a day or so. And Ash is never here anymore."

"Not many people your age left."

She wrinkled her nose. "No boys—at least, none that don't need their diapers changed."

Joshua sighed. "I grew up here. There weren't any interesting girls here then, either."

Jinger's mouth quirked up. She glanced over at Sally, then whispered, "You could dump her and sneak me out of here."

He laughed, a bit too loud because Sterling shifted in his crib. Joshua whispered, "Don't let Sally hear you say that. She's fierce."

He then said, "This isn't ideal here, I know, but there are worse places."

Jinger's eyes were wide. "I *know*! Hank's father—" She stopped cold.

"Go on."

She stared down at her fingers. "It's just that I've listened to thoughts other places, you know. You can't avoid it, really. And there's this boy, Hank over at Kakil Home. His father was locked outside and a Cerik killed him. He's all upset by it. His mother took his clothes and forced him to hide in her room, just so he wouldn't go out and fight the Smileys like he wanted to."

Joshua nodded, making the connections. Jinger had mentioned Hank to Veronica, and his sister had seen the connection to the boy's father in her dreams. That explained it.

He said, "That place is particularly bad."

Jinger looked at him carefully, "It's getting as bad as Rikna was."

"I'm afraid of that. When people feel trapped, they get depressed."

She nodded. "Yes. Hank doesn't know what to do. His sister is missing and his mother is afraid to go outside in the hallways. Neighbors brought them food, but she just sits by the door, doing nothing but make sure that Hank doesn't try to go out and get himself killed."

Jinger chewed her lip.

"Yes?" he asked.

"Well, I've been thinking. When it was bad at Rikna, you came and got some of us out. Can you get Hank out of Kakil Home?"

He sighed. "Something like that is very difficult, you know."

She nodded, "I know. It's just that I know where it's going. Everybody gets depressed and people huddle together for comfort. There's no way out, except...."

He didn't want to put the words in her mouth. He waited.

She took another breath. "People get trapped, and then there's nothing else to do but share each other's thoughts. When you hurt, you want people to comfort you. But it can go too far."

She watched his face. "I know everybody has been watching me since Rikna. When Harmony, Mary and Fancy... attached, they wanted me to join them, even though I was far away." She brushed her hair out of her eyes. "I don't remember it all, but I'm afraid for Hank and his mother. It won't be long for them."

Joshua looked down at his hands, his own memories of Rikna came to haunt him too frequently. "Not everyone at Rikna, even at its worst, joined the hive mind. Some people held on their identity, even with friends and relatives calling them to join. If Hank and people like him can keep their hope alive, they can resist it."

Jinger grabbed his hand. "But do they have anything to hope for?"

Joshua realized his face had gone stiff and solemn. He forced a smile, holding her hand in both of his. "I have hope for them. If they can just hold out a little longer, there is hope." He had no plan, but he had to hold onto his own hopes. She needed that, too.

"But for now, you can help. Maybe better than anyone, you can recognize the signs of attachment. Give us early warning. Pass that information on to any of the adults the instant you sense it."

He hated to wave aside her real concerns with platitudes, but unless things changed—and quickly, Kakil Home would go the way of Rikna. The Names would get yet another example of fixing a U'tanse problem with a ball of fire.

Transcribed

Robert shook his head. "It makes no sense if I don't even have enough power. Not that I don't mind living at Base for a while, but I've been working with Simon on the little subs at Factory, and I'm stuck here until there's a big load to carry across the bay. Planning for an exploratory cruise up to Far Island is just a waste of time."

Joshua tossed him the brush, and Robert went inside the hatch. Knowing he was signing up for cleaning duty, he grabbed another brush and followed.

"I realize we can't go now. It's just that I want your perspective on it. You'll be in charge when it happens. Like you said, you're stuck here. But Base has the best maps of the West Coast. What harm is there in planning a trip, once we have the time and power to handle it?"

Robert pointed at the benches. "Okay. Explain it to me again."

Joshua started on the right front and began scrubbing.

"When we found the entrance tunnel at the seamount, I realized that the Delense had spent considerable effort over time building numerous secret bases. Every one of the ones we've found have been discovered by accident. Doesn't it make sense that there are probably others that we haven't found yet?

"If we cruised up the mainland coast at the correct depth, looking for entrance tunnels or collections of Delense debris, then circled Far Island doing the same, I bet we would find more."

Robert was carefully cleaning the windows, taking his time to get it perfect. "I think you're probably right, but why now? Why not wait until our power supplies are secured?"

Joshua paused to look at him face to face. "Because we have three communities and a growing probability that one of them will be discovered. In addition, Kakil Home may fall apart on us. We just might have to pull off another large rescue. If we had at least one more secret base that we might use at a moment's notice, I'd feel a lot better about our chances for survival."

Robert grumbled, "I'd feel a lot better about this talk of evacuating Base or Factory if we had several more full-sized submarines. It's all very well to consider moving everyone, but the most I've ever carried at one time was just over a dozen people."

Joshua agreed. "You saw the underground dock at New Home. You saw those machines. Somewhere in this world are Delense submarines that can carry them. They would be bigger than this one by far. They might be resting in a forgotten base just up the coast. Who knows what we'll find if we go looking?"

"If they're not rusted away on the sea bottom."

"Like this one? Didn't Aaron manage to re-float this one and rebuild it?"

"Yeah, but it took them years to do it, and they didn't have Cerik boats flying overhead all the time."

Joshua shrugged. "Things change. The over-flights aren't as frequent anymore. After the Faces, Elehadi will lose a lot of incentive to add more human heads to his pile."

Robert shook his head. "I know wishful thinking when I hear it. He may just decide to add the whole Home to his collection, the way it's falling apart."

...

The gentle, almost imperceptible, air circulation was greeted with smiles all through Base. Ash collapsed at the tables and demanded a sweet rice pudding sprinkled with dried strawberries. The cook had seen him on his feet the whole time and provided the treat without complaint.

The Cerik had moved on, vanishing into the high mountains that formed the boundary between Graddik, Dallah and the former lands of Rikna—at least as marked on the map up on the fourth floor. The actual boundary was in constant flux. Over the past six years, there had been no effort to update the map. It wasn't worth the effort.

Pet and his nomads were also moving into the high mountains, trailing the warriors by a day. They were also taking a slower route farther from the coast. Joshua monitored their actions carefully before deciding that they were too far inland to notify Ford.

It was the first time Joshua had seen female Cerik on the move. The smaller shapes seemed to cluster toward the center of the party, with no obvious effort from the males to control them. The difference between their actions in the wild and those of females in the breeding pits of the larger clans made him watch for longer than he usually spent on the nomads.

Was this the original behavior of the Cerik? Or were there two instinctive behaviors among the females—one for travel and another when the clan settled into a new home territory?

Joshua sighed. There were so many mysteries. The small female Cerik who didn't even have language was just one. He'd never solve them all.

…

Cyclops handed him the book, still a loose pile of pages.

"I've finished. But I'll be reading from the Tenthonad library for a while. I'll copy whatever I find particularly interesting."

Joshua checked the small stack of pages and bundled them tight. "Thank you. I was afraid it'd be as long as the Book itself."

Cyclops chuckled. "James bar Bill wasn't a practiced writer like Abe. It's a little stiff to read, but he doesn't waste any words. It's full of valuable information. Certainly the pilots need to read it. James was coached on how to leave the planet and how to land safely by the Ferreer themselves. He probably wouldn't have survived otherwise."

"The Ferreer? How?"

"Read it yourself. I'm afraid I'm a little tired. I stayed up long hours to get this completed before you hurried off on your next adventure."

Joshua smiled. "Adventure? Is that what I'm doing? I thought I was experimenting with how to keep from dying without knowing what I'm doing."

Cyclops nodded, "Or that. Anyway, you're doing a good job."

Joshua left with a glow from the praise, but suspecting his father was just saying what good fathers were supposed to say.

Only a few yards down from his father's room was the Base library. It didn't seem all that long ago that copies were made of several books, including the Book, to be sent off to New Home. Books were terribly scarce among the Free U'tanse. People rescued from disasters never brought their books along with them. The books collected in front of him had been acquired one by one during Festivals, and since his father had gotten involved, by hand-copying books he could *see* with his extraordinary clairvoyance.

The bulk of the written material in this room were logbooks, daily records of crop yields and materials fabricated from Factory across the bay. A large number were their spy records. The thoughts and actions of the U'tanse and the Names in the various clans collected via telepathy and clairvoyance. Joshua's time monitoring Samson the Giant was all in there. Cyclops was insistent on keeping records, and it showed in all these cubbyholes.

But the result was years' worth of practice turning written sheets into a bound codex with the binding clamp and the glue pot. Clamped tight while the glue hardened, he began to read the unwieldy pages.

...

The glue was long dried and his rump was stiff from sitting in the same chair for too long when Lincy walked into the library. She nodded his way and then put a scroll into one of the square cubbyholes.

She was about to leave when Joshua asked, "How long would it take you to copy this book?" He held it out.

She frowned at the binding clamp. "It would have been easier before it was bound, but perhaps three hours." Opening the book and flipping through the pages, she asked, "Cyclops wrote this?"

"Transcribed it."

Lincy was one of the few who was aware of the man's capabilities. "So ... His handwriting is a little shaky, but I won't have any trouble with it. I assume it's urgent. Everything is urgent these days."

"I'd like to take a copy with me over to Factory in the morning, but I'd like to preserve the original here, just in case."

She grinned. "Don't go chasing any *jandaka* now."

He shuddered. "Never."

"I'll have it ready for you before you leave."

...

Joshua flagged down Bernard and sent two coded messages:

"To Patrick, Carson, Den, and Prom: Would like a private meeting noon tomorrow."

"To Ford: Wish to discuss important information with pilots tomorrow. Swimming over early morning. Can tow limited items."

Bernard replied:

"Can you bring jandaka tooth? Prom bragged about it."

...

In the quiet of their bedroom, Joshua told Sally about the Book of James bar Bill.

She raised an eyebrow. "Are you sure you should be telling me this? There are so many secrets these days and it doesn't sound like something I'll be working on."

He shrugged. "No, I shouldn't. But I think you might appreciate it."

So he told her the tale, a bit paraphrased, about the first *tenner*, barely older than Ash, chosen for the task of transporting the attached young girl to the planet of the Ferreer.

Sally asked, "So Abe the Father ordered this just in order to avoid having to kill her?"

"It seems that way. This was an early case of attachment, and they had tried everything to break her out of it and failed. What's amazing to me is that Tenthonad, the Name of the clan at the time, actually permitted it. As far as I know, this is the only time a U'tanse was allowed to fly a boat on his own."

"The Name was the same as the Clan?"

Joshua nodded. "A clan's name comes from the founder, or when a new Name achieves greatness far beyond the original. I'm sure Elehadi wants to rename Kakil after himself, but it'll only happen if he does something that really impresses the other Names."

"Like what?"

"Like wiping out the U'tanse forever."

She shivered. "But I guess it's uplifting to know that there was a time when human lives were actually valuable. It seems like we've fallen so far when all the Names are scheming to get rid of us and there are places like Kakil Home where we're killing each other."

He nodded. "We've got to change that downward trend, somehow. If we aren't valued, we'll never survive. The Cerik are natural killers and they've only put up with us this long because of what we've supplied them."

Pass the Book Around

"Be careful with that bundle. There's a *jandaka* tooth wrapped up inside."

The three Factory dockhands who were helping him out of the water were suddenly much more interested in the tow bag than with waterlogged Joshua.

The swim over had been longer than normal, since he took a different route, sticking to waters shallow enough that he could watch for Delense debris. He hadn't expected to discover anything—the submarine had been making trips through the bay long before he was born. But if he was going to urge submarine pilots to spend more time searching, then he'd better do the same.

Once the bag was pulled up, one of them asked, "Can we see it?"

"Sure." He unsealed the tow bag and pulled it out, unwrapping the jagged tooth as long as his forearm. Quickly drying off and dressing, he gave the men a quick recap of the story of Prom bleeding in the water and attracting the giant beast's attention.

The one with a dark beard said, "I helped pull the minisub out. The sides had these long scars in the metal." He shook his head. "It's a wonder you survived."

Joshua grinned, "I thought so, too."

He stowed his breather and swimming gear in a storeroom, then looked around the dock for any of the people he needed to meet. It was mid-morning and although the makeshift dining area was still cluttered with tables and the cooking gear, there were only two of the cooking crew there, preparing for Factory's mid-day meal.

With a newly bound book in a side pouch, a bundle of spices in his arms, and the tooth slung over his shoulder on lanyards, he headed for the kitchen.

Ciara looked up, eyes wide when she saw the tooth.

Joshua held out the bundle. "Here's the package from Debbie."

She opened the package and sniffed. "Great. With the food supplies from New Home, I needed different ways to make them palatable."

"I'm looking forward to some of your special bug stew, then."

"I'll make something extra for the evening meal, just for you."

Walking through the corridors of Factory with the tooth on display caught everyone's attention, and nobody even mentioned the pouch at his side.

It was fun, showing off the tooth, but the story was spreading faster than he was walking, so people already knew the most of it by the time they stopped him to have a look.

Talking with everybody he met, even some he'd never met before, also spread the news that he was back at Factory. For the few who asked *why* he was back, he commented on the delivery of new spices for Ciara. That was good enough for them.

Prom was already waiting in the private meeting room Bernard had set up for them.

"You brought it."

Joshua set the tooth out on the table.

Prom hesitantly reached out to touch it. "Sometimes I think it was all a dream."

Patrick walked in, followed quickly by Den and Carson. The elder pilot saw the tooth and grinned. "Ah. You called us together so we can go hunting *jandaka*?"

Joshua and Prom cried, "No!" at the same instant.

They laughed. Joshua said, "Den, could you close the door? It's only us five."

The mood shifted to solemn. Closing a door to a meeting was rare and significant. Den closed it and rotated the latch.

Joshua said, "Go ahead, take a look."

The pilots wanted a chance to touch the tooth, as well. When they were done, everyone looked at Joshua.

He shrugged. "The tooth was requested, but it was a bit of a distraction." He pulled the thin book from his pouch and set it on the table. "This is what I wanted to talk about."

Prom stepped closer to the table. "What is it?"

Joshua pushed it toward his hands.

The historian hurriedly opened the pages. "This is a fresh copy of—"

He looked over at Joshua, his eyes wide. "It can't be. How did you get a copy of the Book of James bar Bill? There are no copies, and the original is in the library at Tenthonad Home."

"I can't say."

Patrick sighed, "Believe him. Some secrets are limited to just a handful of people."

But Prom didn't listen. His eyes were on the text. He turned a page.

Den asked, "Can we look at it, too?"

Joshua nodded. "That's my intention, but I think if I tried to pry it out of Prom's hands right now, I might lose a finger."

While Prom read, not even taking time to sit down, Joshua talked quietly with the pilots.

"You heard Prom's narration when he first arrived?"

Carson said, "I did. Patrick was still at New Home."

Den shook his head. "I missed out. Carson was senior pilot at that meeting, but I heard some stuff."

"Okay, then. Prom tells it better, but back in the early days, a young man was given the task to fly into space with an attached girl and deliver her to the Ferreer planet. As part of the job, he had to fly a boat down to the planet's surface and then later fly back up into space. He did this alone, with no Cerik help. Abe the Father ordered him to write a detailed report of all that he did. That's the book."

Patrick looked over at Prom, still reading. "So it's an instruction manual. With that, we can go into space?"

"Maybe. I need you pilots to read it."

Prom sat down. He looked dazed. Patrick reached over, took the book, and started to read.

Prom said reverently, "I've been wanting to read that all my life."

Joshua asked, "Is it what you expected?"

Prom sat down. "I didn't know what to expect. It's roughly what I thought it would be—after all, my mother read it. But for me, a *tenner*, it's so important! I think Ace should read it, too, when he gets back from New Home."

"What didn't you expect?"

Prom thought a moment. "The piloting stuff is beyond me. I don't understand why he did a lot of the things he considered important. But the Ferreer stuff was intriguing. They don't sound like monsters. That's always how they've been portrayed."

Joshua nodded. "They sounded so confident and patient in the book. Not at all like the hive mind that tried to take me over at Rikna Home."

Prom said, "Perhaps it was because these Ferreer, the originals, had a whole planet, multiple planets probably. They were in no danger from a single human. At Rikna Home, the hivers were fighting for their survival, and lost."

Joshua tapped the table, "Now, the girl, so desperate to lose her identity in something bigger—that felt very familiar. That's what I'm afraid will happen again at Kakil."

Patrick passed the book over to Carson after a bit.

"Well?" Joshua asked.

Patrick frowned. "We're going to need more power."

"Why?"

He looked up. "I was thinking that all you needed was to go up for a few miles, and then you'd be in space. Just do the elevate slash and keep going up." He waved his hands in the gesture used by the piloting controls. "But from the book, it sounds like you have to go up like a hundred miles or more and go sideways across the planet for thousand and thousands of miles, gaining speed all the time. That's beyond the range of any of our boats, if I'm understanding it right."

As Carson finished reading, he joined in the debate.

"There's something I don't understand. The air gets thinner as you go higher. I've always been aware of that, because even though we *fixed* boat B, it still leaks air, and I deliberately fly low because of it.

"From the book, it seems the word 'atmosphere' actually means the air around a planet. Before I just assumed it meant the *area* around a planet, like a coast is ground around the sea. So if that's the case, then a boat runs out of air before it reaches space. Since we fly because the engines grab air and pull it round the boat, how does it fly in space? How does it even reach space?"

Patrick said, "The leak rules out boat B for a space-power expedition, then. I guess, from James's explanation, the boat automatically switches methods of propulsion. We've always known the controls were dumbed-down so Cerik could pilot them, after all. In the book, piloting was a matter of choosing a target and letting the machine decide how to get there. That matches a lot of how we fly."

Carson said, "He talks about aiming the boat once he's in space. Is that in the advanced controls only Delense and U'tanse can use? If so, I've never learned it."

Den set aside the book. "Neither have I. There's a lot of stuff in here that I've never heard of before. What did you say earlier, about boat B not being able to go into space?"

They discussed boats and the book for an hour before Patrick sighed. "There's not much more we can do without help. We really need to pull Ace in on this. He's the guy who understands the science."

Joshua reminded them, "Don't forget Betty. Ace is the pure science guy, but Betty knows Delense machines and control systems better than anyone else I know. Together, they're one of our greatest strengths."

Patrick raised his voice slightly. "I agree. Let's table this and go on to our other issue. Prom, have we kept you too long?"

"No, fine. I realize how it is around here. Thanks for letting me read the book. Really, it's something I've dreamed about for years."

When Prom closed the door behind him, Patrick said, "Okay, let's talk about the next power raid."

The Leak

Joshua had to keep himself from smiling too broadly. Things had gone better than he'd hoped. The pilots were now completely on board with the idea of getting power from space, especially now that they had a report written by someone that had seen it done in person. They knew which steps to take. Now it was just a matter of figuring out how to do those steps.

They were still on target for a second power raid—this time, a grain processing center in the Lanana lands far from any shoreline. Joshua had watched Patrick carefully as they discussed the plans. The lead pilot was playing things much more cautiously than before. They were even planning to scout out and map the plant before attempting to leave.

Den's boat A, smaller and able to land on water in a pinch, was chosen as the best craft for the raid. There was room for the crew and five empty cells.

At least that was the plan so far.

Joshua found a quiet place in Factory. The air was a little too sharp with residue from the machines, but no one was around. He settled into a chair and worked his mental list.

Status flags at each of the communities were green with the black circle.

At Base, he could *see* Sally talking with Debbie and gesturing in the direction of the nursery. He could guess where she'd be next.

The Cerik warriors in the high mountains were spread wide, and he wasn't sure how their battle was progressing. Were they taking out Graddik warriors one by one? Cerik battle tactics weren't something Joshua had studied, even if he did have some familiarity with them from his days monitoring Samson.

He scanned for Elehadi, and found him at his Perch. Stakka, his chief telepath, was arguing with him about something. If Joshua didn't already know their long and close partnership, he'd have thought they were on the verge of killing each other. Unfortunately, there was no one around with an unblocked mind so that he could hear them.

Reluctantly, Elehadi jumped from his perch and fell into pace behind Stakka. They were obviously in a hurry.

Joshua pulled out a folded sheet of paper and a charcoal stub in case he wanted to take some quick notes. Something interesting was going on.

The closer the Cerik got to the stream, the more uneasy Joshua felt. This was the path between the Perch and Kakil Home. He resisted the urge to *look* ahead, for fear he'd miss something. At the rate they were traveling, they'd be there quickly.

Soon, he was certain that the Home was their destination. A quick *look* confirmed that there was a large man waiting there for them. And at his feet was a boy, holding his leg in pain.

Joshua switched his attention there.

The man was Roland, the head Smiley, and his mind was open. Joshua scanned the surface thoughts.

He's coming. He'll see that I'm the one in charge here. I can give him what he wants. If I can just get through this before Aarison notices. I should have barricaded his door.

The boy at his feet had no breather, gasping in raw air. Waves of pain boiled off of him every time his broken leg shifted.

Joshua was tense. Were they going to kill the boy? What was Roland trying to do?

<For your Name!> Roland bellowed out, even before Elehadi came to a stop, a breach of protocol that the Smiley probably didn't even know.

Elehadi stalked closer. <What of the injured cub? You wish me to gut him for you?>

Roland stood his ground, bobbing his head, which probably meant nothing to the Cerik. <The cub knows things. He knows about the others.>

Joshua took in a sharp breath.

Elehadi asked, <Which others do you speak?>

Roland looked down at the boy. <The cub spoke of other U'tanse, unknown U'tanse who would come to take him away.> He took in a breath. <Take him away like they took the son of Samson.>

Elehadi hissed.

Roland tensed, <Truly, I have seen it in his mind. He can reach the minds of the others.>

Elehadi turned to Stakka, <Find them!>

Roland kicked the boy. "Go on! Make contact with your Jinger!"

Joshua was up on his feet. He located Paul at Base. He was down at the dock, facing away. He located Ash.

Stakka turning and moved close to face the boy so that they would see each other's eyes. Roland yelled, "Call Jinger!"

Ash was talking with Veronica, trying to calm her down. He turned to face Factory and noticed Joshua, his hands on his head, actually bouncing up and down.

Ash put out his arms to acknowledge. Joshua didn't wait. He sent: "Emergency, tell Jinger *ineda*. Close her eyes."

Ash started to run.

The boy, Hank, in pain and fearing every second that he'd be ripped apart just like his father, reached out for the strange girl who had told him that there was hope.

In Base's nursery, Jinger was walking from the *chitchit* pen toward the cribs when she suddenly stopped still. She felt a familiar call, but as she focused on Hank's thoughts, the wave of pain caused her to stumble and fall.

Stakka *preed* as he caught hold of the distant mind, sensing the female's concern.

Ash raced down the corridor. He reached the ramp and started down to the second level.

In the nursery, Sally saw Jinger stumble, and holding Sterling, moved a step closer to the girl.

Jinger put her hand to her head, confused and distracted by the pain.

Joshua could hear Sally's voice though Jinger's thoughts. "Are you okay?"

Roland, reading Jinger's thoughts now as well, took in a breath.

Ash reached the nursery door and fumbled with the black dots on the circular lock controller.

Jinger looked up at Sally, holding Sterling. "I'm okay."

Roland shouted, <I see her! The one who stole Samson's cub!>

Stakka said, <The cub is there, with the others.>

Elehadi hissed again. <Locate them for me!>

Ash raced into the room, tapping his forehead like mad. Jinger's eyes widened, recognizing the call for *ineda*, and although her skills weren't great, she began to close down her thoughts. Ash reached up and put his hand across her eyes.

Joshua lost his contact with her mind, but through his *sight*, he could see the confusion in the nursery. Sterling was handed off and put back in his crib, screaming. Sylvia helped Sally walk Jinger, her face still covered, out of the nursery.

Joshua turned his attention back to Kakil Home.

Stakka said, <They sensed us. Her mind is closed.>

Elehadi asked, <What did you see?>

Stakka hissed. <There wasn't much. Cubs and females.>

Elehadi turned to Roland, <What did you see?>

Roland straightened. It was his time to prove his worth.

<I saw a U'tanse nursery. It was inside a cave. The walls were stone. The lights were electric. The furniture was well crafted. This wasn't just U'tanse that had escaped Rikna. It wasn't a crude hiding place. It was a place where U'tanse have lived for years. It was a place where they raised their children.>

<But where is it! U'tanse can sense locations, can't they?>

Roland lowered his head. <Yes, but finding a place by thoughts alone is a difficult task. It could be anywhere.>

Stakka growled, <The broken cub is the key. He can reach the female. Through her, we can find more.>

Elehadi asked, <Where is your leader?>

Roland said firmly, <Aarison remains hidden, afraid to show his face.>

Elehadi gestured with his claw. <Take this one inside and keep him alive. We will be back tomorrow, and the day after that. If we find these others, you will have the name you seek. If you fail me, I will cut more than just your face.>

Joshua sagged and held his head in his hands. His stomach churned and the taste was bitter in his mouth.

It's my fault. I should never have told Jinger I had hope for her friend. I should have known she'd turn right around and tell him that. Now Stakka knows Sally's face, and Elehadi knows that we have Sterling.

...

Joshua sent a message to Ash to pass on to the others: *"Elehadi's telepath has seen Sally and Sterling through Jinger's eyes. Roland the Smiley is assisting him, describing what he saw of the nursery. Hank has a broken leg but has been turned over to healers. It is essential Jinger maintains her* ineda. *Stakka knows her mind and can reach it at any time. They will attempt to read everything she knows."*

Ash raced off to deliver the message, stumbling in the hallway, but picked himself up and ran his hardest.

Joshua sighed, holding the wall to keep himself steady. "Now the hard part."

He paced through the corridors, watching every step, until he reached Ford's office.

The door was open and Ford was sitting at his table, pen in hand. The place was a lot more organized now that he'd settled in. There were shelves along the wall, many containing stacks of papers. His workspace was relatively clean.

Ford glanced up to see who it was, and then looked back at his document, concentrating on work. "What is it?"

Joshua slumped down in the nearest chair. "We've had a telepathic leak."

Ford looked up, his eyes fierce. "What? Who?"

Joshua shook his head, brushing his hair back from his eyes. "It was one of the older cuties in the Base nursery. One we rescued from Rikna Home."

"Her name?"

"Jinger."

Ford frowned. "She's the one who was attached, right?"

"Yes. And she was picking up all the distress over at Kakil Home. And not surprising for a girl that age, she befriended a boy. When he was depressed, she tried to cheer him up by saying that we would rescue him."

Ford's frown grew stonier. "In the nursery, she got that idea?"

Joshua closed his eyes. "She got it from me."

There was no response.

He looked at Ford, but the man's face was still and unreadable.

Joshua continued. "I was there, checking to see what she knew about Kakil, and she asked me. She knew Sally and I pulled her out of Rikna before it burned. She asked me to rescue Hank, the boy."

"And you said yes?" His voice was tense, almost strident.

"I said something like that was difficult, but that I had hope."

Ford threw down the pen he'd been holding, knocking aside the ink pot, spilling it across the table and splattering the paper. "So she took that as a yes! Why in the world did you feed her false hope?"

Joshua spread his hands. "At that instant, I realized I had no *reason* for hope, but I still had it. I told her that to cheer her up. I was stupid not to realize she'd do the same for her friend."

"How bad is this leak?"

"Pretty bad. The boy, I guess, attacked Roland, the chief Smiley. He broke the boy's leg, and his spirit. Somewhere in there, the information that there might be 'others' out there who would rescue him was spoken.

"Roland, hoping to usurp Aarison's place, contacted Stakka, who brought Elehadi in. They forced the boy to contact Jinger, and Stakka and Roland rode the connection. They saw Sally and Sterling through Jinger's eyes before I managed to get a message through to them. Jinger had enough *ineda* to close the connection, but not before Roland recognized Sally from the rescue attempt."

"And the boy, did he survive?"

"Oh, yes. Elehadi realizes he's their best bet to break through to Jinger again. Healers are fixing his leg and lungs."

"And the girl, Jinger?"

"She's isolated in a room of her own, Comfort and Debbie are with her now, probably giving her intensive coaching."

Ford gave an exasperated sigh. "So Elehadi knows there's a group of U'tanse who have rescued people before and are possibly willing to do it again. He had suspicions before, and now they've been verified. At the least, he'll shout that out at the Faces and have all the Names up in arms."

Joshua shook his head. "That's already out. Probably everyone in Kakil Home was watching Roland pull his power play. Many of them could ride the telepathic connection like Stakka and Roland. Even if Roland wanted to keep it quiet, everyone knows. They can put the pieces together just like we did.

"All of Kakil Home knows that we exist. They suspect we rescued many from Rikna. They're wondering among themselves if we'll try the same again."

Ford closed his eyes.

"So the whole world knows. So much for living in secret."

"They still don't know where we are."

Ford shook his head. "Doesn't matter. Even if we didn't exist, everyone thinks we do, so the Names have to act. Their whole view of the world is master and slave. There's no place for free U'tanse."

He scooted his chair back and stood up. "I *hate* the idea that a youngster changed everything. I was barely coming to grips with the job of keeping this secret base alive, what with the power outages and hiding from the overflights. Now it's so much worse."

Joshua protested, "She's just a little girl."

Ford faced him. "I was talking about you!"

Ford's Orders

Joshua said nothing. Ford was right. Everything he'd done since he left the nursery himself had led up to this catastrophe. The Free U'tanse had edged out a growing culture of their own, expanding their numbers and reaching out and rescuing the abandoned—all because their existence was secret from the Cerik.

He had been one of the strongest proponents of secrecy. He'd fought for that when New Home was established and trained the semaphore operators in the use of codes.

Was it all going to collapse? How much time did they have before another clue was added to what Elehadi already knew—a clue that would let him send his warriors to slaughter them all?

Ford asked, "So, what are you going to do?"

Joshua looked up, startled out of his thoughts of doom. "What?"

"It was a mistake, a disastrous mistake, to let that girl feed hope of rescue to Kakil Home. But now that they know, they're looking for us to act."

Ford picked up his pen from the floor. "This isn't my job. I ran a factory! I scheduled workers." He waved to the desk. "I can barely handle the paperwork."

He picked up a towel and started cleaning up the spilled ink.

"But you got us into this. You rescued that girl. You filled her head with the idea that we would rescue Kakil. So do it!"

Joshua frowned. "I still don't know what—"

Ford said, "You've been running around all over the place, off on your special projects; making submarines, talking to Cerik nomads, planning trips into space to collect power, and who knows what else. Starting right now, I'm *giving* you a project: Rescue them."

Joshua hesitated, then he asked, "Rescue Kakil Home?"

Ford yelled, "Rescue everybody! Now get out of here. I've got work schedules to straighten out."

…

Joshua walked the corridors of Factory in a daze for a while. What did Ford even mean?

Certainly he couldn't hop into Den's Angel and fly over to Kakil. Or could he?

If there was a rescue attempt, and it failed spectacularly, with the boat captured and the rescuer killed, then maybe Elehadi, and everyone else, would think that it ended there. Then there would be no need to launch a massive search for the 'others'.

He shook his head. Samson took the option to die—to go out in a blaze of glory. He followed his duty to the end, and put a stop to the hive mind that would have taken over the whole world.

That isn't my duty. I'm supposed to rescue everybody. He chuckled under his breath, but it bubbled up loud enough to be heard. He clamped down on it.

That was impossible. Even if all the Cerik went to sleep. Even if Patrick stole all the power cells they wanted and ferried the U'tanse out of their Homes in vast numbers, where would they go?

Maybe there were more secret bases. But even then, there was an economy that kept people alive. Those Homes were more than old burrows. They were now the filtered air that people could breathe. They were the gardens that grew crops that humans could eat. They were the whole basis of human existence on the planet Ko.

As long as I'm thinking big, why not kill all the Cerik? That would rescue everyone.

He didn't even like the idea as wish-fulfillment. Cerik were killers, but not humans. Especially not telepathic ones. There was a reason the telepath *tetca* among the Cerik were not at all respected. A telepath couldn't be a warrior. The feedback from the killing was almost as devastating to the killer as it was to the victim.

He shook his head. Thinking big was getting him nowhere. *Think small.* Who should he rescue first?

...

He'd noticed people looking his way. The idea that there were other U'tanse, perhaps free U'tanse, was spreading across the planet. Gossip in Factory was of necessity limited to speech, but the word was getting around here, as well. How many of them would think like Ford and put the blame on him?

He shook off that thought. It was more important that he clear his head. He couldn't do anything if he was distracted by side issues.

Prom found him near the dock.

"Hey, Joshua. What's this I hear? Is the secret out?"

Joshua kept going and Prom fell in step beside him.

"There was a leak, but what others make of it is something else. I think people realize we exist. It's just a matter of who we are, exactly."

Prom looked up as they entered one of the work areas with a higher ceiling. "Um, does it mean we'll get *flicked* here?"

"No." Joshua went over to a worker.

"Hey, Simon, how goes the repair work on my minisub?"

He looked up, and nodded at Prom with a smile. "Um. I'm going to need a while longer to get Bait back in the water."

Prom winced at the name.

"I'll need it quickly. What's holding us up? I need it working by morning."

Simon frowned. "Um, the hull work will take a lot longer than that." He walked them over to the framework that held it suspended off the ground. "As you can see, I've dabbed a protectant paint over the scratches, but to really fix it, I'll need to buff it down to the bare metal and grow a real coating over it, and that will take three days, at least."

Joshua put his hand on the angry red lines.

"It looks good to me. Will the paint job will survive the water?"

"Yes, but it won't last more than a couple of weeks before it starts to flake."

"Good enough. What about the ballast tanks and stuff you removed to get Cruiser working? Are those replaced?"

"Um. Not yet, but we have the parts."

"Good. I can expect it in the water, fully charged, when I head out in the morning?"

Simon hesitated. "It's still several hours to get it all done. It might take all night."

Joshua nodded. "It's important. New job from Ford. Get help if you need it."

Then he walked away before there were any more questions. Prom hurried to keep up.

"Hey, don't tell me you're really going to try to rescue that kid?"

Joshua's face was solemn. "Eventually. But right now he's getting a broken leg healed. It'll be a lot easier when he can walk on his own. First, I've got someone else to rescue. I've got a lot of people to rescue."

"Are you going to tell me about it?"

Joshua gripped his arm. "When the time is right, you'll be right in the middle of it."

Prom gave him a tight smile. "I've got a feeling this is another one of those things that has to remain a secret, right?"

"You're catching on."

"No *jandaka*, please."

"I'll try to keep you safe and dry. But I do want you to know everything about James bar Bill's book. Do I need to pry it away from the pilots?"

Prom tapped his temple. "It's all up here, every word. I've been going over it time and time again in my head."

"Good. No matter what happens, we're going to need that power from space."

. . .

Quiet time, scanning the planet before he attempted to sleep, took longer than usual. People were talking, chatting telepathically, and unfortunately, some of them were very good at putting the pieces together.

An elder of Sakah Home in the central desert region: *"I remember a woman at the last All-Ko Festival that seemed out of place to me, never explaining which Home she represented. She seemed friendly enough, but never talked about where she was from."*

Someone from Sttegh: *"Yes, I remember her, too. It struck me as odd that she traded a future delivery of copper pipes for two of the Festival girls we were having trouble placing."*

A woman in Dallah: *"That's a problem we're having more and more. The Names can see the value of male workers, but the females, especially the younger ones we trade at Festival, they can't see as anything more than drain on a Home's resources. They're happy to trade them away, but reluctant to accept more in their place."*

In Sanassan Home: *"Just speculating here, but couldn't there be a hidden group of U'tanse, might have been here for years? They could exist invisibly, increasing their numbers by collecting excess females at Festival and rescuing workers abandoned by their Names."*

In Kakil Home, a tired worker: *"If they're the ones who rescued that Rikna girl, I hope they're looking our way. I don't see any other way out for us."*

Joshua finally broke off listening. Some were very close to the mark, but there were plenty of other suggestions. Some speculated it was a hoax by Dallah, just to spook Elehadi. One suggested that the rescuers came from Tenthonad Home—a secret group of U'tanse formed by Abe the Father himself. A young man from Lakka thought they were from Old Earth itself, come to take all the humans back from the Cerik.

Joshua couldn't afford to waste too much time following it. He was just glad there more false ideas out there than good ones. Cerik telepaths like Stakka would be listening in, as well.

He semaphored to Ash: *"Tell Sally to send me blind message about Jinger."*

He watched as Ash delivered the note. Sally left the group that was monitoring the girl and retreated to their room.

Sally moved her arms hesitantly. She wasn't good at semaphore, and without the necessary clairvoyant skills to see him, she was just waving in the room by herself, hoping it got through.

"Jinger upset Cerik was reading her. Ineda *skills rudimentary. Few more weeks training. Sleepy juice for naps and tonight. Angry we won't tell her anything."*

That was about what he'd expected. He'd tried to read her himself and kept getting a few thoughts, even past her *ineda* efforts. She was frustrated by having to stay in a room empty of anything but a bed and a pot, with people watching her all the time. She'd been through the same thing before, when no one knew if she'd broken free of attachment or not.

He flagged Ash again. *"To Sally: I'll need to speak to Jinger in the morning. Alert."*

Sally replied on her own: *"Ok. I'll adjust sleepy juice."*

Joshua thought a moment and flagged Ash one more time.

Theater

Simon sat on a stool next to the edge of the dock. He looked up as Joshua arrived. "Well, it looks like you got some sleep."

Joshua nodded. "Not as much as I wished, but I had to get up early. Is the sub okay?"

Simon waved at the edge. Joshua looked.

"Everything looks in place. Any problems?"

"Not really. I had been holding off getting it ready in hopes that I could get the authorization to grow you a new hull."

Joshua put his foot on the top rung of the ladder. "This is fine for what I need. Save the next hull for minisub D. With any luck, we'll need a regular production of them."

"Same design as Bait here, or more like Cruiser?"

"What's your opinion, Simon? We might need more variety. Think about what it would take to make one that could haul more cargo, more people—and how about one that could make the trip all the way to New Home on its own?"

Simon nodded. "We still have the hull-size limitation, but I've been toying with the idea of two or more hulls side by side. And if you didn't need speed, how about one with an inflatable hull? Put all the tanks in two side hulls and use a flexible bag to handle larger sized cargo."

Joshua nodded, "Put the designs on paper and when we get the time, we'll call Ace in and brainstorm ideas.

"But I've got to get across the bay before my deadline. Thanks for everything."

Simon nodded and yawned. "I'm going to hit the sack."

. . .

Joshua took the straight course, blasting all six pumps. He was protected in the same oiled cloth costume he'd used when rescuing Prom. He bent low to avoid the turbulence. It was the fastest he'd ever traversed the bay. Even the big sub couldn't move as fast.

He entered the underwater tunnel into Base and pulled up to the dock. Hoop noticed the wake in the pool and walked up to help.

Joshua tossed him a line. "Just tie it off. I don't know how long it'll be before I leave."

The dockmaster nodded. "Good to see you. Folks've been worrying."

Joshua didn't need to ask about what. "I'm working on it."

He pulled himself up on the dock and fished the *jandaka* tooth out of his bag. He slipped it across his chest, secured by the lanyards.

Hoop looped the line over a stanchion, watching him. He asked, "Dressing up?"

Joshua struck a pose. "Cerik style. Do I look fierce enough?"

Hoop chuckled. "Enough for what?"

"Impressing a young girl."

The dockmaster, who was larger and stronger, straightened up and shrugged. "I guess."

Sally met him on the ramp. She eyed his costume. "It's still wet."

He nodded. "All according to plan. I want you with me; just agree with everything I say."

She closed one eye and cocked her head. "I don't usually."

"You'll understand, and I'm not working off a script, so just go with the flow."

. . .

Comfort was in the room with Jinger. The girl stood up from her bed when he walked in. She saw the tooth and looked confused.

"Hello, Jinger. Are you okay?"

She looked at Comfort and Sally. "Okay, I guess. I don't like being trapped like this. Nobody tells me anything."

Joshua nodded. "You understand that a Cerik telepath was listening in on your thoughts when Hank called for you yesterday?"

Slowly, she nodded. "He was hurting. And so frightened."

Joshua snagged a chair backward and sat astride it. "Hank was being tortured into contacting you so they could reach your mind. You see why *ineda* is so important now, don't you?"

"Yes," she said timidly. Her thoughts racing and leaking through her primitive block. She was afraid he would listen in. *What do I know, anyway? I'm locked up in a plain room by myself.*

He smiled. "You're locked up in a plain room for a simple reason. What you don't know, they can't read from you."

She winced as he repeated her thoughts back to her. The *ineda* tightened a little bit.

"That's better." He nodded. "I came here this morning for a very important reason. We can't keep you locked up forever. We don't want that. And the fastest way for you to get back to your life is to train your *ineda*, and become so good at it that you're invisible to the best telepaths on the planet."

She said meekly, "I understand."

He spread his hands. "You think you understand, but I've been where you are before, trapped behind locked doors until I learned to block my thoughts. I was in that nursery too, remember."

She frowned, "So why am I locked up here? None of the other cuties know their *ineda*, either."

"None of the others contacted people at Kakil Home and told them who we were. You told Hank I would rescue him, and he told that man who broke his leg. From there, it was just a few minutes before the Smiley contacted the Name.

"Cerik can't tolerate U'tanse rescuing other U'tanse. They'll do anything they can to track us down."

She frowned, "Even hurting Hank."

"They'll *kill* him if they think it'll cause you to leak more information about us. Later on today, they'll try again, and they're willing to hurt him every day to get more."

The faint thought leaked out, *Maybe I should tell them what they want.*

Joshua didn't react and hoped the women weren't showing anything either.

"What really helped me learn my *ineda* was finally seeing what's outside of the nursery—learning why it's so important to lock up every thought."

She narrowed her eyes. "Ash always said you can't ever get out of the nursery until your *ineda* is perfect."

"Normally, that's true. But you're already a special case. You need all the help you can get to make your mind stronger." He turned to Sally. "Could you please come with us?"

Comfort frowned but said nothing as the three went out into the corridor. Sally reached out and held Jinger's hand. "You can do it."

Jinger concentrated on the *ineda* exercises, and just for a moment, all traces of her thoughts vanished.

Joshua beckoned. "Come this way. I'm sure you'll like the garden."

Jinger was wide-eyed as they walked through the rows of plants and squinted at the overhead lamps.

Joshua said, "This place is special. I know you've been worried, ever since that Cerik tapped into your thoughts. However, you should know that there's no way they can get in here."

"Really?"

He nodded. "We're far underground. There's no door to the outside. We grow all our own crops, and our air is sealed off from the outside."

She looked puzzled.

Joshua pointed, "Oh look, there's Cyclops."

Sally's eyes widened, but she forced her face back to normal.

In the center of the garden, there had always been a table for garden workers to eat during long chores. It had been replaced.

Raised above everyone was a large comfortable chair, and Cyclops lifted his hand to greet them. He was dressed much better than usual, with a blue shawl lightly draped over his shoulders. His hair was well combed and the beard that had grown since his accident was neatly trimmed. From his posture in the chair, there was no hint that he was paralyzed from the waist down.

He wasn't wearing the bandage, though, and Jinger's gaze was locked on his blank, eyeless face.

Cyclops faced her and said, "Hello, Jinger. Nice to see you. How is Bella?"

She blinked, and gradually found her tongue. "Okay. He escaped from his cage last week, but I found him under the bed."

Cyclops nodded wisely. "Do you think we should get another *chitchit*, some kind of companion for him?"

Jinger managed to nod.

"Sounds good, then." He turned and waved to Veronica. "Could you remind me to have one shipped in?"

Veronica dipped her head, more a bow than a nod. "I'll make a note of it."

Joshua was pleased at the theater. Jinger might be puzzled, but any Cerik who read this memory would be fascinated and horrified at the U'tanse Name, sitting high atop his Perch. Moreover, an eyeless U'tanse didn't fit into the Cerik's view of the world. Every Name got that way by ripping the eyes out of all the enemies he killed on his way to the top.

Elehadi would be especially disturbed, certain to remember the day he destroyed Samson's eyes and that the U'tanse giant had stood back up, still alive, to continue his duty.

Joshua gestured to Jinger, "Come on, we need to leave Cyclops to his tasks."

He bowed to his father as well. Jinger managed a bobble.

Walking down the ramp, Jinger looked up at the higher floors.

Joshua gestured up. "There are several levels to this place, as you can see, but I'm afraid we can't show you everything. I just want you to realize we're safe here. The Cerik can't get at you."

She nodded, straining to get a look at everything.

When they exited out on the dock, Hoop was there watching. He nodded at Joshua and flexed his own muscles a bit.

"What is this place?" Jinger asked.

Joshua led her up to the edge were Bait was floating.

"There are no doors to the outside, but we need a way to move in and out. This pool connects to the ocean outside through a hidden tunnel. We can move all of our submarines in and out whenever we want."

Jinger looked around the pool, which was much larger than any she'd ever seen back when she was a cutie at Rikna Home. She pointed. "That's a submarine?"

He nodded, "Our smallest one. That's a bigger one over there. They can travel underwater at fast speeds. That's how I came here this morning. Sally has been in it, too."

Jinger looked up at Sally as she nodded and whispered. "I drove it, too."

Jinger's *ineda* was a little weaker, and Joshua could tell she was looking at the scars on the side.

"Are you wondering about the markings?"

She nodded.

Joshua put his hand on the tooth. "The beast who lost this tooth, a *jandaka*, tried to eat me and the sub whole."

Jinger shivered. "What did you do?"

"Some things I have to keep secret. Let's just say I have the monster's tooth and I came out without a scratch. There are other monsters out there in the ocean. We have to be prepared."

He gestured across the far wall. "There are hundreds of other secret bases out there in the ocean. This place is built into a mountain under the sea. It's the safest place to be. Even if the Cerik knew where we were, there isn't anything they could do about it. Rikna Home was destroyed with a large explosion, a *flick*. But here, under the sea and under a mountain, we'd hear the noise but nothing could touch us."

Jinger looked from Joshua to Sally.

Sally nodded confidently. "These were built by the Delense. When the first U'tanse explorers entered the secret tunnel into the seamount for the first time, do you know what they saw?"

Jinger shook her head.

Sally bent a little closer. "Delense skeletons. It was safe inside, but the Cerik were rampaging outside, trying to kill every Delense in the world."

Joshua said, "That's what we're trying to prevent. When the Delense became a threat to the Cerik, all their warrior rage came out, and when it was done, there were no more Delense. If the Cerik read your mind and consider the U'tanse a threat, and then they'll start killing everyone.

"They'll kill Hank, all of his family, the whole of Kakil Home. And then the other Names will start to do the same. Only you, with a solid *ineda*, can help prevent the slaughter of everyone on the land."

Jinger nodded. Joshua couldn't read a thing past her block.

A Strategy of Hope

They walked Jinger back to her little room. She promised to work harder on her *ineda*.

Sally and Joshua then returned to the garden, where Debbie was directing her helpers in disassembling the Perch.

His mother asked, "Well, did you spin your tale?"

Joshua helped lift the chair off the table and onto the cart.

"I have hopes. If she really does tighten up her *ineda*, that's great. If she weakens, either from lack of training or because they're hurting her friend, then they'll get an interesting story."

Sally chuckled. "Base is really under the ocean, built into a seamount, and it's just one of hundreds of other secret bases."

Debbie raised her eyebrows. "Thinking big?"

He shrugged. "There just might be a lot more bases. We've only explored a very small portion of the world.

"I just wanted the idea out there that we were too powerful, too well-entrenched, to destroy. Knowing where we are is useless, because not even a *flick* will affect us.

"At the very least, I want Elehadi to think that torturing a boy and probing into the mind of a little girl, is just not worth the effort. In a way, I hope to rescue them in place."

He gave Sally's hand a squeeze. "Pardon me. I want to run up and check on Cyclops."

. . .

"How'd you like your Perch?"

His father was stretched out on his bed, his face bandage back in place.

"Oh, the visit to the garden was welcome, but I didn't like being up that high. When you can't catch yourself if you fall, it's a little nerve-wracking.

"Still, I've asked if we could put some wheels on a chair so I could move around a little more. I sympathize with Jinger, cooped up in her room."

Joshua sat. "Well I thought you did a great job playing the Name of all Free U'tanse."

Cyclops shook his head. "I understand what you're trying to accomplish: If secrecy has failed, then manage the information that leaks. I'm less certain that it'll accomplish what you want. The Cerik are expert hunters. They're used to prey that try to leave false trails."

"I'm not just talking to Elehadi, you know."

Cyclops tilted his head.

Joshua nodded. "Last night I listened in to U'tanse speculation. A lot of ideas were circulated. Some true, some false. But what I got from them is that the U'tanse are hungry for any kind of hope.

"And hope is what we've got to give them. Yes, Elehadi or some other Name might decide to squeeze harder, and I don't really have any power over that. But when it comes down to it, either the Cerik will *flick* us all, or the hopeless U'tanse will convert to a hive mind. Either way, we lose.

"Giving the people hope will hold off the day when a Home rebels and is *flicked*, or when attachment gets out of hand."

Cyclops considered it.

"Hope is a fickle thing. I hoped that my eyes could grow back. They never did. I hoped that I could get over my fear of the water. It hasn't happened yet. I hope that my spine will heal and I can walk again, but that hope is fading."

His son said, "Yet, you still hope. I can see that in the way you talk. What hope hasn't failed you?"

Cyclops *looked* off somewhere. With his *sight*, it could have been anywhere in the world.

"I ... hope that you succeed. I hope that the children in our nurseries will grow to adulthood and have children of their own. I hope someday to live without fear."

A Strategy Of Hope

He pointed at his son. "Those hopes haven't failed me because I can see progress. Yet, for the rest of the world, if you spin the tale of rescue, you will have to deliver. They will have to see progress, or they will lose that hope.

"When false hope collapses, it's bitter and taints the spirit. You can't let that happen."

...

Right on schedule, Elehadi and Stakka approached Kakil Home.

Joshua *looked* into Jinger's room. She was sewing something, working quietly. Her *ineda* felt okay.

Paul walked up, momentarily distracting Joshua from his monitoring.

He handed him a strip of paper. "Message from Factory."

"Thanks." Joshua glanced at it. It would take a few minutes to work the code.

"How is Ash holding up?" he asked.

Paul shrugged. "He's taking a nap at the moment. It's good to have someone to deliver all the messages. His semaphore is pretty good, too."

Joshua nodded distractedly. He'd exchanged quite a few messages with the boy lately.

"Umm." Paul shifted his footing.

Joshua focused his eyes on the man. "You have something else?"

Paul tried to smile. It didn't hold. "Um, people I've been talking with think it was reckless to let Jinger out of seclusion. Her *ineda* isn't that good."

Joshua looked back down at the paper. "I know. I took a gamble, and we won't know how it turns out for a few days yet. When I have time, I'll apologize."

Paul turned. "Okay. I guess you know what you're doing." He walked off.

Joshua began decoding the message. *I don't know what I'm doing. I'm just guessing.*

The text of the message was: *"From Patrick: Den, Wender, Anra and I heading out in Angel."*

He sighed. So, they were leaving for the next raid. He'd intended to be part of the group, but they couldn't wait for him. Anra for the healing, and Wender, he guessed for the heavy lifting, made a good group.

One more thing to monitor. It was all he could do. He looked, and Angel was still hidden behind Factory's tall camouflage draperies. Everyone was on board, probably waiting for the status flag to signal when they could leave. Angel was the only boat of theirs that could float on the water, which made it perfect for this kind of quick launch.

. . .

Joshua felt sick, watching Roland strip off Hank's breather and slap him repeatedly. The boy's face was fierce as he shouted, "No, I won't!"

Somehow, Jinger's friend had recovered the bravery he'd lost the last time when his leg was broken. Roland demanded that he contact the girl, but Hank closed his eyes tightly and suffered the blows.

Joshua could see that Jinger's needlework was idle in her fingers, and tears ran down her cheeks. But she was repeating the *ineda* exercises for all she was worth.

Even then, the block was erratic. She couldn't listen in to Hank's silent cries and block her own thoughts at the same time.

Elehadi and Stakka watched silently. Time passed.

Roland glanced at the Cerik, then gripped the boy's ear. He leaned close and whispered, "I'll do more to your sister, and then your mother."

Hank's determination wavered. He grit his teeth, and muttered, "I should have killed—"

Roland's slap sent a wave of blackness through his thoughts, nearly to unconsciousness.

Jinger whimpered.

Roland shook him back to alertness, facing the killing anger in the boy's eyes. He raised his hand again.

Elehadi said to Stakka, <How long do we watch this play?>

<The cub resists, for now.>

Elehadi's voice rumbled lower, <We will return again. Heal the cub.>

Roland clenched his fist, barely able to control his frustration. He forced out a call, <For your name.>

. . .

Joshua quickly checked on Angel's progress. It was at high altitude, over the mountain range that separated Sanassan and Lakka lands, descending toward the facility that took metal sheeting and produced the ubiquitous tow carts that were used all over the planet. During their planning, they had confirmed that they were a week away from metal delivery, and the previous load of carts had been picked up a month earlier. As with many of the Delense factories, it ran unattended.

Joshua hoped they scanned the area well before entering. He didn't know if any of the party had semaphore skills, or even if they were looking for messages. He couldn't help them no matter what.

Roland returned Hank to the healers. The Smiley didn't even see the looks of scorn in their eyes as they turned their hands to the boy's new injuries.

Joshua shifted in his seat. It appeared Elehadi and Stakka were heading to the private meadow. That would give him ten minutes or so.

He hurried over to Jinger's room and knocked on the door. Comfort let him in.

The girl looked up to him and blinked away her tears. He didn't say anything; he just handed her a soft cloth to wipe her face.

"Hank..." she started.

"I monitored it. He was very brave."

"I should have done something!"

"A strong *ineda* will make their efforts useless, and they *know* that. The Cerik gave up on it today. You just have to hold on and keep your mind firm."

She nodded, no matter what she really thought.

Comfort brought her a drink of water and Joshua left.

He had to get back to monitoring Elehadi. No matter what he'd said to Jinger, Stakka had used her distress to tap stray thoughts. He had to find out what they had discovered.

Return

That's a different Ba. Joshua was surprised that he even noticed. It was very easy for most people to identify another human by their thoughts. Over the time he'd spent monitoring the Cerik, he'd gotten the taste of individuals' thoughts as well, when they weren't blocked by *ineda*.

But the Ba were such a totally different species that their minds had very little in common with the creatures that walked upright and had eyes to build an image of the world around them. He couldn't communicate with a Ba mind to mind, for one. The flat, subterranean, aliens were only able to talk via the shared language of the Cerik, voice to voice.

And yet, if a U'tanse knew what a Ba mind *felt* like well enough to make the connection, they did share one common thought process—listening.

It was the basis for the secret alliance between the Free U'tanse and the escaped Ba.

Both humans and the Ba were captured during the exploration phase of the Cerik civilization. Several species were taken, either as prey or as slaves. Ba were perhaps the latter, used by Cerik to haul large items on their flat backs. They were not common, and few Names owned them anymore. Since the trips to other stars had stopped, there were no new Ba to be had.

Perhaps the Cerik didn't realize that so many had escaped, and that they still bred in the wild. The only ones Joshua had heard of among the Cerik were very old, kept more as trophies than as workers.

They had been trained to take orders in the Cerik language. Not one of the Names realized that they could also speak.

Elehadi had struggled with keeping his counsel with Stakka, his most trusted advisor. How do you keep rival Names from listening in on your war plans? His solution had been to keep a private meadow, surrounded at a distance by guards to keep any spoken words from being overheard. The two Cerik, their thoughts protected by *ineda*, and their speech protected by distance, could then confer in private.

But a Ba moved in, under the patchy shrubs and low ground-covering plants, close enough to the surface to hear every word.

Joshua listened in to what the Ba could hear through its senses. It was much like hearing it himself. Whatever the Ba thought about it, if anything, made no difference. With his human *sight* adding details to the scene, it was as if he was hiding in a tree, listening.

Elehadi asked, <What did you sense? I dislike watching the U'tanse damage the cub for fun. He should kill it and be done with it.>

Stakka said, <For your name. I was able to taste the thoughts of the female. She was disturbed, as well.>

<Was there anything useful?>

Stakka kept his claws still as Elehadi paced.

Then telepath reported, <There were flashes of memory. Images of a great underground burrow, and she no longer feared for herself.>

<She doesn't fear your skill?>

Stakka hissed, lightly. <She no longer fears the claws of a Cerik. She struggles with her limited *ineda*, but it is getting more complete. She is being trained.>

<Anything else? This prey is slipping out of your *dul*.>

<I have her scent. Perhaps she will drop her guard soon.>

Elehadi made a dismissive swipe through the air with his claw.

<Then what about Graddik? Are the warriors in place?>

<The three parties delivered into the Graddik foothills have all taken up their positions. The main group is collecting on the Rikna side, and Graddik's forces are coming together to form a line.>

Joshua listened in to the battle plans. It seemed Elehadi was ready to cut off Graddik's mountain forces, eliminating that threat to his conquered Rikna lands and to take a part of Graddik's lands as well.

Elehadi wanted to arrive at the Faces with another military victory, just to prove that even with his restricted power deliveries, he was a Name to be feared.

···

Joshua panicked as he searched for Angel and its crew. It wasn't in the sky and it should have been at the cart factory by now.

Instead, there was a different boat at the facility, strangely shaped, a triangle rather than the softly curved loaf shape of Angel and the two transports. He could *see* two Cerik inside, but what they were doing was beyond the limits of his clairvoyance.

But where is Angel?

If they had been confronted, the Cerik would be chasing them or standing around, gloating over the kills.

Did they turn back?

Searching for a single boat in the sky when you had no idea of its course was nearly impossible. That's one of the reasons Ford's job of keeping Factory's activities from being discovered by a random overflight was so difficult.

Patrick or Den was looking ahead before landing and saw the other boat. If they immediately went to ground, where would they be?

Joshua followed their course in his imagination. *Den would be flying. It's his boat.* Joshua remembered that Den tended to steer to the right. So, they would look down and see...

It took several attempts, but he found it. Angel was resting on a small pond, about the only flat place in those hills, nestled up under some trees.

Everyone inside was safe. They were just waiting for the Cerik to leave.

He checked back at the cart factory. The triangle boat was still there, on a flat landing pad right up against the side of the building. Something about the wall made him look inside. There, resting up against the wall, were three large power cells.

They're charging them directly, just like we did the New Home's power cells. Positioned that close, with the factory's cells set to charge, the pilot in the boat could push power through the wall. The boat's power controller was doing the same job as the hand-held device Ace had built for him.

But it's probably a lot faster.

Does that funny boat have that much power in its cells?

He strained to see the internals of that boat, but it was beyond him. But the idea was possible. He'd never observed Tenthonad delivering power before. Did they always use the triangle ships? He thought power was brought in by delivering whole power-cells.

In fact, he knew that was the case! That's how Rikna Home received its power. That was what Samson overloaded to *flick* the burrow into an exploding ball of flame.

So, power was delivered in two ways, depending on the destination. So many of the Clans had just a few boats and a few small operations.

How did the Clans charge their boats? Did the triangle boat land beside them and charge them up? Why was this new information?

Perhaps the Free U'tanse are out of the mainstream. Maybe some guys at Factory already know this, but just never thought it was worth mentioning.

Soon, the triangle boat lifted off in a cloud of dust. Joshua followed it. It was traveling almost due east. Tenthonad lands were on the East coast.

Not long after that, Alpha blasted high in a cloud of water vapor and spray and continued its mission.

...

Hoop shrugged, "Oh, I've seen triangle-shaped boats, but my job was herding runners. I never had anything to do with the odd-shaped craft. They were rare, but had nothing to do with my job."

Joshua smiled, "From herder to dockmaster, hmm?"

"Not that big a difference, really. Managing the unruly, loading and unloading, and keeping the opportunists out of the storage bins."

Joshua winced. "Not me, surely."

Hoop eyed him in sorrow, "Ever since you left the nursery, you've been in my storage rooms, treating everything there as your personal property."

"Oops."

Hoop shook his head and walked off.

Joshua had tracked the craft all the way to a sheltered landing area two days' walk up the coast from Tenthonad Perch and Tenthonad Home. There were about fifteen of the triangular boats, with most of them underneath spreading canopies. As far as he could tell, there were no U'tanse workers there. From the number of warrior's huts, there could be as many as fifty Cerik guarding the place, although he didn't see that many.

Hard to see from overhead and well-guarded. All the rare triangle boats could be right there.

...

When Angel was safely back, being pulled up to Factory's dock and out of sight behind the draperies, Joshua settled down in his room. Sally was at the garden, helping Debbie, and he didn't want to bother her. Perhaps it was time to sleep.

A quick check over at Kakil Home showed Hank sleeping as well, his new cuts mending under bandages.

Joshua sniffed his distaste when he saw Roland in his bed with a girl. It wasn't Hank's missing sister, because he'd already located her, bound and gagged in a nearby chamber. Everyone knew where the missing girl was, but no one was brave enough to confront Roland in order to rescue her.

It would be easy to write off everyone in Kakil Home as beyond saving, if they didn't already feel that way about themselves. The Smileys were quick and ruthless to anyone who defied them, not caring who else would be hurt. In a telepathic community a cut or a wrenched shoulder was felt by many, not just the boy who needed to be healed.

Joshua was about to turn away, to scan someone else on his list, when Roland started to gasp and thrash in his bed. The girl hopped up, her hands across her mouth.

"Healer!" Roland forced out. The girl nodded, snatching up her robe and racing into the corridor.

Aarison stopped her. "I'll take care of it." She nodded and raced on.

Roland's eyes, already wide in his distress, locked onto Aarison face, healed of its scar, as he entered the chamber.

"Oh, you seem to be struggling," Aarison said, his voice faking concern. He sat down beside the naked man and snatched up his thrashing arm.

"Hmm. Your heart is racing." Aarison shook his head sorrowfully. "That's bad."

He reached into a pouch and pulled out a small bottle. "Did you know that when I was young, I wanted to be a healer?"

He peered at the bottle carefully. "Of course, that was a child's dream. A man can't be a healer. It's in the girls' genes. Still, I searched the library and found a number of books, written by healers for other healers. Not everything is done with the mind, you know."

Roland couldn't breathe, couldn't make his arms move, only his eyes followed his will.

Aarison tipped the bottle up against Roland's lips.

"There are many potions described in those books. Some derived from Old Earth plants, some from local plants or creepers. They can do may things."

Roland kept his lips compressed. Aarison pinched his nose. In his distress, Roland couldn't keep his mouth from opening.

As the colorless fluid dripped into his mouth, Aarison smiled.

"Some can cause the heart to race. It's useful for some conditions. Interestingly, it has little effect touching the skin; only when ingested. You could put it on your hand and never notice. Or you could put it on Caniele's breasts as she slept. It would be harmless, unless someone shortly *intended* to suckle on the girl's breasts."

The fresh dose of the potion hit Roland hard. His eyes rolled up.

Not thirty seconds later. Porter, another of the Smileys, showed up. He looked at Aarison, sitting over Roland's body, and froze.

Aarison said, "It appears poor Roland had a bad heart. Why don't you get Ned and Eric and dispose of the body? Also, will someone please release Darla, the daughter of Kurt, and get her back to her mother? That's not how we treat our girls in this Home!"

Several people had listened in, as Joshua had done. Quickly, everyone knew Aarison had poisoned Roland.

But isn't it better this way, many thought.

The man's a poisoner, thought others. *How many other people has he poisoned?*

A Trade

Sally put her hand on Joshua's shoulder. He blinked.

"Sorry, I didn't know you were here."

She sighed, "I've been watching you for half an hour, I guess. You're always off in your own world."

He took her hand and kissed it. "Not my world."

He gave her a quick summary of the events at Kakil.

She frowned. "I don't like that place."

"I don't, either. And yet, I'm supposed to rescue them somehow."

He sighed loudly. "It's not the powerless people I should judge, I guess."

She nodded. "It was Roland. He was a bad man. I'm not sad he's dead."

Joshua shook his head. "Roland got that way because of the leadership of Aarison. Aarison got his power through the manipulation of Elehadi, who sees no value in the U'tanse. They and others at Kakil Home have let their worst sides come out, but the same conditions could happen anywhere."

"At least Aarison is better than Roland."

"Perhaps. If Aarison was the 'name' and Roland was his 'second', then they just had a very Cerik struggle for power where Roland tried to usurp the leadership and Aarison put him down. Is either of them good?"

"Aarison played out a rather public execution, putting the rest of his Smileys in their place, and at the same time, rescuing Darla to get the people firmly on his side. It's all a power play. He could have easily poisoned Roland without showing his own hand in it. He needed to strike fear into his underlings."

Sally nodded. "So we're back to a Home tainted with evil. If you rescue them, I'm not sure I want them as my neighbors."

"I'm not sure we're that much better. I *think* Ford was on the brink of ordering me to quit my efforts. Our own safety is everything to him. Instead, he let his better instincts rule and told me to rescue everyone. At least, he gave that order even if he doesn't think it's a possibility."

"Maybe Cyclops should be put back in charge."

Joshua smiled. "I wouldn't mind, but why the change of heart? Didn't you say he was a man who drove everyone too hard?"

She put her arms around him. "I just don't want everything on your shoulders. It'll burn you up and leave you a dried-out husk. I want a loving husband and someone who will play with his children."

"Children?"

She cocked her head. "Been thinking about it. Don't you think Sterling will need a brother?"

. . .

At the appointed time, Joshua *watched* as Elehadi and Stakka approached the Home. Aarison stood beside Hank's litter. Neither of them wore breathers.

Elehadi growled, <Little name, I see you have crawled out of your hole.>

Aarison's face twitched. He still felt the scar Elehadi had left, even if it had healed nearly invisibly. He shouted, <For your name!>

<And the other one?>

<I had to remove him. Cubs and females were being hurt.>

Elehadi nodded. Succession killings were proper business.

Stakka said, <Make the cub contact the female.>

Aarison turned to the boy. Quietly, he said, "Hank, they've asked you to contact Jinger. Please. I've rescued your sister and given the order to protect your family. I'm not going to hurt you.

"But our Name has given an order and we *must* obey. If you don't do what *I* ask, then they'll quickly kill me and turn to the next man with a fist. So please, make the effort to contact Jinger."

Hank hesitated, then nodded. He closed his eyes and reached out, forming his mental image of the girl that had tried to help him.

His eyes tightened, and he visibly strained. After a bit, his eyes opened and he gasped, "I can't reach her."

Stakka moved his claws in a subtle gesture.

Elehadi growled, <I can't waste this time.>

To Aarison, he hissed. <I won't tolerate more failures. Forget the cub.>

The Cerik turned as one and headed off.

Aarison waited until they were out of hearing range. Then he turned to Hank, handing him a breather. "It appears they don't need you anymore. So, let's get you back to the healers, okay?"

...

Elehadi grumbled on the way. <I thought I'd broken him.>

Joshua was glad he'd followed their progress, rather than assuming they'd stay silent until they reached the private meadow. They were talking, and even though both Elehadi and his telepath had solid ineda, the warriors they passed had open minds. It was hard to skip through the minds of one passing warrior after another, but one would hear a sentence, and then Joshua would have to listen in through the ears of the next.

Stakka said, <And it seems the others don't resist him as much.>

<Who is his new second?>

<Perhaps one called Ned. There is another with a fresh scar called Eric that could also make his move.>

<Any result with the female?>

<Just flickers of thought. More leak through her dreams than when attacked directly.>

<Anything useful?>

<I believe I saw her Name on his Perch. I heard his voice as he talked. He had no eyes.>

Elehadi paused and Stakka hurriedly came to a halt, as well. A warrior cleaning his claws paused to stare at his Name.

<No eyes?>

The telepath crouched lower. <Yes, no eyes. No scar, just... no eyes.>

...

Joshua hurried up to the map room just as soon as the Name and his telepath stopped discussing their battle strategy.

He pulled the detailed map of the Graddik mountains from its slot and spread it out. Joshua placed markers to designate where the forces were positioned. Half of the battles were already underway, and Graddik's Name was heading to the peaks with a transport full of reinforcements.

Joshua could see that Graddik was falling into Elehadi's plan. In that terrain, there was hardly any place a transport boat could set down. Either the warriors would have to leap out the hatch one by one, or the boat would land at a place Elehadi's forces had already secured. Either way, they'd arrive into waiting claws.

It might take a day for the issue to be settled, but unless Graddik managed to deliver a miracle, Joshua suspected Elehadi's plan was solid.

There are side-effects for us.

Joshua flagged Bernard at Factory and sent a best-guess of the battle plan. Every available boat from both Graddik and Kakil were going to be concentrated in the mountain region for the next day and a half.

All the flights over Base and Factory would vanish for that time period. Perhaps longer, if it was a great Kakil victory and the boats moved to Kakil Perch for a celebration.

Factory went into action. Patrick's Candy, boat C, was moved into the water and headed off toward New Home.

Joshua relaxed for a moment. The second power generating pump for Factory had been fabricated at New Home and was just waiting to be transported. With the additional power cells from the raids, Ford had just been waiting for clear skies to get the new generator moved to Factory and into service.

That'll bring Ace and Betty back to us, as well. We really need their input on the space power project.

Joshua started putting the map markers away, preparing to roll up the map, when an annoying thought intruded.

He paused and *scanned* the mountains.

"Uh, oh."

...

Joshua ran down the corridor and snagged Ash by the arm.

"What?" the boy asked.

"No time to explain. Any new nightmares?"

"Um, no."

"Follow me with your *sight*, in case I need help."

He looked seriously puzzled. "Okay."

Joshua raced on. He quickly changed into this water suit and jumped into the water. He unhooked the line and pushed off in Bait, ignoring the people who yelled at him.

I'm going to get in trouble for this.

Navigating by *sight* to keep his head down, he raced for the stream that formed the half-way mark between Base and Factory. It wasn't very deep, so he couldn't take Bait upstream. He found a shading tree and tied it off. From then on, he'd have to be on foot.

I'm glad Pet is a creature of habit.

One of his regular hunting trails passed very near the place where Cyclops and Joshua last talked with the Ba. That encounter had led to the fall that destroyed his father's spine.

Joshua smiled at himself for thinking like a Cerik as he identified Pet's location and estimated where he would be in a few more minutes. From there, Joshua searched out an overlook.

His heartbeat was racing as he waited in the shadows, like a hunter. He was often calm when racing into action, but afterward, his body rebelled. His arms were shaking and his breather hissed, pulling air in so rapidly. He forced himself to breathe deeply. *I need to practice my* kadan.

Barely visible, he saw a shadow move fifty feet below him, beneath the trees.

Joshua forced himself to move. He'd never faced a Cerik voluntarily in his life. It was crazy. But he had to do it. He stood up where the light would catch him. The *jandaka* tooth was bright against his chest.

<Hunter,> he shouted, <I have information you need!>

Still not visible, the Cerik paused in his shadows.

<U'tanse-that-swims? You are upsetting my prey.>

<You need my words more than meat.>

The Cerik shifted position and was visible in the sunlight.

<What are these words?>

Joshua made his play. He shouted back, <I will trade you the words for a live *chitchit*.>

The rhythmic hiss could only be called derisive laughter. <A *chitchit*?>

Joshua said, <I have caught *chitchit* before, but I'm in a hurry. Meet me where the stream meets the ocean. Bring a live, uninjured *chitchit*. I can't wait long.>

Before Pet could reply, Joshua backed out of the light and hurried down the steep path. *I hope he doesn't decide to hunt me instead.*

As he raced, he worried. *He might just ignore me. If so, Ford and all the others were right, and I should never have tried to communicate with Pet.*

But if we can make this trade…

It was joyful, despite his panic, to splash into the stream and race to untie Bait. He pushed it around, got in and waited.

It wasn't very long before Pet arrived. He approached the shore, only twenty feet away. He was holding a wiggling *dul*, the net used to hold live prey.

<U'tanse-that-swims, what are your words?>

Joshua told him. He detailed the battle already started, and more specifically, when and where the Kakil warriors would be headed.

<That is where you've hidden your nomads, isn't it?>

Pet growled. <You know too much.>

<There is more that I can tell you.>

Pet tossed the *dul* his way. It was on target. Joshua barely caught the scratching beast—beasts—without being knocked out of the sub.

He grumbled, <The others will complain about moving again.>

<Are you their Name or not?>

Pet didn't answer, ignoring the question. Joshua suspected no Name had been decided among them.

<What is that thing?>

Joshua laughed, and hoped that Pet understood the human action. <This takes me across the ocean and under it, where the great *jandaka* live. I call this one 'Bait'.>

He had translated the name. Pet gave another rhythmic hiss.

<Are those teeth marks?>

Joshua slapped the tooth. <That one learned better.>

Pet still hesitated. Then he said, <You who know much, do you know a safe place to move my nomads?>

A region with occasional border skirmishes was one thing, but this region was becoming a more intense battle ground, and one harder to hide a nomad clan.

Joshua said, <I will find one. Then we will trade again. South along the coastline is best, but Dallah watches the mountain passes, as well.>

Pet turned and before he left, he asked, <Where will we meet?>

<I will find you.>

Pet hissed and left. No Cerik liked being the prey.

Planning Session

Too much full-speed travel in the minisub had drained its power. Joshua was still a half mile from Base when he pressed the button and nothing happened. He cruised quickly to a stop, adjusting the ballast so Bait rode high on the surface, to keep from drowning the two *chitchits*. Carefully standing on the unstable platform, he put his hands over his head.

Ash responded. Joshua sent: *"Please ask Robert to come tow me. I'm out of power."*

The reply came back a couple of minutes later: *"From Robert: Serves you right. Be there soon."*

When the Alpha rose out of the water, Joshua waved. It edged closer, and then the hatch opened. Robert looked out. "Need a line?"

"Yes, but take this first." Joshua heaved the *dul* at him. Robert caught it, but quickly shouted as he brought it inside.

"What is that?"

"A couple of *chitchits*. Keep them alive."

Robert grumbled, then closed the hatch with a loud clang.

Joshua attached the line between the subs and waved. As the larger sub turned around, heading toward Base, Joshua brought Bait down below the surface so it wouldn't bang against the top of the tunnel entrance.

...

It was two days before Robert towed him back to Factory, where both Alpha and Bait could have their power replenished. Joshua had ridden in

Bait, making sure the little sub kept the same depth as its larger brother. So close to shore, they didn't need to leave any revealing wake like they had on the trip to New Home towing Cruiser.

It was good he was already in the water when they ducked under the draperies and entered Factory's dock area. It was crowded. With boats Angel and Candy resting in the water beside the largely unused tub, a water boat that always rode on the surface, there was little space for the submarines.

Joshua swam free, detaching Bait and letting Alpha settle into its dockside position before he hand-towed Bait into place beside it.

It wasn't the record for the number of craft docked at Factory. One time Boat B had been there with them, forcing Candy, resting on its raft, to be hoisted up onto the dock to make room for the others.

Carson was back at New Home with his boat, waiting for more power cells to arrive to recharge the large transport.

Once dried off and dressed, Joshua attempted to report to Ford. The man waved him off. He hadn't fully adapted to sitting at a desk doing paperwork and needed to be in on the action. Ford was busy with a crew working to get the turbine dismounted so that the new pump system brought in from New Home could be installed in its place. Restoring Factory was within sight, and that made it his highest priority.

Joshua was okay with that. He really didn't want to have to explain his trip ashore to trade with Pet. If he could let that slide by, all the better. He left a sheet detailing the battles raging in the mountains.

The conflict between Kakil and Graddik was winding down, with Kakil having won back the Rikna lands and some of Graddik's side of the mountains. How long that would stay would likely depend on whether Elehadi could get his power deliveries restored. Several of his boats were stuck on the ground until they could be charged up. He'd committed more power than he could afford in order to win the border conflict.

Joshua didn't mention the nomad clan he was following. They had slipped into Dallah territory, hiding in caves, actually nearer to Factory than before, but Ford was only interested in significant threats, the major clans with boats.

Prom tracked him down. "There's a meeting this evening, when Ace gets free of the installation work crew."

...

Ace had charts. Joshua thought they were pretty, but he didn't understand them at first.

"I finished reading the Book of James bar Bill and then had to go back and read it again slower," he said, turning to the first of his charts.

"James describes the curve of the boat lifting off and going into space. From the timing and the details he gives, this is what I plotted. You go straight up at first, and then as the air thins out, you start moving sideways. It forms a curve so that when there is no longer any air, you are moving mostly sideways."

Den asked, "How do you move it all if there's no air to grab?"

"The beam that grabs the air can be told to push against the ground. I know you can adjust that from the control pad. On the boat James used, it was obviously programmed in, since the Cerik pilot did nothing other than set a target on the display and the boat did the rest. What we don't know is whether your boats can do the same or whether we'd have to control the direct push with the pads."

"Pushing against the ground would make you go up."

"So you push against the horizon, not straight down."

Ace changed charts. "So I took some details from the Book, like the estimated size of Ko, and using the formulae laid down by Abe the Father, I calculated the speed we'd need to travel. Any faster than that, and we keep going up, never to return. Any slower, and we'd fall back down to the ground. But exactly at the right speed, we can keep going forever without using the engines anymore."

He had to explain the process several times before they got it. He took a metal disk, usually used to hold down curled papers, and threw it across the room. He tossed it farther and farther each time, explaining how the boat would 'fall' around the curve of Ko, and keep going, with no air to slow them down.

"And that's what those starships are doing. They are falling around the planet, several times a day, and they'll stay that way forever, using no power. For us to reach them, we have to do the same, go just as fast and reach their altitude. Only then can we enter a starship's airlock."

Patrick asked, "But we can do it, right?"

Ace gave a short nod. "Maybe." He pulled out a sheet of paper with a table of numbers.

"I took the estimated weight of each of the boats, and using the speed we'll have to reach, I guessed at the power needed.

"Angel can't do it. It's the smallest, but its power cells have too little capacity to reach 'orbit'—that's the term Abe used.

"Breezy is unusable because it leaks."

Joshua asked, "Breezy?"

Patrick said, "Carson finally gave in and gave boat B a name. Breezy for the sound of the leaks at high speed."

Ace put his finger on the third column. "Candy has the power cell capacity, but that's using my guesses, and with not a lot of excess."

Patrick nodded. "I'd expected to use Candy, but are you saying it'd take a fully charged cell to make it into space?"

Prom grumbled. "That sounds like a losing game. Take a fully charged boat into space, just to recharge it and come back home again. You don't gain anything."

Joshua said, "Maybe that's what those triangle boats are for. Maybe they have the extra storage capacity to fly back and forth into space and return with a useful charge. It looks like Tenthonad is the only clan that has them, and they're stored at a special location deep in Tenthonad lands."

Prom nodded. "Maybe that's how they maintain their monopoly on power cells. They have the only boats that can make it up there."

Den asked, "So do we go steal a triangle boat?"

Joshua shook his head. "The place is heavily guarded. We'd never get close to one of them without being overwhelmed."

Ace put up a diagram. "So we modify Candy. We use the empty power cells we discovered at New Home's remote factory to add power cell capacity several times over."

. . .

There was so much to do. Joshua wanted to spend the rest of the evening planning their trip into space, but Patrick insisted that a higher priority was the third power raid. Until they could be sure of having the power to run the fabricators to make the new internal structure for Candy and to power up the boat to full capacity, even after the alterations, they had to stay on task.

"Patrick," Joshua flagged him down after the meeting ended.

"Yes?"

"I think I'm dead weight on the power raids. You've got a good crew already. You proved that with the second raid. However, I do have one big worry."

"What is it?"

Joshua faced him squarely. "Disasters can happen, no matter how good the crew. Should you not return from the next raid, we'd have only Carson, a single pilot remaining."

"You want me to keep it to one pilot?"

Joshua shook his head. "No. A backup pilot is essential in case one of you is injured. If there was only one pilot, a broken arm or leg might kill all of you because you couldn't fly away quickly enough.

"What I want is to be trained to fly a boat. Not just me, either. Train two or more. Right now there are probably twice as many people who can pilot a submarine than we have subs in the water. It would be good to do the same for the boats."

Patrick said, "Maybe that's because subs are easier to drive than boats."

Joshua chuckled. "You can have that argument with Robert. There's a difference. Submarines are all manual. You have to pull every lever and steer constantly by hand. From what I've read in James's book, boats are automated so even Cerik can fly them.

"I'd like someone who has experience with boats walk me through it so I don't have to learn it all by trial and error while I'm in the air."

Patrick frowned at a memory. "Yeah, that's how I learned. I guess you're right. Catch me in the morning. I'll show you how with the power turned off. It'll get you started at least."

Poisoner!

Joshua was waiting at the dock the next morning when Ash sent him a message: *"New sketch. You were facing a dozen Cerik beside a mid-sized boat. Rocky terrain."*

Joshua asked for more details.

"Veronica said tense situation, no more."

As usual, there was no hint at when this would happen. Joshua was also worried about the mid-sized boat. Although Ash had never left Base, he had *seen* Angel, Breezy, and Candy, and had chatted about them over a meal a week or so ago. Either Veronica's sketch wasn't detailed enough for Ash to identify which boat, or it was going to be a different boat entirely.

Joshua sighed. *As usual, just enough information to make me worry.*

Patrick arrived as promised, and Joshua tried to put the vision out of his mind. But it was there as Joshua concentrated hard on memorizing the hand strokes that controlled the power and flight of the boat. Patrick was very careful that only the controls were lit up and the engines were left idle.

The pilot growled. "We don't want you trying to fly Candy around on the inside of the dock area. I'd get very angry if you put some dents in her."

...

Peace under Aarison didn't last long. Joshua was notified by Ash: *"Jinger told Comfort she fears something bad is happening at Kakil Home."*

Joshua hurriedly found an out-of-the-way corner to avoid being disturbed and probed the Home.

There was a crowd in the corridor. Porter, one of the Smileys, was poking a stick at two half-dressed girls that were tied together. They were young and so similar Joshua thought they might be sisters. They stumbled when poked and moved a step farther down the corridor. Joshua was puzzled by the crowd. Everyone was horrified, but no one was yelling. No one was trying to stop it.

Several of the crowd were comforting a woman in tears, kneeling on the floor. *The girl's mother?*

Joshua dipped into the chaotic thoughts. He picked up the girls instantly. Nelly and Kelly's thoughts were one. Attachment was the big fear among the crowd. Even Porter's was filled with terror, trying to keep as much distance between himself and them. He was pushing them in the direction of the airlock.

Where is Aarison in all of this?

Joshua searched down the corridor and found him in his bedroom, panting hard and holding onto the arm of a third girl about the same age as Nelly and Kelly. There were clothes littered on the floor.

Aarison had *ineda* up, but his block was wavering. A memory broke through; the two girls holding each other tightly, backed up against the wall, screaming "Poisoner!" in unison. Aarison shook it off. He focused on the activity out in the hallway. Part of his mind was counting steps.

Aarison was monitoring the crowd, as well. As Porter moved the girls within sight of the inner airlock door, Aarison gently, but firmly pushed the other girl away. "I think you'd better return to your room, for now."

The girl, a little dazed by what was happening, nodded and grabbed up her robe.

Aarison hurriedly fastened his ornamental tunic and went out into the corridor. He reached the crowd.

He shouted. "The girls are attached! Is there a chance to heal them?"

A half dozen voices called out, "No!" One man called out, "We have to get rid of them!"

Porter froze, his stick still keeping them away.

Aarison let his head drop in a sorrowful expression and waved his hand.

Two men hurried out of the crowd to open the airlock doors.

Joshua's face tightened. Aarison's act would get rid of the girls, and yet he could put their blood on the crowd.

It was all his fault.

The mother wailed louder. In seconds, they forced the girls outside and the outer door was barricaded shut.

The girls both raised a right hand to beat on it, but perhaps the fresh scars on that door made them realize it was a bad idea. Together, they started running toward the row of feed storage sheds a few hundred yards away. They didn't say a word. They didn't need to.

A Cerik hunting roar echoed off the walls. Whether the guard had heard the noise or caught the girls' scent, he was on the way. First one girl, then the other, glanced to the side and checked behind them. They shifted course, aiming for the second storage shed rather than the closest.

Landing right in front of them, the Cerik spread his claws and roared again.

The girls separated, one to the left and one to the right, out of his range.

The hunter took a step toward the left girl. The one on the right screamed, causing him to look her way. He took the challenge, and no sooner had he shifted his stance than the girl on the left yelled.

Angrily, the Cerik kept after the one on the right. His claw cut through her torso, below the ribs. Both girls tumbled to the ground, but the left girl struggled to regain her footing. She took a few, faltering steps, but by that time, the hunter stopped her, too.

The hunter severed their heads for trophies, but left the bodies where they fell.

Joshua felt cold as he proceeded to do followup monitoring. He needed to know if Elehadi was behind any part of the slaughter.

It took fifteen minutes or so before Stakka noticed the bragging of the guard. From the way he talked, he had no idea the girls were attached. Stakka passed the word to Elehadi, but the Name wasn't interested. He was listening to the reports from *tetca* leaders in the recent battle.

Joshua rubbed his forehead. The girls' deaths weren't ordered by the Name. This was human evil, spawned by his schemes of course, but fed by human greed, lust, and hopelessness.

How can I stop this?

...

When Joshua *looked* over at Base, he could see that the news had spread, just by people's postures and the looks on faces.

Hopelessness spreads.

It was probably the same in every Home. There had been more violent death at Kakil recently than in all the other Homes combined. How many people wondered if it could happen to them?

Across the bay, Sally found an empty table and sat down. Joshua wished he could reach out to her.

That's exactly what so many other people are doing right now—reaching out, hoping to share their pain.

So many telepaths that much closer to attachment.

Free U'tanse were lucky that way, he guessed. *Habitual* ineda *keeps us apart. It also keeps us lonely.*

Joshua put his hands over his head. It took a few minutes, but Ash *saw* him and acknowledged. Joshua sent:

"I need you to do some things for me, since I'm not there to do them myself.

"First: go to Jinger and give her my sincere appreciation for the alert. It was very helpful.

"Second: go to Sally and tell her I'm watching over her.

"Third: I appreciate your help, Ash. I realize I'm keeping you running.

"Finally: do anything you can to keep spirits up at Base."

. . .

With Angel as the boat of choice for power raids, due to its ability to land in tighter quarters and on water, and with Candy winched up onto the dock so that the alterations could be started, the dock looked relatively empty.

Joshua walked the dock area by preference, since he could keep up a faster pace than he could manage in the labyrinthian maze of Factory's corridors. He chatted with the workers when they had time for him.

The ladder to the cliffs outside was nearly completed. The man he'd met when they were first starting the project was still there, looking up the tall climb and scribbling notes.

Joshua nodded, "Hello, Ewan. What are you up to this time?"

The stonemason blinked. "Oh, Joshua. Just trying to figure how much cable to have fabricated for the winch."

Joshua peered up to the bright crack between the cliff face and the camouflage draperies. "For lifting cargo?"

"Right. I've climbed the ladder a couple of times, and just taking a light line with me was a killer. We're going to need a motor-driven winch to move much of anything."

Ewan showed him the details. A hinged tripod would keep the winch mechanics hidden in a small cave chipped into the rock face, out of sight of any passing Cerik. But if it was needed, two strong men could climb the ladder, hoist the tripod from its recess, and then secure it to an outcropping just behind the cliff. From there, bags could be raised and lowered.

Ewan said, "Just a simple pulley at the top, with the winch motor down here. I need cable for a bit more than twice the height of the cliff, and a winch spool large enough to hold it."

Joshua complimented him on the design and then went on with his walk.

This is my job today—keep talking with people about ordinary things and help them avoid dwelling on the disaster that Kakil Home has become.

He looked up to the top. Maybe someday he'd like to climb that ladder, but it looked a little too high today.

...

Larson, the Factory dockmaster, was yelling at one of his workers down inside the tub. A power cable, a couple of inches thick, draped from the dock across the tub's deck and disappeared into the hatchway.

Joshua asked, "Anything I can help with?"

Larson looked at him. "Have you been on the tub before?"

Joshua smiled. "All the time when I was first out of the nursery. Robert showed me all the details. I helped recover it the time it broke free in a tsunami."

Larson nodded. "Yeah, I think I remember. Anyway, could you help Fingers with the charging cable?"

"Sure. Getting it charged back up?"

Larson frowned. "Ford's orders. Everything has to be kept charged for as long as the power situation is improved. 'Better the power where it can be used than sitting in a power cell gathering dust.'" He shook his head. "Busy work for me."

Joshua stepped aboard the tub. It was their original water boat, and still the only one they had if you didn't count the rafts that Breezy and Candy needed for landing pads. Raised from the seabed back before he was born, it had an electric motor for propellers, just like Alpha the submarine, but its power system was complicated. Charged by an electrical cable, it had to be converted for storage in a small power cell, and then converted back to electricity when it needed to be used.

Down in the interior, Fingers was making do with a hand-crank light, at the same time trying to fish the thick cable through the cluttered space. There was no sunlight to help. Factory's dock was dark since they'd added the draperies, and tub had no juice to run its own lights.

Joshua climbed in and said, "The last time I was down here was in daylight. Do you want me to feed the cable or hold the light?"

Fingers handed him the light with a three-fingered hand. "If you can keep this thing working, I'd be grateful."

They got the cable connected and after yelling to Larson, the power converter started humming. Joshua tapped a button and the dim internal lights came on, gradually brightening. Fingers gave him a nod and a smile.

Cut

An ordinary day, working with people doing ordinary tasks helped Joshua's spirits and, it seemed to him, those of the people around him. He probably hadn't really helped anyone get their work done any faster, but that hadn't been his intent.

Every few minutes, Joshua directed his attention across the bay. Twice Sally had been looking blindly in his direction, and sent: *"I'm thinking of you."*

He was glad he'd been watching in order to catch it, and resolved to be more consistent at it.

Grateful there was no immediate crisis to be watched, Joshua collected a bowl from the kitchen and found a chair in the corner where no one was likely to come chat with him.

He sipped the broth. *Ciara has outdone herself this time.*

His attention slipped across the ocean, northeastward toward the southern tip of Far Island. He'd neglected the place long enough.

There had been one lone entry in the Tales of the Cerik about Far Island. It had taken root in the public consciousness.

The Tale of Kooru
Kooru, a powerful Name of his time, discovered a strange beast washed ashore and his Delense told him of a new land that had appeared in the sea. The beast must have come from this Far Island.

The Name ordered his Builders to make him rafts with which he could take his warriors across the ocean and conquer this new land. The Delense cut down a forest and made three great rafts; one for Kooru and his Perch, one for his warriors, and one for the Builders. Winds blew them for many days until they reached Far Island. But as they arrived, Roostata the tsunami washed them ashore, smashing the great rafts and killing many of his warriors.

Kooru raged on the barren rocks, growing hungrier by the day. He ordered his surviving Delense to rebuild the rafts, but finding no trees, they could only build one from the remnants of the original three. Kooru slaughtered and ate his Delense, as the raft drifted for many days on the ocean, until he returned to his lands, vowing to never look at the ocean again.

Joshua was surprised to see the forested peaks of Far Island. He'd intended to hunt for abandoned Delense burrows, possible new homes for rescued U'tanse, but the lush lands overlooking the sea attracted his attention. From the tale, he'd expected a barren landscape. The island of New Home had no forests. There were certainly small wooded areas and many different varieties of plants, but it was nothing like this.

...

Patrick described the next target. "Sanassan's lumber mill is just the final step in the process. U'tanse workers chop the trees down in the northern stretch of the Western Mountains. They put the downed trees in the river, where they float to the mill. After that, the process is automated. Trees feed into chutes where they are trimmed and sized. Board lumber is produced according to the requests fed into the control panel. Some of it is baked in ovens, it looks like."

Wender said, "That makes sense. Back when I was at Keetac Home, we ordered board lumber from Sanassan, and it was all dried out."

Joshua asked, "Are we sure that we won't run into any Tenthonad power deliveries again?"

Patrick shook his head. "We don't know their schedule, but now that we know what to look for, we can take precautions. Not that it was all that bad last time. We drained four cells' worth."

"Speak for yourself," Den frowned. "I was panicked to find myself sharing the sky with that triangle thing. It was twice Angel's size, and I bet it was all power cells inside."

Patrick said, "Anyway, the Sanassan transports will be finished loading a large shipment tomorrow, and after that, the place will be running itself. We need to slip in after they leave and drain what we can."

That meeting ended, and as Wender and Anra left, Ford, Ace and Prom arrived.

The next meeting started.

Ford said, "I thought I ought to see how things are going."

Ace described the construction. "The new internal supports are almost complete. We'll be able to carry two large power cells and sixteen standard cells and still have cargo space left over for a crew of four and their supplies. I've checked Candy's air capacity, and it should last a day and a half. Within that time, we'd need to get up into orbit, make contact with a starship, tap the planets for power, and get back down to the surface."

Den raised his hand. "I'm not sure I can hold it for a day and a half."

The group laughed. Ace tapped his sheets. "I've got a workman's pot on the supplies list. I just hope Candy's air circulator keeps the air filtered, or it'll get a little ripe in there."

Patrick reached across the table to look at Ace's papers. "Are these power cells accessible to Candy's engines? I mean, if your calculations are off and we run out of power half-way up, do we fall to the ground?"

Ace shook his head. "Not directly accessible. We'll have the transfer harness you use for your raids. I suppose you could move power that way."

Den frowned, "Transfer while in flight? While falling? I don't like that idea."

Ace waved his hands. "No, that's not it. When you're in orbit you're not really flying. It's just very controlled falling. No tumbling. No screaming. None of that. We'd check the power levels when we were stable and make any transfers then."

Joshua asked, "Will there even be any power in those cells on the way up?"

Ford said, "That'll depend on how smoothly Patrick's raids go. But I have a different question. Who is in this crew?"

Joshua looked around the table. Everyone was considering the question.

He spoke first. "You need a pilot. Candy is Patrick's boat, it would be best if he flew it—he's most familiar with its quirks."

Ace said, "I'm going. I probably know more about the science of getting us to orbit and then getting us back down again. Flying in space is going to be entirely different from normal piloting."

Joshua pointed to Prom. "We have to have our planet expert. He's been working on this for years longer than we have."

Ford said, "That's three. Who else?"

Prom said, "I'd recommend another pilot, if for no other reason than the length of the trip. People have to sleep."

Joshua realized that he was suddenly out of the picture. It was a surprisingly painful shock. Whatever he'd learned about piloting a boat, Den or Carson were the obvious choices. Carson was still at New Home and hadn't been in these planning meetings since he left. Den was it.

Ford waved his hand. "Think about it some more."

. . .

Ford waved for Joshua to follow him as they left after the meeting.

"I was a little surprised you didn't make an effort to join the crew."

Joshua shrugged. "When we were thinking about which skills were needed, I suddenly realized I didn't make the cut. It's vastly more important that we learn to tap energy from the planets than it is for me to go on that first trip. I'm expecting an angry Name will realize their power has been stolen any day now."

"Hydro power is now up to eighty percent, and Betty is still tuning the system. We could live without space power and without the raids."

Joshua shook his head. "Not really. Base and Factory could live that way, if we closed our eyes and stopped listening to the other U'tanse across the planet. We could never make enough excess power to keep New Home thriving. And we could never pull off rescues like Rikna Home again. We'd dwindle away."

Ford stared ahead as they walked. "It's hard for me to imagine a day when we could really rescue all the U'tanse."

Joshua nodded. "I know. U'tanse live in a bubble of filtered air, their Home. We don't really have a bigger bubble for them to live in. Yesterday, I spent hours scanning Far Island, looking for more undiscovered Delense bases, like we've found here and at New Home. I was sure I'd find them."

Ford looked his way. "No luck?"

"No. I think I found one, maybe. There was an access tunnel near a bay, but it had collapsed. I think they tried, but Far Island has active volcanoes all along its length. It looks beautiful. But forests and streams are one thing, stable rock layers for the Delense to tunnel through is another. If humans could live in open forested land like that, it'd be a great place to move to, but we can't."

Ford nodded. "You're not the first person to turn his sight toward that place. Cyclops had mentioned it once. One of the crew rescued from Dallah decades ago was interested in using lava flows to run a power plant. He wanted a place where no Cerik lived to try it out, but nothing ever came of the project."

"I wish I'd known. But I guess I need to keep looking. I *know* the Delense have more bases. It's only logical."

"You need more bubbles for all the people you're going to rescue?"

"Partly." Joshua sighed. "I want more bubbles so that if the Cerik come hunting, they can't pop them all."

"And space power will help this?"

Joshua smiled. "It can't hurt. If we had endless power, we could fabricate a lot of submarines, so we could maintain regular traffic out of Cerik reach. We could reactivate all those tunneling machines we found at New Home. We could build our own underground bases, if necessary. As more Delense technology gets discovered, we could develop a more complete economy of our own, independent of whether a Name was in a bad mood or not."

He laughed, "At least, that's my hope. The bigger the hope, the better, because when we lose it, we're on the down slide to oblivion."

A Bigger Trade

"No!" yelled the woman. "You can't leave me!"

Joshua's eyes opened. He took an instant to remember where he was. *Factory, the room where I sleep.* He stared at the open doorway. His room was barely more than a storage closet with a narrow metal-frame bed. He sat up, trying to figure out where the voice came from.

Common politeness kept him from using his *sight* to scan the nearby rooms. Yet, the voice nagged at him. He wished she would yell again, so he could identify her.

There were few enough women at Factory that he probably knew them all. It was strange he couldn't identify the voice.

Was it local? There were plenty of places on the planet where men and women had fights in the night. Half asleep, could he have been confused? He'd be happy enough to ignore it. There was enough anger and dispute on the planet that he couldn't afford to take it all on.

But if it was local…

He shook his head and did a quick scan of his list. All the flags showed green. Nobody seemed awake.

Even at Base, where no sunlight had ever touched the floor, people stayed linked to the cycle of day and night. Enough of them were clairvoyants and were aware of when the sun rose and when the moon climbed in the sky to keep everyone on the same schedule.

Sally was asleep, curled up in their covers. He was glad they'd gotten past the days when she yelled at him. She wasn't timid about expressing her opinions.

Footsteps. Joshua faced his doorway. Ace hurried past. A moment later, Betty followed.

Betty? Could it have been she? Come to think of it, he'd never really heard her speak above a whisper. Certainly, she'd never yelled.

Were they fighting? Joshua nodded. Ace had told her about the space flight.

…

Mystery solved, he dozed back off. Their dispute was not his to worry about.

But he didn't sleep well. From time to time, he drifted back into awareness. He *looked.* Daylight on the east coast. He counted the triangle boats at Tenthonad; three less than his previous count.

Later, dawn came to the desert in Sakah. A cluster of Cerik were surrounding a wide, fat *hork*, defending its pool of water.

Then finally, the red sun shone on the West Coast. Joshua checked a few battle sites, but many were cleared out, with nothing left but *lulurs* and *ska* covering the dead bodies. A pack of *haeka* were tearing apart some others.

He checked Pet's cave. The females and smaller males were huddled in the darkest recess. The warriors were elsewhere. Joshua began searching for them.

Pet had favored hunting trails, but since they moved into Dallah lands, Joshua had never seen him too far from the caves. The hunt didn't last long.

Side by side with the other warriors of the nomad clan, they peered over rock ledge at a boat landed in a meadow. One by one, three warriors with necklaces of severed claws crept out of the boat's hatchway and sought the cover of the tree line.

Joshua peered inside, confirming the pilot watching until the others vanished.

Pet gestured to two of his warriors and they vanished into the vegetation. Pet conferred with the other four. The nomad with a wicked-looking trophy claw dangling from his shoulder gestured his disagreement.

Pet slashed out instantly, tracking a cut across the other's chest. It wasn't deep and the foaming blood hardened in seconds. The tension was plain in them all. The battle for leadership could happen right then.

But they were facing an enemy. The warrior with the *haeka* claw moved a few feet back.

Pet gestured, and they swarmed down the slope and into the open hatch. The pilot didn't last a second.

Joshua *looked* at the scene of Cerik surrounding the mid-sized boat.

I'm supposed to be there. It was right out of Veronica's warning.

...

Joshua threw on his oiled-fabric suit and snatched up his breather and the *jandaka* tooth. He raced down the corridor toward the dock.

The crew were already loading into Angel, preparing to leave on their power raid. The camouflaged draperies were already spread for their departure.

He ran up to the side.

"Patrick, it's an emergency, I need a lift."

"What?"

"Just as soon as possible, I need you to carry me to the Dallah side of a certain mountain pass and drop me off. You can go on to your raid."

Wender asked, "And leave you there?"

"It's important, and I don't have much time."

Patrick asked, "Did Ford approve this?"

Joshua waved his hand, "In general. Honestly, I don't have the time to talk about it. If I could get there in time by hiking, I'd already be half-way up the ladder."

Patrick frowned, but he said, "Everyone, get in."

Joshua squeezed in after the rest of them. With the load of power cells and the four of them, it was a tight fit.

The crew on the dock pushed the boat a few yards away from the dock.

Den said, "Don't anyone move. I've got to balance the engines just right."

The whine began and water turned to spray all around them. The thrusters in the rear were stronger, and Alpha began moving faster through the gap in the draperies.

Once they cleared the opening, the whine dropped in pitch as they climbed higher.

Den asked, "Where's this mountain pass?"

Joshua leaned closer, pointing to the map display. "There's a party of Dallah scouts moving through *this* area. I need to get *here*."

Den gave one nod, his eyes tracking the dot that marked their current location. "Keep your *sight* working. Warn me of any Cerik."

Patrick asked, "Okay, explain."

Joshua looked him in the eye. "My pet Cerik has just taken a boat as a battle trophy. I'm going to trade him out of it."

...

As soon as the voices settled, all of them objecting to his irrational statement, Patrick said, "This is just a ploy to come along on the raid, isn't it?"

Joshua shook his head, "No, I've got a chance at this! This Cerik has talked with me before. I've even traded with him. And every time we've talked, he has gained more status. He's on the verge of claiming his Name, and he knows I can help him do it."

Anra said, "You'll end up dead."

Joshua looked at Patrick. "How many of us would risk that to get us another boat?" The pilot had risked his own life dozens of time and seen what Joshua could do, working with him since he had become an adult.

In the end, it was Patrick's decision. He was in charge of the raiding party, and he more than anyone knew just how important it was go gain another boat.

They dropped him just on the other side of the ridge, hoping their engine buzz wouldn't be heard. Joshua had to climb to his destination.

Joshua crept low as he followed the same rock ledge where Pet and his warriors had hid earlier. The roars and hisses of the nomads echoed in the little meadow.

From what he could hear, Pet was claiming the boat was a great prize. The warrior with the *haeka* claw claimed it was the work of a cub, claiming more than he could hold.

<Dallah will come for it. And then what? Will you defend it with your claws? They will take it back, and then come for us. We need to be far away before the scouts return.>

Joshua's heart was pounding. *I'm crazy. You hide from Cerik. You don't confront them!*

He adjusted the drape of his *jandaka* tooth, certainly much more impressive than a *haeka* claw. Maybe the others wouldn't know it came from a sea creature, but any tooth that size would command some respect from the hunters.

Standing, he yelled, <Hunter! I have found lands for you and your clan! Do you have anything to trade?>

Pet roared, <U'tanse-that-swims!>

Two of the others crouched to leap at him. Pet snarled them back.

<I will speak to the one who has lands!>

Pet's adversary shifted slowly to the side, where he could make his own attack without fear of being stopped. Joshua didn't even need to read his thoughts. It was plain in his actions.

Joshua yelled, <I have found lands wider than Kakil, empty of Cerik. These lands have forests, and clear water, and more *doonag* than I've ever seen.>

<Doonag!> was whispered by several others. It was a marsh-living prey, about a third the size of a Cerik, mentioned many times in the Tales. No one in living memory had seen one on the mainland. Joshua was just guessing that the beasts he'd seen along the streams on Far Island were *doonag*, but that was as good a name as any.

<Lands empty of Cerik? How can that be?> called out one of the other Cerik.

Joshua waited. He was talking only to Pet, and they needed to see that.

Pet shifted his stance. <Tell me more of these lands. Where are they?>

Joshua spread his arms wide. <To the west lies a great land, it stretches from near here to near Sanassan. There are great peaks, and many volcanoes. Vast forests have grown where the lava has grown cold. Rain soaks the western slopes, but it is drier on the eastern side. Have any wondered why Kakil has weaker rains than Dallah? That is why. Far Island steals the rains from Kakil. *Doonag* live along the riverbeds, but that is hardly the only prey.>

One of the other warriors said, <Kooru went to Far Island, only to return. It was barren rocks.>

Joshua paused again, waiting.

Pet raised his claw. <Speak, U'tanse-that-swims. What about the Tale of Kooru?>

Joshua made the little-crouch gesture of respect. <Kooru was the only Name brave enough to risk the ocean. He had great warriors and great Builders. But no one can tame Roostata. What he saw was for his eyes only, but the tale he told kept all Cerik from ever challenging his greatness. Perhaps the forest have grown since that day, but whatever the reason, the *doonag* have enjoyed their peace because of the Tale of Kooru.>

Pet asked, <How can I get there? Do you want me to fly across the ocean in this boat?>

<Are any of you of the Rear-Talon?>

Joshua knew that none of them had the training to fly. That was what they'd been arguing about.

Pet growled, <No.>

Joshua had been waiting for this moment.

<Long before Ghader took Builders under his Perch, Cerik and Delense would speak together and sometimes help each other. We U'tanse have been called the new Builders, and we too can trade. If the Name decides, I will carry the whole clan safely across the waters to the lands of Far Island. In trade, I will take this trophy you've just won, but which you cannot use. Do you consider this *soso*?>

Pet took a deep breath when he said 'Name'. It was time. A word surfaced in the hunter's mind, one that he had tasted in his dreams for a long time.

He screamed loud enough to echo from the rocks. <I am Rukan! This clan is mine!>

The other roared his challenge and pivoted his stance to attack Pet.

Rukan was already in the air and caught the challenger off-guard. They tumbled on the rocks, but the battle was over in the first half-second. Rukan ripped the eyes from his challenger's head and ate them.

Joshua stood silent as the rocks. Blood scent was in the air, and any Cerik was a deadly danger.

<I, Rukan, Name of this clan, consider the trade *soso*.>

Joshua, as well as any human could, bowed to the Name.

...

There were traditions and protocols every Cerik grew up with. Joshua was in a better position than almost any other U'tanse, having monitored Samson daily when the giant was being groomed as a *rettik* to Elehadi. There was a way for a U'tanse to walk when in the presence of Cerik warriors. You could not act like prey, yet unless you were ready for battle, you could not challenge them in any of the little ways they could read.

The U'tanse had no rear talons to rake across the ground when gesturing respect. The fingernails were ridiculous substitutes for the claws of any Cerik. The massive legs of a Cerik bent in different ways than those of humans. Still, Samson had managed. Joshua was very glad of his *jandaka* tooth. It set just the right tone.

Joshua walked slowly up to Rukan.

He's no longer Pet. Forget I every thought of him by that name. Rukan. Rukan.

The name was simple and easy for the Cerik to say, one that many could remember and yet one that had never appeared in the Tales. Rukan could grow his own legends.

The Name gestured and they changed positions, with Joshua's back to the boat.

He spoke respectfully to the Name. <You must collect all of your clan and get them to the place where I took the *chitchit*. Females should be bound and warriors expect to travel in *erdan* until we arrive at Far Island.>

Joshua scuffed his feet against the gravel, and then backed into the boat. He didn't take a deep breath until the hatch closed.

Rescue Everyone

Joshua almost stumbled over the body of the Dallah pilot still sprawled on the floor. He stepped over and stood at the piloting position.

There's no seat. Just a bar for a Cerik's rear talon.

Remembering the lessons from Patrick, he held his fingers together and chopped through the air. The display lit up. Holding position, he activated the power to the engines. Outside, Cerik were moving back as the air was kicking up dust. He had to do this right. If he crashed on take-off, Rukan's position would crash as well.

To lift off, slowly bring my left hand up to here.

The outside display showed movement. The ground dropped away, a little too quickly. Joshua adjusted his rate of climb. The boat was very forgiving. The Delense had designed the craft to be flown by impulsive predators with no fingers and no real understanding of how anything in the system worked.

Now, before he got too high, he had to direct the boat to a safe landing area.

He slashed through the air with his hand and the display changed to something like a map. It was a three-dimensional view of the ground below, with water and mountains clearly visible. Pointing with all fingers together, he stabbed at a location closer to the shore.

Joshua frowned. *What are all those lights?*

His eyes widened, remembering something Den had told him long ago. There was a communication system on the boats, something called a shouter. Pilots could talk among themselves that way, but there was a side-effect.

Every time a shouter was used, it placed an identifying mark on the map display so that the pilots could locate the other boats.

Joshua stared at the five bright dots on the map. *Those are all Dallah boats, and if I can see them, then they can see where I am, too!*

He couldn't go to Factory, then. Nor any of the other places where he might lead Dallah warriors. But he couldn't just hover in place either. The power would run out eventually.

He chose a random spot on the coast and drifted that way.

I need help.

Bernard was looking his way. He'd made a spectacle at the dock, probably. Making sure that the boat would continue while he stepped away from the controls, he signaled to Bernard: *"To Ace: Shouter system reporting my location to other Dallah boats. How do I turn it off?"*

He wasn't sure anyone knew the solution, but Ace and Betty had a better grasp on how Delense control systems worked than any other U'tanse. If it could be done, they had the best chance to figure it out.

Joshua settled down on a relatively flat stretch of beach. The map still showed the Dallah locations, but they hadn't moved.

Relieved of his attention to the piloting, he checked on Pet ... Rukan. The nomads were still at their cave, but at least none of the others had attempted a challenge. He was still running the show.

I'll need to be at the mouth of the creek to meet him.

Spray on the water caught his attention. It was Angel, come to meet him.

When Patrick stepped out, Joshua asked, "So, you didn't go on to the raid?"

Patrick shook his head, not looking happy. "We'll go another day. I could hardly leave you stranded in case your plan failed."

"Well, it may have." He quickly explained the situation.

Patrick nodded. "I knew about that tracking business. As far as I know, the dots fade away eventually, but if you want to keep them active, you can, just by using the shouter again. When Dallah's Rear-Talon name calls for a report, it'll be refreshed."

"You still have the power-transfer harness. If we drained the boat's power, would that stop it?"

"I don't know. The engines take the bulk of it. The controls are the last to fade. Let's just wait to see if Ace comes up with anything."

Joshua frowned. "I've got to get back to Factory. It's urgent."

"I'll say it is. Ford probably wants to fry your ears for trying a stupid stunt like that."

Patrick thought a moment. "Let me look at the controls."

He almost tripped over the Cerik body, as well, but he checked the status of the boat.

"Okay, I'll stay here, ready to move it in case the Dallah dots start heading in this direction. You can go on back to Factory. But first..."

The two of them managed to drag the Cerik pilot off onto the pebbly beach. Scavengers would be after it shortly.

...

Ford could barely speak from his anger. "How could you— What kind of a stunt was that?"

"I got us a fourth boat, once we get past one last technical hurdle."

Ford opened his mouth, closed it and then tried again. "What made you risk your life on this stupid chance?"

Joshua straightened a little. "Your orders."

"What? I did no such thing."

"You said to rescue everybody. That's what I'm doing."

Ford stared at him, again speechless.

"Rukan's little clan of nomads is being squeezed on all sides in this border war between Kakil, Graddik, and now Dallah. They have no place to hide anymore, and as soon as any of the larger clan groups find them, they'll be slaughtered.

"I saw the chance to get them to safety, and at the same time trade my help for the boat they'd just captured from Dallah. They get transported to safety, and we get the boat. What's more, we establish a Cerik trading partner. It's something we've never had before. It's something we can use to rescue more U'tanse, when the time comes."

Ford said weakly, "I never said to rescue Cerik."

Joshua spread his hands, "Where do you draw the line? You said everybody. I've been monitoring Cerik since I started watching Samson. I'll admit, I never shed a tear when one Cerik kills another, but they *are* people. So are... so are the other captive races, the Uuaa and the Ba. In a way, we're the aliens. The Cerik are the people."

Joshua lowered his voice a little. "I can't rescue everyone. You knew that when you gave the order, but when I see a chance, I have to take it."

Ford sighed. "I guess. You are *crazy*... but I do understand."

"Then I need your permission to take the tub." He turned his head, seeing off into the distance. "Rukan and his group have left their caves and are already making their way here."

"Here?" Ford leaned against the table and looked off in the same direction, even though his sight wasn't able to resolve what Joshua saw.

Joshua waved his hand side to side. "Not Factory. The mouth of the creek. It's in Rukan's regular hunting grounds and it's a place he knows. Believe me, he has no idea Factory and Base are here. I just show up in his path as if by magic. But I need to be through the draperies before they arrive."

Ford asked, "Why the tub?"

"It's large enough, barely, to hold their little clan. And I couldn't risk one of our pilots on this. I trust Rukan, but his people are still very dangerous. At worst, I'll dive off into the sea and let them starve. We may lose the tub, but we haven't used it in years." He shrugged. "It's a gamble, but I have to move fast."

...

A scout appeared at the creek when Joshua was approaching the shallows. The thirty-minute ride from Factory had given him much needed experience steering the tub. When the figure appeared out of the line of shash, he was practicing moving at the slowest possible speed.

Getting them into the tub in the first place was going to be difficult. Cerik wouldn't wade out to the water boat. There was even the chance that they would panic and his trade with Rukan would fall apart. Cerik hated the water and the ocean was a pitiless monster that would swallow them whole.

Others started to appear as he crept closer. Joshua was scanning the shoreline looking for anything that he could use as a dock.

His first choice, a line of boulders that the Cerik could easily navigate failed when the tub's hull began scraping the rocky bottom before he could get close enough.

Cerik were following him as he moved farther northward, finally stopping beneath a twelve-foot rock outcropping. The wind was helpful, pushing the hull up against the granite. There was an ugly scraping noise every time a wave lifted the hull.

<Rukan! Get your clan on this raft!> There was no word in the language for this kind of water boat.

There was a fight, and from Joshua's viewpoint, he couldn't see any of it. But then one of the warriors appeared at the top of the rock, and then dropped into the metal basin with a clang. Another warrior followed, then another.

Shortly, the bound cubs and females were shoved off the rock and dropped down on top of the others. When the floor space was all covered shoulder to shoulder with angry Cerik, the last ones had to jump in anyway. Minimal blood was spilled, luckily. Joshua noticed one of them was wearing a necklace of claws. Had he been one of the Dallah scouts and taken the *uuka* oath to avoid slaughter, or was the necklace just a trophy collected from one of the scouts?

Rukan leapt directly to the platform where Joshua was piloting the water boat. He shouted out deafening orders, until they all settled down into their trances. The cubs were too young, not understanding much of anything. The small females had no comprehension of language at all, but being captive and forced into tight quarters was familiar.

Joshua turned the tiller and applied power. With a long scrape, the tub crested a larger-than-normal swell and pulled away from shore. Squeals came from the large-net *duls* where the cubs and females were confined. Warriors were crouched beneath the gunwales. No one wanted to see the ocean around them. Only Rukan had his eyes open, watching Joshua's every move.

It was going to be a long trip. If a storm hit, or even worse, something like the tsunami of Kooru's Tale, then it would be all over. He was packed with shoulder-to-shoulder killing machines who were more frightened of the water than his father.

Telepathically, the water boat was a quiet rumble of *erdan*, the trance state of predators waiting out a long night, or the unknown delay between migrating herds. This was the best state for them, not thinking about the water.

Joshua spoke. <Far Island is off this way.>

Rukan didn't reply. Joshua focused back on his navigation. He locked the tiller and tapped the power lever to make sure it was still full on. The steering controls were simple and crude, but they were all that the tub needed.

He closed his eyes and pretended that Rukan wasn't there. He'd catch what naps he could. No telling when he'd need to be alert.

...

By night time, even Rukan had slipped into *erdan*. Joshua checked their course every thirty minutes or so, unless he dozed off for longer.

He watched the stars. Unseen up above, there were other places, other things to see. Even written as a technical report, the Book of James bar Bill told of things that had stirred his imagination. There were windows that looked out over the whole planet, and collections of starships, things so large he couldn't compare them to boats or tubs.

The sky was so clear out here over the ocean, with air washed of much of the volcanic ash and fumes that obscured the distant vistas on land. He stared at the blackness, straining to see anything until moonrise, when it was all washed out. Luckily, the moon was only mid-sized, which meant the chances for quakes were slim. While he didn't mind the idea of someday being a character in one of the Tales, he'd rather not share it with Roostata, the demon tsunami.

...

<What is that noise?> asked Rukan.

Joshua startled out of his light doze. His stomach growled.

<There it is again.>

Joshua hesitated. They were all hungry, and he didn't want to bring the subject up right then. He had biscuits wrapped up in a supply bag down in the hold, but he'd never had the chance to dig for them. He'd have had to elbow several large Cerik aside to open the floor hatch.

<It's a U'tanse thing. Ignore it. It'll go away.>

Claws tapped the tiller. <What's this?>

Joshua checked their course. He unlocked the tiller and moved it a couple of degrees before locking it again. <This directs our path over the water.>

<How soon?>

<Before the sun reaches its peak.>

...

It was noon when Joshua cautioned Rukan, <Don't wake them all up yet. We need to find a good place to approach the land.>

Rukan stood tall, watching the hundreds of *ska* flock around a white rock. Waterfalls cascaded down the steep face of the southernmost mountain. Trees obscured the slopes everywhere he looked.

<So this is Far Island.>

Joshua nodded. <The land of the Rukan clan.>

An hour later, Joshua found a sloping beach where he could ground the tub well enough that the hunters didn't need to get their feet wet. Unfortunately for them, the panicked females and cubs had to be dumped over the side and hauled to shore by their *duls*.

Rukan sent scouts ahead. Only moments later, there were the cries of successful kills. The promised *doonag* were plentiful. The Name was presented a captured beast to kill for himself.

Joshua declined a taste. <Not today. But soon enough, I will seek you out for another trade.>

Storytelling

Bernard signaled: *"You're going the wrong way. Set course for New Home."*

Joshua apologized for not keeping in touch: *"Hard to signal with Cerik at your elbow."*

Bernard replied: *"Everything blew up here. Sanassan attacked Kakil. Raid called off. Angel and boat D to NH, Candy when sky clear. Unsafe to return tub."*

Joshua scanned the area himself. It seemed like the whole of the West Coast was in it. Everyone who had boats had them in the air. There was no reasonable chance of getting the tub back under the draperies of Factory without being seen.

Making sure he had the correct course set, he checked in at Base.

Ash updated him: *"Pretending normal. At least we have power. No dreams. Planting new crops."*

He found Sally in the map room. Cyclops was sitting in a wheeled chair and she was copying papers. He was glad she was finding things to do. The next time he got home, he expected a severe scolding for taking too many chances again.

...

It was murder, traveling at the tub's slow speed while events were happening at a nerve-wracking pace. If he turned the throttle up higher, he'd be out of power before he reached New Home.

Before Kakil had taken over Rikna, it had done the same to another smaller clan, Runa which had separated the Kakil and Sanassan lands to the north. Perhaps inspired by the border clashes between Graddik and Kakil in the south, Sanassan moved warriors into the former Runa lands, taking over half the prime grasslands Kakil had gained earlier. Elehadi was in a bind, with his best warriors defending against Graddik, and not enough charged boats to ferry them to the north.

The minor clans in the area, Lanana and Keetac went to the air, ready to drop defenders where needed. In the south, Graddik, which had just suffered a loss in the mountains, realized its best chance was to move into Kakil lands near its border with Lanana, now that Elehadi had to focus on Sanassan.

None of the battles are near the Perches, only at the borders. The Homes are relatively safe.

But that could change. Battle lines were unstable things. And it didn't protect U'tanse workers caught in remote locations.

Someone at each of the Homes would know where their remote workers were. *I should have researched who that was in advance.*

Sitting at the tiller of the tub, worrying about the flash of lightning he could see off to the west, there was nothing he could do about events across the sea.

Will I make it to New Home before the storm moves in?

He glanced back at the deck. A good hard rain would wash all the stink away. He should be grateful for that, at least.

. . .

Like before, someone on the shore was waiting for him, this time waving a large, pale gray flag back and forth. The rain was coming down hard, and he felt sorry for the woman who had that duty.

New Home didn't have any dock like Base or Factory, at least none that a surface-riding water boat could use. Instead, they had chosen a rock outcropping for him. He edged in slowly, fighting the choppy waters.

He tied the bow to the rope they'd provided and dropped an anchor off the stern to keep the tub from swinging around and slamming against the rocks. He used his food bag to protect the hull from scraping too badly against the rock at the bow, but they'd need a better way to dock the tub before too long. Metal was tough, but not when it was being beaten against the rocks and the tub already had a corroding scar on the side from when he had loaded Rukan's clan.

When he climbed ashore, they made a dash for the airlock. Luckily, he was dressed in his water proof gear, but she was drenched. Inside, he told her to keep the towel. She needed it more than he did.

Hurriedly drying her hair, she said, "Thanks. I'm Stenny."

He nodded. "Holana's apprentice. I've exchanged a few messages with you. Sorry I didn't recognize you in the rain."

"One of them. She's got two of us working for her now. Braidy is on duty, so I was sent to flag you in."

Joshua *looked* over in the direction of Holana's chamber. "Did the name come first or the hairstyle?"

Stenny chuckled, "The name. Her mother looked the same."

...

A good meal was first on his priority list, then he tracked down Patrick.

The pilot looked tired, and his hair, although it always had been gray, now looked even whiter.

"You're not the only one who has hair-raising adventures," he grumbled.

Joshua handed him a rolled up chewbread with a savory paste inside. "Tell me. I love stories."

He shrugged. "At first, after we moved the body and you flew off in Angel, I just sat around, airing out boat D. Believe me, that thing is a mess. It must have been used to ferry Cerik around for decades. There wasn't a surface on it that didn't have scar marks from some claw. And the stink— you can't imagine."

Joshua said nothing. He had ridden in boat D, and what's worse, the tub before the rain.

"I sat outside most of the time, but I didn't go far. I had to be ready to move in an instant. I kept the map display up and watched the dots. One of them kept calling for an update, the voice getting angrier each time when I didn't respond. I was sure he'd be coming for me soon enough.

"I *watched* you from time to time, hoping a little that Ford would beat your head in for hobnobbing with the Cerik nomads. Little did I know you'd head right back out and load 'em all up into the tub. I was really angry with myself for not spending the time to learn semaphore. I know some of the signs, but not enough to make myself understood. I really wanted the story.

And I wanted to know when they were going to send me help."

He bit into the chewbread and worked on it. When he swallowed, he continued.

"Finally, Angel showed back up, and to my surprise, Ace and Betty came out. Den gave me the scoop. Betty had wanted to dig into Candy's controls systems to discover the way to turn off the tracking, but the metalworkers were putting the final touches on the internal bracing and it wasn't safe to be in there while they were depositing the corrosion resistance on the bare metal. Time was critical, so she decided to come to me. Ace had to go with her, of course.

"I barely said hello, when she walked past me and started tapping away at the control pad. The map display vanished and it was all Delense squiggles. She can read that stuff, but it's nothing to me. Ace complained of the smell, but she never noticed."

Patrick took another bite and worked on it. He mumbled over the last swallow. "Thirty minutes, I guess. Then, when she restored the map, it was like every boat on Ko was showing, and I had no idea how long it had been that way!"

Joshua asked, "Angel was still there beside you?"

He nodded. "Right! I threw Den out the door and told him to get back to Factory, then I looked at the map and told him New Home instead. I tried to get Ace and Betty to go, too, but Ace wouldn't have it. 'No,' he said, 'we have to make sure Betty's changes don't have any side effects.'"

Patrick shook his head. "Well, I didn't have time to argue. I waved Den off, and then started the engines on boat D. I asked what Betty had done. I was still worried they'd track us. Ace said she made it so that the boat didn't send tracking information anymore. Although, he said, we couldn't send voice messages out, either."

"So, it's possible?"

"Yeah, I asked, once we were in the air and out of sight of land. She seems to think that the boat could be modified to only talk to certain other boats. And, it might be possible to separate the tracking from the voice. Ace said they'd taken the fast and easy solution. Betty wanted to look at the Delense commands more closely, but Ace had insisted on the fastest solution."

Joshua nodded. "We'll probably want to remove tracking from the other boats as well."

"She's already done it. At least on Angel and Breezy. Candy's still back at Factory."

Joshua frowned. "And all the pilots are here."

Patrick gave a tired chuckle. "Almost. I gave Wender the same introductory training I gave you. I didn't realize he'd be taking my Candy up for his first flight, or I'd have done a better job of it."

The Scold

Otto dropped his cup and the clatter turned every head in the room his way. The elder's face looked shocked and angry. "He did *what?*"

Patrick, sitting across the table from him was amused. He gestured to Joshua, "He rescued a bunch of Cerik. Took them off to Far Island and turned them loose."

The leader of New Home faced Joshua and slammed his hand down on the table. "Why?" He sounded as if he couldn't believe it. "They own the whole planet. We barely own this little island of ours, and now you've released them on an island that's far larger that we U'tanse could have used for ourselves? Why do that? Why turn on your own people?"

Joshua felt his stomach turn. He shook his head. "That's not how …"

He looked at the other people in the room. Shocked and angry faces told the story. None of them understood. The Cerik were the enemy, the killers.

"We're never going to own this planet by ourselves. We'll need Cerik who can work with us."

Someone said, "Work *for* them."

Joshua said, "*That* has to change! I just took the first step."

Derry, one of the younger of New Home's elders, said, "There's a reason nearly every Home is run by a group of elders. Every new generation thinks the world is broken and it's up to them to change it. But things this serious have to be thought out first."

Otto put up his hand. "This is just reckless! Joshua, you've done a lot of good things for us, and we're willing to help you try for this power-from-space thing, but *please*, anything as significant as turning Far Island over to the Cerik has to be agreed to by *all* of us. You've taken a serious step that we may never recover from."

Joshua clenched his teeth together. This was not the time or place to argue it out. Far Island had never belonged to the U'tanse in the first place, but if he said that out loud, he might be banned from doing what he needed to do. Otto's scolding was about the best he could hope for right now.

Joshua nodded to the elders and walked out of the room. So much for his hope of getting an update on New Home's progress. He couldn't pretend to be a representative of Base and Factory when they thought he was dangerous and irrational.

He had to get out of there, away from the stares of so many people passing judgement on him. The airlock was close, he paused behind the inner door.

His heart was pounding; the sudden turnabout had shaken him.

Perhaps they can't see that Far Island was just worthless land to humans. But maybe Otto's people, spending so much time out of doors didn't see it that way.

Yes, we need more lands, more places to live, but....

He shook his head. Maybe he could convince them, but maybe not.

Having Rukan as an allay will be worth it, eventually. I'm sure of it.

But Otto would never believe that.

The storm had passed so he went outside.

The ground was wet, but there were many workers out there as well.

"Hello, Joshua!" waved one of the girls he'd met on a previous visit. He dredged his memories for a name to match the smiling face. She wasn't wearing a breather. Some of the girls here had gotten so good at regularly healing their lungs that they ventured out for short times without them.

He nodded, "Anna. How are you doing?"

She chuckled. "Better than you, I think. Otto yelled at you?"

The telepathic grapevine was in full force, he realized, even thought New Home had gotten better at *ineda* training than they had been originally.

"Perhaps not *yelled*, but I'm avoiding him right now."

"Anything I can help you with?"

He paused his pacing. "Do you have a local material that can take regular impacts without wearing out?" He explained about the tub, rubbing up against the rocks.

She shook her head. "Everything wears out. But maybe ... we use some pretty thick shash rope."

After a couple of hours' work, he fashioned a net of the thick fibers and *kel* branches to wrap around the rock. The tub seemed to be able to bump up against it without scraping the rocks or smashing the net to pulp.

He tried to shake off the instinct to hide the tub. At Factory, it had always been hidden behind the draperies and one of the reason it was hardly used anymore was that it couldn't be hidden out on the water. But here at New Home, it hardly mattered. The landscape was covered with fields and storage huts. On the island, no one hid from the Cerik. If the island was discovered by a Cerik boat, the tub would hardly attract any attention. Perhaps New Home needed to build a dock for it. Taking it back to Factory would be hazardous right now. It might even be more useful to keep it here permanently, although he wasn't the one to make that suggestion. Not now.

He sent Anna back inside before he finished the net. She wanted to help, but he didn't want her to risk her lungs.

I'll need to find some way to express my gratitude that won't be misinterpreted.

It was easier to work with women co-workers when Sally was with him. His wife gave off her own protective waves that they seemed to understand. It was ridiculous to always have to bring up Sally's name in conversation to remind them all of her.

...

Back inside, as Joshua was changing out his breather's filter powder, Holana tracked him down.

"Candy launched in the middle of the storm and got away unseen. If the pilot stays on course, he should be landing over at Sally's Crater within the hour."

He was happy to see her. "So, the place has a name, now."

The long-haired semaphore operator nodded. "Doe started calling it that. Anyway, Hugo said you'd probably want to be there."

Joshua nodded. "I guess I'd better throw together a snack bag for the hike."

"Oh, no. A whole work crew is going. Carson will be ferrying everybody on Breezy, so you'd better hurry. I'll show you where they're gathering."

He nodded and sealed up the air-filter. After he made sure his breather was working properly, Holana led the way.

He asked, "*Two* apprentices now?" She was a good teacher. Sally had gotten training from her as well.

Holana grinned. "It was your idea, right? And Otto is in favor of it so we can communicate easily between Home and Crater. I've been asking around, trying to find all the women with the necessary distance *sight* for the job." She tilted her head. "I've also made no secret of my intention to move to Factory eventually."

"I'm sure Bernard would be happy with that idea."

"He knows."

"Come to think of it," Joshua mused, "Bernard has never started training his own apprentice like he was supposed to."

...

Joshua resolved to keep a low profile. With his reputation tarnished and his judgement called into question, it was the best way. This wasn't his project anymore. He'd done his part in getting it moving, but now the effort had its own momentum.

Holana wished him well, but she hurried off to take care of her part of the job. She was just the messenger who called him in.

Breezy had landed on the other side of the New Home main burrow among some fields. There were more than a dozen people collected around the area, loading carts into the boat. The power cells they needed for Candy's trip into space were stored down in the depths at Sally's Crater. They would have to be hauled up one by one on the carts the hard way, with muscle power. He glanced around for towing harnesses to help pull the carts up the slope, but he didn't see any. He was tempted to mention how useful that would be, but it wasn't his operation. Someone else was in charge.

Patrick was there with Hugo and Jenta. Carson was directing people as they wheeled the carts into place.

Patrick turned to Joshua. "I'm sorry about that. I didn't realize I'd get that reaction from Otto."

"No. I should have predicted it, and I wasn't going to hide it anyway." He waved at the boat. "What can I do to help here?"

Hugo handed him a crate. "You can take this. We've got a lot of work yet to do."

Everyone loaded up. Patrick, Hugo, and Jenta sat together. The women found places to sit among the carts. One old man looked familiar. When Joshua saw that he was missing his right hand, he remembered.

Shortly after they lifted off, he said, "Hello, Franklin. Good to see you."

The wrinkled face peered at him. "Do I know you?"

Joshua smiled, "We've probably never met in person, but I know you—carpenter at Rikna, right?"

He gave a grumpy nod. "Used to be. Been useless for a long time. Probably in the way here, but they asked for volunteers. Didn't really explain what for."

"Well, I'm glad you're here."

Joshua didn't want to brag about what he did for Rikna. If the man didn't recognize him, all the better. But it was good to see someone who would have died in that disaster still holding in there, still trying to help.

I've got to be like that, even if they don't want me around.

Some of the girls were watching them talk. There were whispers, but Joshua didn't even try to listen.

...

Carson yelled, "Wender is coming. I've got to lead him in. Everyone hang on and try not to let the carts hit you. And try not to distract me, either."

Franklin stuck his foot out and forced his shoe against the wheel of one of the carts. Joshua followed his example. If the wheel couldn't turn, the cart would be less likely to shift. Some of the others did the same.

The engine's buzz shifted, and the boat swayed in the air. Joshua took a harder grip on the railing against the wall. Out one of the windows, he could see Candy pass by.

There was a sinking feeling in his stomach as they moved lower. But quickly, they landed. The engines went silent. A few seconds later, the other buzzing noise ended, as well.

Patrick gave a loud sigh. "He made it. I'm so glad."

Joshua spoke to the ceiling loudly, "Good going, Wender!"

The others spoke his name as well.

The hatch opened and everyone spilled out.

When Candy's hatch opened, the first-time pilot was wide-eyed as a group of women reached out for him, calling, "Wender! Wender!"

Back on the Team

Prom poked his head out the doorway and was greeted by a couple of smiling ladies, himself. Wender managed to pass a bundle of papers over to Patrick. Patrick shook his hand, probably thanking him for not hurting his boat. The greetings lasted a few minutes, but quickly Hugo took charge.

Both boats had landed close to the tunnel entrance inside the Sally's Crater. People were hauling the carts from Breezy and two people at a time started down the sloping tunnel into the darkness.

Joshua got in line to help, but Prom snatched him back.

"Hey, Patrick is calling a meeting. You'll want to be in on this."

It took a bit for everyone involved to gather in a side chamber a little ways off the main tunnel. Ace and Betty had to be called up from working on the power cell fabricator.

Patrick handed Joshua a folded sheet of paper. His face was dark. "Read this."

Joshua moved closer to the lantern and opened it up.

To Joshua:

We never had a chance to discuss this at Factory, but there's more to selecting a crew for a project than having the people with the right technical skills. I'm recommending to Patrick that you be in charge of the flight into space. I don't know how you'll juggle your crew, but I've come to realize that I trust you to get into trouble and get back out of it with your skin intact. That's a talent a little more important on an exploration like this than just having a backup pilot, with all due apologies to Den.

So go up there, get the power we need, and get back safely.
Ford

Joshua folded the paper and put it away. He'd have loved to have had that recommendation back at the beginning, but things had changed. He wasn't going to push for this. It was more important that the flight go off without a hitch. Nobody had trained for this. No matter who sat in the fourth seat, there were going to be unknown problems to solve, and Den's flight experience might just make the difference.

When Ace and Betty arrived, Patrick made room at the bench for them.

"Okay, we're all here." Patrick said. "Wender asked to be let out of this." He smiled and added, "He said, 'I'm just a dockworker and I never signed up for all this excitement.'"

Carson said, "Sounds like he did a good job at it."

Patrick nodded, "I agree, but he's right. He did just volunteer for the power raids, and he stepped up to take on even more, but he hasn't been in on any of the space flight meetings and it was his choice."

He held up a sheet of paper. "Ford added his crew suggestions, so what we have to do now is finalize who's going up on the flight, and nail down some other last minute details."

Prom raised his hand. "I thought we already made that decision; Patrick, Ace, Den, and me."

Patrick nodded. "Yes, but things have changed."

Ace said, "Unfortunately, it's become very clear that either Betty comes with us, or I have to stay behind. We're not going to be separated." They clasped hands.

Patrick said nothing as everyone thought about it.

Joshua said, "It actually makes good sense to include Betty."

Patrick said, "That's what I was thinking. We should have included her from the beginning. Considering what she's capable of doing with Delense control systems, having her along when we try to understand the starship makes her essential."

Prom said, "But there's only room for four people, didn't you say?"

Ace nodded. "Yes, but that's with our original design of two large cells and sixteen smaller ones. We've taken a look at the designs again. If we only took fourteen of the smaller ones, Betty could squeeze into the remaining space. We even fabricated an empty shell that will fit into the framework to hold the place for her. I think she's more valuable to the trip than the two power cells."

Betty sat frozen, not meeting anyone's eyes as they all talked about her. Ace squeezed her hand from time to time, but she stayed quiet.

Den was quiet, too. He didn't look at Joshua, and Joshua suspected Patrick had mentioned Ford's recommendation to him.

Den hadn't really talked to him about going on the flight, but he'd seemed upbeat about the idea. As much as Joshua wanted to be up there himself, he knew Den felt the same way.

The junior pilot's voice caught slightly as he asked, "Um, does that re-design account for the change in food, water, and air five people will need?"

Ace nodded. "Yes. It'll be a little tight for her, but she's not the same shape as power cells, so we added a storage area in that space, as well."

Den nodded. "Okay, just as long as Joshua and the rest of the crew don't run out of air, I'm okay with it."

Prom asked, "Joshua? He isn't on the list, is he?"

Den kept a straight face. "Ford recommended Joshua, so that means I'm out." He sighed. "I was half expecting to be bumped off the list at any time anyway. Carson had more experience with transports, so he might have been a better choice than me. And I'm okay with Joshua filling in as backup pilot. He did okay with boat D, didn't he?"

Joshua said, "Ford isn't really in charge of this. Patrick has always been the leader of the pilots. And we're really a joint operation with New Home as well, and I certainly won't be on Otto's list."

Ace asked, "Why is Otto mad at Joshua?"

Patrick said, "Joshua rescued a bunch of Cerik and took them to Far Island."

Ace's eyes went wide. "Really? Why?"

Joshua put up his hand. "I'll explain later in great detail. But for right now, it's not important. For many people, my actions have called my judge-ment into question. If that means I'm grounded, then so be it."

Prom said, "Hmm. If anyone's going to make this decision, I think it should be me. This has been my project for years now. All of you are new-comers. I think Joshua ought to come. He saved my life and he's been a hundred percent for this project from the beginning. No objection to you, Den, but we've barely said a few words together. I trust Joshua a bit more."

Patrick said, "While I will occasionally roll my eyes at Joshua's antics, I do feel inclined to accept Ford's recommendation."

Joshua said, "This might well be a life or death decision, so I won't go unless it's unanimous. Ace, Betty, what do you think?"

Ace frowned, "I really want to understand the Cerik thing, but I'm fine with you coming along."

Joshua said, "Betty?"

Her eyes flickered up just an instant. She nodded.

Patrick said, "Okay, the final crew assignment is settled."

Carson reached out and took Den's wrist when he attempted to stand. "Hey, don't leave. I don't want to be the backup, backup pilot by default. I've got a girlfriend now, and she just might object."

...

The meeting went on to discuss other last minute details. An hour into a review of James bar Bill's flight and how it translated into what Candy was capable of doing, Patrick brought up a point.

"Speaking strictly as a pilot, a couple questions I have that have never been addressed keep nagging at me. Where are we going? And when do we leave?

"I understand about how fast we climb and how long we accelerate, but I have no idea which direction we should be heading once we start."

Prom looked at Ace.

Ace shrugged, "We're going into orbit, but Patrick's right, I don't know which of many thousands of possible orbits we'd be attempting."

Joshua said, "Well..."

They looked his way.

He shrugged. "I understand that we're going to try to find a starship. And after that, figure out how to tap power from the planets, right?"

Prom nodded. "That's what James reported."

"Well, when I was on the ocean, traveling to and from Far Island, I had two nights of exceptionally clear skies—well, one and a half before the storm clouds started moving in. With nothing to distract me, other than the stink of a Cerik's breath, I did a lot of looking at the stars.

"Before the moon rose, there were easily two dozen stars in the sky at the same time."

Prom said, "Two dozen! I've never seen skies that clear."

Joshua nodded, "And there was this other thing. It moved across the sky so fast it was only there for a minute or so. It was a faint light, and a little fuzzy. I thought it might have been a flock of *ska*, only so high that it appeared as one fat dot.

"The only problem was that *ska* don't fly that fast."

Ace said, "But a craft in orbit might. It might even be several of them, clustered together, only so high that they merged together."

Prom asked, "Okay, which direction was it traveling?"

Joshua thought back. "In the same direction the moon travels. If it was different, then it was just off a small angle."

Ace was leaning forward. He had his pad of paper and a pen in hand. "Now, think very carefully, when did you see it?"

"The middle of the night."

"No, more exact. You said the moon came up, so it was before then. By how much?"

Joshua closed his eyes and tried to recreate that moment in memory. "Two hours. And a bit, maybe ten minutes. Oh, and it passed close to the star I thought might be the planet *Katranel*, if that helps anything."

Prom and Ace retired from the meeting, concentrating on the details of that dot in the sky. Joshua had to estimate his position in the sea. Prom had the rise and setting times of the moon and also the planet for the next several years memorized, but only in relation to his observation point at Kakil Home. Ace had the equations to put it all together.

By the time the meeting ended, Ace brought Joshua a list of times on a sheet of paper.

"Tonight, you need to stay up and find the darkest place you can to observe the sky. From fifteen minutes before to fifteen minutes after these times, search the sky for that dot again. Ideally, I'll want the exact moment it's highest in the sky. If you can find it twice, that'll be great, because it'll tell us how high its orbit is."

Joshua timidly took the paper. "I wish I'd paid more attention the first time."

...

Ash was facing his direction, on watch duty when Joshua attempted to send a message to Base.

"*To Sally: You've heard I did something controversial, rescuing the nomads. If it's any excuse, it was all triggered by Veronica's dream. Honestly, I'd do it again, because I thought it was the right thing to do. I was surprised that people didn't understand. You can beat me up over it when I get back.*

"*But in a day or so, I'll be going on another trip, and you know which one I'm talking about. It'll probably be more dangerous than taking a water boat trip with a bunch of Cerik. Yet, I wish you were coming along with me, because I don't think there's anything we can't solve when we work together.*

"*Don't you worry too much. I'm coming home shortly, and believe me, I'm ready to get started making Sterling's little brother. Maybe I'll even stay home enough to play with them.*

"*You stay safe, and don't worry about all these New Home women here at Sally's Crater. You're my love and they all know it.*

"*Joshua*"

Orbit

Prom pointed to the left. "And that's a red star. R3 in my list. I'd love to give them all names, but eventually we'll get the star picture James bar Bill made after his journey, and I just didn't feel like making the effort. *Katranel,* which is *that* one, has a name because it's the bad luck star in mythology, but most of the others don't have Cerik names."

Joshua said, "Names are good. I can't wait to see what boat D is finally called."

"You traded for it. Maybe you own it. You name it."

Joshua chuckled. "Individuals can't own boats. They're too valuable an asset for anything but the community. I've toyed with the idea of having my own minisub, but that'll be sometime far in the future."

The clock in his head was getting closer to the time. His eyes scanned across the stars. There were more than a dozen out tonight.

Prom sighed, "The skies really are clearer out here. I wonder if that's always the case."

Joshua kept watching the sky. "There are no volcanoes on this island, and the wind is generally from the west, maybe west-southwest. The air over Kakil Home was always contaminated by the volcanic ridge on Far Island. I can imagine it's always clearer here. The air has come thousands of miles without a volcanic plume adding its smoke and ash, I suspect."

He blinked, and it was there. "Prom! Near your B2 star. Can you see it?"

"Where!" Prom pulled off his breather so he could see without the goggle lenses. Then, "I see it! I see it!"

"Shush!" Joshua was focused on the fast-moving dot. *Seeing* brought it much closer than his eyes could resolve.

It bloomed into his mind, a vast, unblemished metal shape, curves rather than angles, complex, like a cluster of *janji* eggs, only huge, and of differing sizes.

But it was just one of several. There were five others, all together arranged as two triangles, each five times as far away to its nearest neighbor as its own length.

And then it was gone.

Joshua blinked. There were just stars in the sky.

"Prom, did you see it?"

"Yes. I took notes. I've got its track through the stars and the timing."

. . .

Joshua had to keep his head down, stepping through Candy's constricted space, helping to hold the last power cell in place as Lacruse, one of Hugo's assistants, finished tightening the straps designed to keep it from shifting. There were too many people in the confined space. With the air circulation shut off, it was stuffy inside. What's worse was that the hatch was open to the outside and it was all raw air.

Patrick leaned against the display, arms crossed and frowning. "It's never been so loaded. I hope it lifts off properly."

As the workers finished and emptied out, just Joshua and Patrick were left. Joshua asked, "When do we leave?"

Patrick shook his head. "I'm waiting for Ace. Apparently it's not just a matter of taking off and chasing the starships, we have to take off at the right moment and once we get up there, they will catch up to us."

"I don't understand."

"Neither do I. This is not the way I learned to fly. It's all by the numbers, so I have to wait for Ace to figure it all out."

Prom showed up at the hatch. "Ace has the solution. We need to leave in forty minutes. Best take the opportunity to use the camp's pot while we can."

. . .

Lifting off was normal, if crowded. Patrick grunted as he got used to Candy's response. "Not too bad," he muttered.

Joshua's seating position just gave him a glimpse of part of the display screen. There weren't windows everywhere, like on Breezy. The climbing kept going on, and the engine pulses dropped below the buzz to just a throb, and then not much of a noise at all.

Ace was closest to the pilot, where he could keep track of their course.

"Okay, we're through the thickest part of the air. Now it's time to shift course for the east. That's it. Just keep moving the target pointer eastward, a bigger gap each time."

Joshua remembered the passages that James had written, describing what he'd seen his first time up, watching the Cerik pilot, just as he was watching Patrick. It was comforting to see the same actions being followed.

Patrick said, "We're really not pushing the air anymore, are we?"

Ace said, "No. And down isn't down anymore. The boat has tilted so that we're pushing at the horizon, rather than at the center of the planet."

He raised his voice, "Everyone, keep a grip on your seats. It feels like we're falling, but we're safe. Don't get disoriented."

Joshua looked back at Prom, gripping his notepad fiercely. His eyes were wide but glazed, as if he was in a trance.

What kind of a trance would a tenner *have? No* sight, *no telepathy, just his own imagination.*

Joshua closed his eyes. He tried to reach out and get a feel for his own location, and it was hard. The ground was whipping by below. They were already over the continent. *So fast!* With no air to slow them down, they could just keep accelerating, getting faster each passing second.

Every time he turned his head, he felt dizzy. Ace had warned them. He kept concentrating on the seat in front of him.

He resolved to wait out the time without trying to follow their path and without trying to make sense of the part of the screen he could see. After all, they had to travel thousands of miles, if he understood the mechanics of their flight.

But not too long afterward, Ace said, "Okay, that's it."

Joshua asked, "What's going on?"

"We're in orbit. Until we locate the starship, we just have to wait."

Locate the starship. Joshua nodded. He could do that.

He reached out with his *sight*, remembering that it should be behind them. The image came quicker than he expected. "*That* way." Joshua pointed to the rear and off to the left.

Patrick and Ace adjusted the display. "There!" Patrick pointed.

"Put a target on it!" Ace urged.

Joshua felt everything spin as the boat adjusted its orientation on its own. The ship seemed above them now.

The display screen showed the image he'd seen before only in his mind. Prom gasped. "What's the size of that?"

The image of the closest of the starships grew larger in the display.

Prom said, "Docking."

Ace nodded. "Request the docking."

Patrick made the criss-cross slash with one hand and then the other that the book said sent a signal to the starship to begin the docking maneuver. The starship would open a hatch and pull the boat into an internal loading area.

The boat shifted slightly, and then stopped.

A harsh Cerik voice spat, <Entrance rejected!>

...

Joshua shook his head. "No. I don't *see* anyone inside. It's cold and dark. It has to be an automated response."

Prom said, "The voice sounds identical each time."

Patrick said, "Well, my arms are getting tired from making the docking slash. Let's try a different starship."

Joshua held onto his chair as they shifted. He noticed Betty's hair drifting around her head as she peered out of her cylinder. She was watching it all.

The second starship reacted the same. <Entrance rejected!>

Prom said, "That's exactly the same voice. Are they all set up the same way?"

Patrick grumbled, "After all we've been through to get here, it's ridiculous to stop because the door is locked."

"Maybe," Joshua suggested, "Tenthonad set a lock on them to keep the other clans from coming up here. It's a way to protect their power monopoly."

"Why are there locks in the first place?" Ace was frustrated.

"History," Prom said, "These starships used to be owned by various clans. It was just a way to keep raiding parties from coming in and stealing from them. Probably when Tenthonad finally took over, they set all the locks."

Patrick growled, "We can't be sure. We need to check every one of them."

He set the target for the next. When they moved closer and signaled, it replied, <Entrance rejected!>

Betty's voice caught their attention. "It's cold."

Joshua had noticed that himself. He'd been shivering.

"Sorry," Ace said. "I didn't realize we'd be hanging out here outside a starship for so long."

Joshua said, "Whenever I *see* into those starships, it seems they're all cold and dark."

"Right. We get some warmth when the sun shines on us, but when we move into the night side, we get colder. If Candy was painted black, it might be better."

Prom rubbed his hands together. "Then we have a time limit to solve this problem. Otherwise we have to go back down, where the air would surround us and keep us warm."

Ace said, "It's not as simple as that."

Patrick nodded, "Yeah. It took a lot of power to get us up here, but it'll also take a lot to get back down. We're at less than half power now. I'm going to move us to the next target."

But by the time they'd checked the sixth star ship, they were all sick of: <Entrance rejected!>

Betty stuttered. "Freezing."

Ace said, "Come on over to the control pad. Maybe you can find some way to warm the boat."

She nodded and wiggled free of her cocoon. With no weight, she was floating in the air. Prom and Joshua helped push her up to the front. Ace gave her his seat and hovered in the air beside her, up against the hull.

Patrick leaned back as the display shifted over into Delense text. It wasn't too long before the air began to hiss.

Joshua chuckled, relieved. "It feels like it's warmer. You did it."

Prom sighed. "That's good to know. I didn't dress well enough for this."

Betty was still tapping on the control panel. Text on the display moved. She whispered to Ace.

He said, "The boat sends an identity code when requesting entrance, and she sees how to change the boat's code, but there's no way to know what the correct code is."

"So we're locked out and there's no way to get the key?" Patrick asked.

Joshua said, "Not unless we hijack a Tenthonad boat, I guess."

A voice shouted out, echoing inside the tight quarters, <Kakil intruder, leave immediately!>

Prom jerked, drifting up from his chair. "What is that!"

Ace translated for Betty. She tapped on the control panel. The screen shifted to a map. All six starships were visible, as was another small dot, approaching fast.

Patrick said, "Why did he call us Kakil?"

Joshua said, "We got this boat from the Kakil-Rikna war. Maybe its identity code still marks it as Kakil."

Prom asked, "Do we reply?"

"Probably not. He can't look inside, can he? He won't know we're not Kakil warriors."

<Kakil, leave immediately or I will knock you down!>

"Can he do that?" Prom struggled to hold himself down.

Patrick looked at the display. "Um. Maybe. If he …"

Just then, there was a hard shove and the boat started spinning. Joshua could feel himself pulled against the side of the hull. Patrick was thrown forward and hit his head against the railing. He looked dazed.

Betty, after a startled squeal, pulled herself back to the control panel and tapped. They jerked again.

Patrick yelled, "What did you do?"

Betty didn't answer. But the spinning had stopped. The display showed that they were farther from the starships, but their retreat was slowing. Then, they started back. The other boat, a triangle-shaped one, had positioned itself between them and the starships.

<I will burn you up in the fires of *Koee*!>

Betty was still working. Ace had one hand holding her into position and braced himself against the hull with the other. The display had split in two, part text, part showing the map. Then she paused, her hands unsteady over the control panel.

Ace whispered, "Betty?"

She reached over in front of Patrick and waved her hand. Screaming loud, she yelled, "Die!"

Then she was back, tapping away.

<U'tanse! What did you do? I will gut you. I will smear your blood over the face of Ko!>

Ace looked nervous. He didn't translate the Cerik threat for Betty, nor the progressively incoherent screams that followed.

He whispered to her, and she whispered back.

Ace cleared his throat. "Betty sent a docking-acknowledged code back to the other boat, over the shouter signal. It seems that when a starship accepts the command to dock a boat, it sends a different code to the boat which locks the engine commands, so a boat pilot won't accidentally damage the starship while docking. The Tenthonad is locked out of his own controls."

Joshua asked, "What was that earlier threat? Fires of *Koee*?"

"*Koee* is the spirit of the land," Prom said. "Volcanoes, maybe."

Patrick rubbed his head, wincing at a smear of blood. "But what do we do? Can he release the lock?"

Ace looked at Betty. She shook her head. "U'tanse stuff."

Ace nodded. "His claws can't work the control pad, even if he understood how. It was put there for the Delense only."

Joshua said, "But you can, right?" Betty nodded.

Joshua thought, "So, if he were reasonable, we might…"

Patrick pointed, "Look!"

In the display, the triangle ship was clearly visible, as they slowly approached. Joshua let himself drift higher so he could see what Patrick pointed at.

There was a puff of vapor. The hatch opened, and the Cerik launched himself at them.

Ace said, "He's crazy."

Joshua said, "He's a warrior. His boat failed him, but that doesn't mean he can't fight."

Naked to space, arms wide and claws extended, he sailed at them with death in his eyes. Every one of them had heard tales of Cerik clawing through metal when they were angry or frustrated. U'tanse had spent generations repairing machinery that Cerik had tried to claw into submission.

Joshua tensed as the warrior came closer and closer without any intent to slow down.

And then, he hit. The body twisted slightly and drifted off.

Remote Control

"What happened?" Prom asked. "Is he dead?"

Betty had her arms across her face, blocking out the sight. Ace had his arms around her shoulders.

Patrick said, "I *think* he's dead."

Joshua said, "He couldn't last long without air. He might have lost consciousness by the time he hit. I didn't sense any reaction from him." He shook his head. "I can't read any thoughts. He'll certainly be dead shortly, if he isn't already."

Prom said, "Hey, good going, Betty."

Ace looked up with a frown and shook his head. Prom nodded and did the zipping his lips gesture.

...

For the next several minutes, nothing changed. Betty showed Patrick how to do more precise engine controls with the control panel than could be accomplished with the hack and slash Cerik gestures. They brought themselves stationary in relationship to the starships and the slowly rotating triangle ship.

"The other ship has the right docking code. Can Betty reach in through the shouter system and pull it out?" Joshua asked.

She shook her head.

Ace said, "No, it looks like only a few ship-to-ship commands can ride over the shouter signal, but we can't really dig into its system like that."

Prom said, "The empty boat has the right code, and Betty could turn its controls back on, but there's nobody there to control it. We're stuck here with no entrance code. What's the chance one of us could jump through that open hatchway and survive the experience?"

Patrick looked at the triangle boat. "Little to no chance. Neither boat has an airlock. So not only is the triangle boat unlivable, but opening our hatch would kill us all, as well. There is air in Candy's tanks, but opening the hatch, closing it again, and refilling the cabin with air would take far too long. It just won't work."

Joshua closed his eyes and reached into the other boat. It was strange, staring at the lit up display on the triangle boat. He could actually look back at Candy on the screen, although it was just a small image.

The interior of the triangle boat was divided into sections, a central hub and three lobes, but it was all empty: no cargo, no other passengers.

What was he here for?

Joshua asked, "He called us Kakil. For him to know that, the starship had to tell him, right?"

Ace frowned. "Um. Yes, I think so. We didn't use the shouter first, and that's the only other way I can think of for that information to have gotten to him."

"So, we signaled the starship. The lock said no to us, and at the same time reported us to …"

"Tenthonad clan, obviously."

"Yes, but to some boat on the ground, or was he already in orbit?"

As Ace thought, Joshua continued, "Because I think I *see* another starship on the triangle boat's map screen."

"Other than these six?"

"Yes. It's a lone dot much higher above the planet. I think maybe he was on board that starship and when the alarm was given, he was the first to respond."

"The first. You mean there will be others?"

"If the alarm got all the way to the ground, then certainly Tenthonad will send more warriors. We threaten their monopoly. We will have to be destroyed."

"Is there any way to tell?"

Joshua shrugged. "I know where the Tenthonad park their triangle boats. If there are any missing, then it's likely they will be heading our way."

Patrick said, "Check for them. I'll see if I can make this map system respond."

Joshua nodded and closed his eyes. He was having difficulty seeing things on the ground because of the speed at which things moved, but he needed to locate that landing area.

Familiarity let him find Base first. With that anchor, he moved his focus across the continent. Across the Western Mountains, across the Lost Mountains, and then across the Third Mountains, into the deserts of Sakah, and northeastward into Tenthonad lands.

He found it. The area was swarming with warriors. The canopies that had been covering many of the triangle ships were pulled aside.

"They're still on the ground, but they're coming in force. It looks like there will be a dozen or more coming to visit us as soon as they can take off."

Prom said, "We need to get out of here."

Patrick said, "And go where? Like I said, I don't really know if I have enough power to get safely to the ground, and there will be Tenthonad after us. If the first one knew we were Kakil, he might have had enough information to track our signal. Candy was at Factory when Betty neutered the other boats' shouters. We never had time to do that once Wender brought it to New Home."

Ace said, "Lucky. Betty's lockout trick wouldn't have worked if we'd done the alteration."

Prom asked, "The other starship. Did he lock the door behind him when he came for us?"

Joshua chuckled. "He's a Cerik. They don't make that kind of tactical error."

Prom shook his head. "There has to be some place we can go. Are you sure we can't just drop back into the atmosphere? Why does it take a lot of power to go down? Doesn't make any sense."

Ace said, "We're falling now, but we're going so fast sideways the planet's curve falls away from us before we get there. To reach the atmosphere, we'd have to push off something, like the starships, or the moon, and that takes power.

"Then once we get to the air, we're still going so fast that we'll heat up by friction. I doubt the hull would hold up to that.

"No, the only way to go down safely is to gradually slow down, using the engines, making sure we never get too deeply into the air layers until we've already slowed down. It's going to take power to do it right. It's all spelled out in the book James wrote. It'll take time, and power, to do it right. One wrong step and we'll burn up."

Betty said, "*Koee's* fire." Every time she spoke, it caught everyone's attention.

Joshua realized what she was saying and it suddenly made sense. The warrior was going to push them into the atmosphere too deeply for them to control it, and they would burn up.

"Betty, I think it's on you."

She looked back at him, puzzled.

He nodded. "It makes no sense that the Delense would lock themselves out, in the case of a dead crew on a boat. Surely there's a way for them to regain control. The starship takes control of a boat to dock it internally. Dig into whatever systems you can reach. Can you make the triangle boat do something to help us?"

She shrugged, but turned to the control pad.

Joshua tried to locate that other starship with his *sight*.

It took several probes, guessing at the direction by trying to understand the location of the starship on the triangle boat's map. It twisted his sense of direction to work in this way. It was nothing like finding his directions on the surface of the planet.

But he found it. It was a huge maze of chambers inside, many lit up and with the feel of having been used. There was even a chamber with runners walking around. Somehow, inside the starship, the feel of ground beneath your feet was preserved. The poor runners, food for hunters who had to live there, had no sense they weren't in just another pen down on Ko.

But there was no other Cerik. Had they left a lone warrior to guard the place? Inside the docking area were three other triangle boats, all powered down. But there was space for six.

Betty's voice, as she said, "Oh," woke him out of his vision.

She whispered to Ace. He said. "She's found something. If the triangle boat is in the right location, she can cause it to call for docking."

Joshua nodded. "That's it."

…

It took time to get everything adjusted. Using Candy's engines, they nudged the other boat into position, just outside the docking port of the nearest starship. Candy was right behind it.

"Do it."

Betty tapped the pad. Patrick activated the shouter and said, "Go", sending Betty's signal the other boat over the call.

Both boats shivered. Patrick muttered, "I hope our engine controls are still active."

The large hatchway on the side of the starship slowly opened up. Lights from the internal docking area showed the landing pad within, only at a steep angle from Patrick's perspective. The triangle boat began tipping up, matching its bottom to the inside dock. Using the control pad, Betty attempted the same, following inside only a couple of feet behind the empty boat. With the tilt, everything looked normal.

"Did we make it?" Prom whispered.

Patrick said, "Maybe." They pushed forward, nudging the other boat with a clang as the hulls tapped together, and then he scooted past to find Candy a spot of her own.

There was a thud. "Candy's down."

Prom asked, "What?"

Joshua reached over, his face plastered with a wide grin, and gave him a bump on the shoulder. "There's weight. Can't you feel it? Fake weight."

Ace slid down against the hull to the deck. "Oops. Should have seen that coming. They must use attractive forces, inside, just like the boat's engines."

Prom nodded. "James told of running around inside the starship. I just didn't think about it."

The outside shook, as short-lived winds rushed through the docking area.

Patrick said, "It's air. Probably mixed like raw air, but we should be able to breathe."

Joshua said, "And we have to hurry. The Tenthonad warriors are on the way."

Lock the Door

Prom led the way, following the details from James bar Bill's book etched in his memory. "This is the corridor to the control center."

The passageway was ceramic-coated metal, unlike the mud or stone they'd grown up with. Joshua could easily see which wall was against the external hull by the gentle outward bow. The interior walls were flat, except for the seams which smoothly joined the other surfaces in a four or five inch curve. When he sensed the other chambers, it reminded him of how soapy foam formed interior cells with flat joining walls. Had they created huge eggs and then blown some kind of metal interior structure that same way?

Patrick hunched over walking stiffly. "I hope there are heating controls. It's worse than freezing in here."

Joshua noted the ice crystals on the walls. "Yes. I agree."

He was glad the automated systems recognized their presence and lit up the corridors ahead of them. Hunting for light switches might have just been too much to handle.

Ace and Betty walked huddled together. Of them all, only Prom seemed unaffected. *The grand reveal of his dream must be keeping him warm.*

Joshua felt a little safer, now that they were inside the starship, but it was an illusion, he knew. The coming ships all had the unlock code, and as soon as Cerik roamed these hallways, they'd be dead.

The starship controls were their only hope.

The display was twice as tall as he was and even wider. There was a scarred perch where a Rear-Talon pilot typically rested, waving his claws to control everything.

Betty went straight for one of the circular Delense control pads. She nodded to herself, and Joshua was relieved. If she understood what she was seeing, that was a good sign. Ace was by her side and Patrick started testing his boat commands on the ship, seeing if they matched.

Prom whistled in surprise. He waved.

Joshua walked over to where he stood. At first glance, it appeared to be a different kind of display screen, but he couldn't interpret the lights on the black background.

Prom waved his hand at it. "Isn't it magnificent?"

At first, all he could see were dots of light, then Joshua shifted his head. Suddenly, he understood and a shiver that was more profound than that from the cold went down his spine. He whispered, "Are those stars?"

The scholar nodded, his eyes shiny. "Thousands, for sure. Perhaps ten thousands."

Joshua moved closer to the glass. It was just a window, he realized. A window out into space.

Prom mused, "One of them shines down on Old Earth."

"How could we ever know which one?"

He just shook his head, then waved to the side. "Move over to this side." Prom moved back.

Joshua took his place, and at the far edge of the view was a wide reddish curve: the edge of Ko. There was a sliver of darker blue, part of the ocean. And a thin haze edged it all, the barrier of air that kept life alive and the majesty of the stars out.

...

Ace yelled, "We've got warm air flowing, but it'll be a long time before everything thaws out. Keep moving if you want to stay warm."

Joshua tried to locate the boats coming toward them, but they would just be tiny points in the vastness of space. Even if he looked out the window, he wouldn't be able to see them until they got close.

He frowned, then walked over to Ace and Betty.

"Can you control the lights?"

She nodded.

"Ace, can you calculate how long it'll take the Tenthonad boats to reach us?"

"It really depends on where we were in the orbit when they took off. I'd say anywhere from twenty minutes to an hour or so. And that's just a guess."

"So, if we turned off all the lights on the ship before they arrived, they wouldn't know which one we were in, or even if we managed to enter. All they'd know is that the Kakil intruder and their own guard's boat were missing."

Patrick said, "They'll still check. I know I would."

Joshua looked to Betty. "Can you change the door lock code so they can't come in?"

Ace said, "She's been looking. The lock section doesn't seem to be anywhere in the station maintenance controls. I was thinking we could bypass the code stuff and just force the door shut."

Joshua frowned. "What about a diversion? Betty, can you control anything on the other starships? If we were dark and a ship on the other side of this cluster had its lights on, they'd certainly hunt there first."

She looked back to her control pad.

Patrick had a map display much larger than anything they'd seen before. The cluster of six ships was shown, and off on a different path altogether, the lone starship the Tenthonad warrior came from was marked.

"Why is it there in a different orbit?" Joshua asked.

Patrick shrugged. "I was going to ask Prom, see if he had any idea, but he's wandered off."

"That station is warm and active. It has prey animals for a long stay. That's where Tenthonad has been working. It's probably the ship they use to pull power from the planets. These six were just in storage."

Joshua looked down at the curve of the planet on the map. There were dots.

He tapped the display down in the lower corner. "These are the ones we need to worry about."

Patrick counted in a whisper. "Nine boats coming for us. You said they had more?"

"Yes, but that's a nice round number for a Cerik. The guard reported to them, probably, and then went silent. They probably know a single Kakil boat is here, and nine attackers is just overkill. They want us dead, quickly. But they're not desperate. Otherwise, they would have sent them all."

Patrick grumbled. "I guess it's nice to know they sent nine Cerik to kill me."

"Nine boats' worth. I saw groups loading up. I don't know how many warriors there are on each boat."

Joshua asked, "I don't suppose you can fly this starship? Run away from them?"

"Honestly, I'm been too frightened to try. It's not like this thing is set up to fly through the air. I don't even know where the engines are on this cluster of eggs. Now that we've walked through the corridors, I don't even know where *we* are in the ship."

"But the controls are the same?"

"They have to be, don't they? Cerik flew them, even after they killed all the Delense. So it's hack and slash controls, but do the gestures mean the same thing? I don't suppose we could get one of those attackers to come in and demonstrate it for us?"

Joshua wrinkled his nose. "Not likely." He looked at the dots rising from the planet. They were getting closer, and moving fast. "I'm going to track down Prom."

It didn't take long. Prom was sitting cross-legged in the corridor in front of another window. He had several sheets of paper spread out on the floor, marking dots. He was trying to map the stars.

"Prom, we need you in the control room. The attackers are coming."

Frustrated, Prom looked at his pages. "I guess the stars will still be here later, right?"

"Probably."

He laid his pen aside and got to his feet, glancing back as they went to the control room.

Ace looked up. He had moved to a different control panel from the one where Betty worked. "Good news. The air coming out of the system is now filtered. The Delense controls can mix the air in any proportion."

Joshua nodded. "You read the Book?"

Ace grinned. "Yes. I hope it doesn't come down to hand-to-claw combat, but if so, the Cerik will bleed a lot more freely."

Bred in the raw air of Ko, the Cerik blood clotting mechanism depended on some of the very chemicals in the air that the U'tanse filtered out. Father and Mother used that to their advantage in an early battle for their existence. The U'tanse never mentioned it where a Cerik could overhear, but it was there in the Book for all U'tanse to read.

Prom had drifted over to the large map display and was chatting with Patrick. Betty was working intently.

"Did you find a way to light up another starship?"

Betty looked up, glanced over to where Ace was working, then forced herself to speak. Joshua had to listen carefully to her soft, tenuous voice.

"I found the cluster controls—applies to all ships in the cluster. Lock code is there."

"Great. Can you change it?"

She nodded. "To what?"

Joshua frowned, considering it. "Something the Tenthonad boats can't enter. Something U'tanse maybe?"

"Delense script icons?"

"Will it accept that?"

She nodded again.

"Okay. Do it then."

She tapped. Joshua could see just enough to observe what she was entering. They were the simplest of characters: a square, a circle, and a triangle. Three simple codes a U'tanse could enter on a control panel, but something no Cerik could manage with his claws.

"Done."

He breathed out a deep sigh. "Good work. We've locked them out, for now."

As he turned to go, she gripped his sleeve.

"Yes?" he asked.

"Twenty-nine."

"Twenty-nine what?"

"Ships in the cluster."

"Here in orbit?"

She shrugged.

"Oh."

There weren't just these six in storage and the one lone ship off in the funny orbit. There were others, all in range of the cluster controls. Were they all empty?

"Hmm. So, if there is another ship in the cluster and it has a U'tanse on it, that person could change the access code back?"

She shrugged again.

Patrick called, "They're getting close!"

Joshua nodded. "Okay, it's time to go dark. Cut the lights."

Ace tapped the command and all the lights went out. Patrick gave a slash command, and the large map went dark.

Prom said, "Back to the windows. We can see out that way. But let me collect my papers."

Fires of Koee

The triangular boats appeared as a regular line of dots, appearing over the curve of Ko.

"Can they see us in the window?" asked Patrick.

"Not yet," Ace said. "The boat is bigger than this window. We can't see more than a dot. They may not even be able to see the window yet. But when they get closer, we should step back out of the light."

Joshua remarked, "That's a nice formation."

Patrick nodded. "They probably need to line up like that to keep from getting in the way of each other's pushing beams. It's telling that they know how to do it. It means they've been flying groups of boats up into space on a regular basis."

"Probably up to that lone starship."

Patrick nodded. "Prom explained it to me. The lone ship is in an orbit that gives it several days lined up between the moon and *Katranel*, the other planet. While it's lined up like that, they can run a power collecting beam and fill the ship's huge power reserves. The boats dock and fill their own power cells from the starship."

Prom added, "Then they can just fly the big ship back to an earlier position in the special orbit and do the whole cycle, all over again. That's the power collecting system for the whole of Ko."

The line of dots expanded into a line of triangles, slowly approaching the cluster of ships.

<Intruders from Kakil! Prepare to die!> The sound echoed from the control center.

Joshua chuckled, "I guess no one turned off the shouter?"

Prom asked, "Why are they waiting?"

Joshua reached out, listening for thoughts. There was the usual churn of blood lust from the warriors, but there were some calculating thoughts, as well. The commander sent a shouter command to the other boats.

"Step back," Joshua waved. "They're going to do a close flyby to see if they can tell which ship we're in. Don't the sunlight shine on you."

Three of the boats stayed where they were. Joshua pointed to the one on the left. "That one has the *tetca's la*. He's giving the orders."

One of the boats moved close, a silent blade passing by, blocking out the view. It was close enough to see a Cerik face through the boat's window.

Prom asked, "Did he see us?"

Joshua shook his head. "No indication of it. There are plenty of other windows to check."

It was a tense moment, waiting in the dark, hearing nothing but the faint passage of the warm air.

Then, there was a loud bang, and then a scrape.

"What's that?"

Joshua took in a sharp breath, and then winced. "They touched the hulls. The boat pilot can hear the air circulation. He's reporting to his *la*."

They waited ten long seconds. "That's it." Joshua could see the command boat move. "He's going to attempt to dock. Pray that Betty changed the right code."

Boats were moving, collecting back on the docking side of their ship.

The command center spoke in Cerik, <Entrance rejected!>

Prom chuckled. "Glad to hear it this time."

<Entrance rejected!>

Patrick said, "That's going to get old."

The boats started moving in different patterns, more like a flock of *ska* circling a dead body.

There was a shove, and they all staggered. Prom stumbled to his knees. "What was that?"

"Push beam," Patrick said, his voice tense. "They can't get in, but that doesn't mean they can't hurt us."

Joshua asked, "*Can* they hurt us?"

Ace said, "Possibly. This starship is a collection of eggs connected together. If a beam hit one just one of them, it would put a lot of stress on the connection points. With luck, they could cause a tear in the hull and leak all the air."

Prom complained, "But that would destroy the ship!"

Joshua felt the anger from the Cerik commander. "To them, they only need one ship. These are derelicts to them. It would be worth it to lose the starship if it wiped out the infestation—us."

"But if Betty changed the master code, they're already locked out of all of them. They've lost."

"They don't know that."

Ace suggested, "Maybe we should retreat to Candy."

Joshua shook his head, but in the dark, they probably didn't see. "No, we have to find a way to stop them before they damage the ship."

Betty tugged at his sleeve.

"You have an idea."

She whispered, "Yes."

"Come on, then."

She held on to his sleeve, as he walked back in the darkness. He didn't know how good her sight was, but obviously his was better.

Ace called out, "I'm following." The *tenner* walked with his arm outstretched, touching the wall.

Joshua led her to the control panel she'd been using. She tapped.

The lights came back on. Patrick and Prom hurried to the map display.

Ace came up beside Betty. They whispered. He nodded and moved to the other control panel.

Another shove, and Joshua reached for the wall to hold himself upright.

Patrick had the map on, showing the swirling ships, looking almost as real as if they were looking out a window.

One of them abruptly darted toward the ship. There was a loud scraping noise. Then it tumbled away.

"What's happening?" Patrick called.

Ace was focused on his controls. "Betty and I are pulling the power out of the boats, one by one." He leaned closer to his command pad. "The starship's beam can overpower their systems."

"There goes another one," Prom pointed.

Joshua walked closer to see. As power was drained from a boat, it lost the ability to adjust its course. Some of them hit each other. One more glanced off the hull of the starship.

The commander ordered a retreat. Three of the boats pushed away, dwindling in size.

Ace groused, "Lost them. They're out of charging range."

Joshua ordered, "Locate the others. Where are they?"

The map display had them all. One of the still-powered boats began its careful drop out of orbit, returning to the planet. The other two were shifting course toward the lone ship in the charging orbit.

"We'll have to keep track of those two. Once they realize they can't get in, they might come back for another attack."

Patrick frowned, "Would they attack that ship?"

"They might, but there's nothing we can do about it. What about the derelicts?"

Six boats were drifting, out of power. Joshua could feel the panic coming from them.

Joshua pointed at the farthest of the lot. "Patrick, can you … somehow, pull that one back closer?"

"Maybe. Why?"

"Boats are irreplaceable." Which was true. Nobody had discovered the factory where they were made, just places where repair parts were fabricated. But he didn't want more deaths than were necessary, either.

Patrick timidly made some familiar slashes. Some markings appeared on the map. "Ace, can you help me figure this out?"

Ace hurried over. Together, they puzzled out the controls. The boat was drifting still farther. Others were drifting off, as well. One of them passed between two of the big ships and was sent spinning.

"What was that?"

Ace looked. "There are small, low-powered beams that go from starship to starship, maintaining them in this cluster of six. I could turn it off, but then the big ships would start drifting off as well, or run into each other."

The push and pull beam controls were decoded, but not before the farthest boat started moving away faster.

"What's happening?"

Patrick frowned. "It's caught the wisps of the upper atmosphere, I suspect. It is slowing down, moving out of range too quickly for us to deal with."

Prom was at the window. He yelled. "I can see it. Come quickly."

Joshua ran over. Prom pointed. It was a faint dot in the sunlight, but just as it moved into the shadow of the night side, Joshua could see it glow red, and then brighter against the dark landscape below.

Prom asked, "Is that the air friction Patrick was talking about?"

Joshua nodded. It flared still brighter, and they lost sight of it.

Prom whispered, "The Fires of *Koee*."

...

Using the beams from the starship, they collected the five remaining boats together.

"What are we going to do with them?" asked Patrick. "They'll kill each other, you know."

Joshua nodded. One crew had already turned on each other, and those not killed immediately collapsed, having used up all their air.

"Ace, can you feed a little power back into one of those boats?"

"Yes, but why? If they have power, they'll just try to kill us again."

"Try it. And show me how the shouter controls work."

Ace turned the power back on. Joshua yelled at the boat. <Are you willing to accept *uuka*!>

The call came back. <I will never give *uuka* to U'tanse!>

Joshua shrugged. It had been worth a shot, but such a thing was too big a step for a Cerik.

<Are you willing to pledge *uuka* to the Cerik Name Rukan!>

...

The others watched as the drama played out. Of the twenty-two survivors, eighteen accepted *uuka*, and the others were killed by their boat-mates. Ace fed enough power back to the four boats that were now part of the Rukan clan to reach Far Island safely.

Patrick shook his head as they left. "That's crazy. They could have turned on us the instant we gave them the power."

Joshua shrugged. "And Ace could have pulled their power again. Believe me, there are some advantages to have a Cerik clan as an ally."

"If they go to Far Island, like you told them. I really doubt it."

"Dead or alive, they couldn't hurt us. Alive, they might be of benefit."

Ace said, "It's been kind of interesting for me. There's a lot about Cerik culture I wasn't aware of."

They all jerked when the command center spoke again. <Entrance rejected on Lokaan by Tenthonad thirty-three!>

Prom said, "That's what happened when we attempted to enter here. I guess Lokaan is the name of that other starship?"

Joshua nodded. "Now we know. Good job, Betty."

Prom looked at him sideways. "We've won, and you don't seem very happy."

"We've indeed won control of all the starships. We have taken the power monopoly away from Tenthonad."

He looked at his four companions. He forced a smile.

"But now, we have to face the fact that all power is shut down across the planet. No one realizes it yet, but when the clans contact Tenthonad and ask for a freshly charged power cell, it won't be delivered.

"Boats will stop flying across the sky. Wars will go back to the way it was before, with warriors hiking across the hills to get to their enemy.

"And every U'tanse Home will start to go dark. Every Home will run out of power to refresh their air. And if a Name can't get power to fight his neighbor, he certainly won't worry one bit about getting the power to keep his U'tanse alive."

Joshua sighed. "If we own the power monopoly now, we'll have to find a way to keep power flowing."

The Sting

<U'tanse-that-swims, are you there?>

Joshua hurried to the control center.

<Rukan! Your voice carries far, up into space itself!>

The rumble of satisfaction echoed in room. <My new Rear-Talon has told me that you wished to speak of a new trade.>

<Ah! Then you have accepted the new clan members?>

<Some of them. I made them take *uuka* with my claw at their necks. The idea of speaking the oath to a U'tanse did not taste well to a few.>

<Choose your Second well.>

Rukan made a hissing roar that said much. <Sometimes I think you think too much like a Cerik and not enough like the U'tanse.>

<My right-eyes say the same. What do you think of my boats?>

He hissed. <Your boats? I see them resting on my land, under my claws.>

<Boats with power enough to carry your shouts, but not enough power to fly where you wish.>

<You want to come take them from me? Even if I have no wish to fly anywhere, yet they grace my Perch.>

<There's nowhere you wish to fly? Not even to the City of the Face.>

There was silence. After a minute, Rukan made a low growl. <What is this trade you wished to talk about?>

…

It was more difficult than they expected to find a dining table on the ship. Candy's food stores were moved aboard, and they sat on perches next to a flat workspace.

Joshua chewed on the tough biscuit. "Now that they've left, we have to make a visit over to the Lokaan ship and see if they've damaged it. But as soon as we can, we need to get Candy and the power cells down to our people."

Prom said, "We still haven't pulled power from the planets ourselves. We just used the power from this ship and what we pulled from those boats."

"I agree. It's very important we own the whole process, but things are going to blow up, politically, very soon now and we have be prepared. If you could do the task yourself, I'd leave you up here to tackle it, but as great a historian as you are, and as important as your help has been in cracking the power monopoly, we need people like Ace and Betty to work out the details."

Ace cleared his throat. "Betty and I won't mind being up here by ourselves until the next crew arrives."

Patrick rolled his eyes, but Ace wasn't looking his way. Betty didn't raise her eyes. She concentrated on eating.

Joshua said, "I agree you need to stay here. Someone needs to be up in either this ship or another that can control critical systems, just in case the Tenthonad show up with a new plan for re-taking the ships. I wish there was more then five of us."

Patrick asked, "Are you up to taking the triangle boat back yourself?"

"That *is* why we have a backup pilot, right?" Joshua smiled. "Ace has the return procedure written out for me."

Prom frowned, "You don't mind if I ride back with Patrick?"

Joshua laughed. "That's fine. Candy goes back to Factory. There's no landing raft for the triangle-shaped boats, so I'll go to New Home. By this time tomorrow, every fabricator we have will be running at full power. I'll certainly leave enough power in... boat T1 to make a trip back up to recharge."

Patrick raised his hand. "With more pilots?"

"Right. Although we'll be training a lot of people on the job. We need to have as many of these T-boats flying as possible before people realize Tenthonad's power has dried up."

"I wouldn't put it past them to try to *flick* our landing sites."

"That's why Betty is shifting every one of our boats to the alternate tracking system she worked out. The only ones left on Tenthonad's shouter maps will be the ones on Far Island. I've mentioned the risk to Rukan, and I just hope he's taken my advice and moved them away from his Perch."

Joshua grinned, "Free U'tanse have been hiding from the Cerik for all our existence, and those skills will still be necessary, even if we have to get a little more visible."

...

Joshua felt like he did the first time he snuck out of Base and swam ashore to see what it was like to step out on land and see the open sky above. He kept one hand on the center pole by the perch and swiped his hand, adjusting the angle the T-boat was making with the horizon. He was flying the new and unfamiliar craft, and it was responding to his every whim. He could fly it anywhere.

He glanced at Ace's sheet. Only, *anywhere* was restricted to a corridor through the atmosphere that kept him slowing down from orbital speed without risking the Fires of *Koee*. Ace said it was better to fly a little lower on the way down. *"When speeding up, we wanted to be high above the air to avoid wind resistance. When slowing down, it's better to have a little wind drag to help us."*

He particularly liked the flat, triangular shape of this boat. It cut through the thin air like the wing of a *ska*. The loaf-shaped boats could never match a T-boat's speed and agility. Not that he'd gloat about it too much to Patrick, Carson, or Den.

And the power capacity was enormous. One of these craft could easily deliver power to a factory and still have capacity enough to get back into orbit to charge up for more. He suspected they were designed for planet-to-orbit use. This was the only type of boat in the starship's docking bay.

Perhaps Father and Mother rode up from Old Earth in one of these.

Prom was excited about investigating every room in the starships for clues to the travels they made. *"There have to be logs and records of some kind, or if not, then maybe artifacts."*

If they found clues to the home worlds of the Uuaa or the Ba, then they needed to see if it would be possible to return them.

Although, I can't see how to fit one of the adult Ba into the boat. Supposedly, they arrived as children. They hint that they remember the home world of Ba on Ba on Ba, but is that personal memory, or some kind of racial memory?

Joshua reached up to adjust the path again. Suddenly, the hull jumped up and threw him to the side.

What? The world had tilted. The impact had sent the boat spinning. The center pole was above him.

Dizzy from the spin, he had to focus on the screen to see the dot that marked the other boat. "Where did they come from?"

The shriek of the wind told him the T-boat was knocked askew, no longer cutting smoothly through the air.

It had to be a Tenthonad attacker, trying to knock him for a tumble in the most critical part of re-entry. He pulled himself across the perch and stretched for the control panel.

I have to get the boat under control!

He had to climb up the floor to reach the center pole. He cradled it under his arm and made a flat slash. The T-boat hummed loudly, grabbing the air around it to stabilize itself. He almost got the floor under him when there was a second slam, and Joshua could only hold on tight.

The attacker was climbing straight up, trying to reach his altitude.

The closer he gets, the stronger he can push, unimpeded by the column of air between us.

I can't die. I have to fight back!

He made another flat slash.

He had to get his boat stable. The hull was getting warm. The view out the real window showed air glowing red. His tumbling had increased his wind drag drastically. He was dropping too fast and he would burn if he didn't pull out of it.

But the attacker was stable and he could shove him again.

I'll knock you down! But how? The slash-push needed a target, marked on the display. He wasn't stable enough to center the target.

But maybe time was on his side! He was racing across the sky at enormous speed. The Cerik had just come straight up to attack him, there was no way this encounter would last more than a few more seconds. He just had to keep the Tenthonad from giving him another uncontrollable tumble.

And he was coming up very fast. Was he going for a close killing push?

Too close. And then he remembered something else Ace had told him.

Joshua centered his view on the control pad and tapped the third button on the circle, and then the fifth. The shouter activated.

<If you survive,> he yelled, <tell your Name that it is useless to attack us. We have a poisonous sting!>

The metal hull was creaking, as the air slamming roughly against the hull fought the boat's attempt to stay stable. Joshua climbed back upright, using the center pole. The attacker's boat drifted to the middle of the display and with a stab of his fingers, Joshua marked it, then tapped the charge function.

There was a display he'd seen before—symbolic bubbles of power flowing his way. He was rapidly draining the power from the attacker.

Should I stop it? I'll kill him.

Serves him right!

Joshua's hand hovered over the buttons, watching all the power drain from the attacker.

Ace had said, "Think of it like two buckets of water, connected at their bases by a hose. Each bucket has a valve. Open both valves and raise one bucket higher than the other and water will flow to the lower bucket. Betty's shouter code will turn on the valve on the other boat. Your boat will do the rest, draining their power."

The bubbles of power stopped coming. The Tenthonad boat was drained.

I couldn't let you kill me. My people need this power.

But could he watch as the attacker fell to the ground, boat and pilot lost to the fortunes of war?

Just a second to decide.

Joshua tapped one button and then another. A single bubble of power shot back to the other boat before it fell out of range. If the pilot was skilled, he'd make it to the ground alive.

He hadn't really needed his long taunt. Betty's "Die" had done just as well to transfer the command code. But as long as he was talking, he might as well pass on the message. Maybe it would make it back to the Tenthonad commanders.

They would try to attack again, he was sure of it. As long as the U'tanse stayed on their toes, and they had people like Ace and Betty to give them the technological edge, they *should* survive.

But now, he had to get back into the proper path. He was sweating from the heated air around him. He slashed, and his T-boat gained altitude into thinner air.

The attacker had climbed up from the east coast, and that's where it was falling back. But Joshua's boat still had to travel across the wide ocean and find that tiny dot where the people of New Home lived.

. . .

People in the field panicked when they saw the strange boat appear overhead. Joshua kept his approach straight and level, slowing down and settling down on the landing pad next to the fabrication area.

Hugo was peering out the access door when he opened the hatch.

"Are you ready to accept a charge?" Joshua yelled.

Hugo's face relaxed when he saw who it was. "How much do you have?"

"More than you'll ever need!"

City of the Face

Joshua stood on the metal raft, his arm resting on the hull of his T-boat. The endless waves in all directions reminded him of the stars from space. They both were so vast that it was impossible for the human mind to feel their size. Where was that point, he wondered? Did his mind start to blur the feeling of distance once something was beyond his arm's reach, or was it how far he could jump?

Time is like that, too.

He'd imagined that this day would come, but it alway seemed so distant.

But now it was close, and his heartbeat seemed to race faster, like counting the seconds was too slow.

But they were waiting for him down below. Events far off in the center of the continent at the City of the Face were moving at their own pace and wouldn't wait for him.

Joshua walked to the edge of the raft and stepped over into the transport sub where Sally was waiting for him. He sealed the hatch above and checked the airflow.

This was fresh out of Factory's submarine workshop. There was comfortable seating inside and room for four passengers. The outer dimensions were designed to easily navigate into the access tunnels the Delense favored.

Joshua checked the cables running off the edge of the raft and into sea. Everything was secure. The sky above was clear, and the winds were mild.

Sally asked, "Are you done? You checked it when we got up and last night, as well. One would think you're nervous."

"Possibly. There are so many ways today can play out. I don't want anything to go wrong."

She took his hand. "Sit down. Something *will* go wrong, but at the end of the day, we'll be in better shape, no matter what happens."

He sat down in the pilot's seat, checked the seals and the air. "Okay, we're going below." He turned the valve, and the ballast pressure adjusted. Water crept up over the canopy and the colors all changed. The view of the raft from below showed myriad dancing bubbles, air trapped between the floatation tanks.

Sally reached past him and flipped on the lights. The deeper they got, the darker it was. The entrance to the seamount base loomed like a giant dark mouth, glowing with an internal light from deep within. The cables from the raft led the way into the entrance.

There were hands to lift them out as they docked. Debbie said, "Cyclops is ready."

Past the bones of the Delense, past the sealed hatch a Factory crew had opened only with great difficulty, Joshua and Sally walked into the first of many interior chambers.

Sally sniffed. "They still don't have the air fixed."

"It's good enough. People can breathe it. It's another bubble where U'tanse can live."

The lights were brightest on Cyclops, sitting on his throne.

"It feels a little warm. Do you have lights on me?"

Joshua said, "Yes. You look most impressive, from a Cerik perspective."

"I liked the garden better."

"It's not like you'll be living here. It's just a one-time thing."

Cyclops smiled, shaking his eyeless head. "That's what you said the first time."

Joshua was proud of his father. The very idea of transporting him to the undersea base had to have been difficult for him. The new submarines and careful use of sleepy juice had eased the transport for him. The more difficult struggle was coming out of the dark and showing himself to the world.

Joshua sat on the chair prepared for him, down beneath his father's 'gaze'.

"I need to check on how things are going."

"Just signal me when I need to speak."

Monitoring had taken a lot of Joshua's time the past week, *viewing* the City of the Face. The moon was approaching the peak of its phase and size, and when the Large Full Moon shone down on the City, the Faces would begin.

Preparation had started the week earlier. Rukan's warriors had arrived, claiming the abandoned High Perch of Rikna. The pen for Rukan's feast was repaired.

Workers from other clans were there as well, making their own preparations. U'tanse weren't allowed in the area within the week leading up to the Faces, so there were only Cerik present, and a *new* Name prompted the most gossip. Over the past hundred years, clans had gone extinct, usually through conquest. New ones hadn't appeared in anyone's memories.

Still, there was little doubt he was legitimate. A Name had to have females, land, and warriors. When Rukan's warriors arrived in their own boat, it was deemed sufficient. Some minor clans, too poor to own a boat, needed to have neighboring clans bring them to the Faces.

When a second boat arrived, bringing dozens of the fabled *doonag* for the feast, gossip reached a frantic pace.

Joshua had been expecting a reaction from Tenthonad workers. The T-boats were obviously taken from Tenthonad, as were some of the Rukan workers. The *katche* was in effect from the moment the first feast prey arrived for the first clan, so it was unthinkable for Tenthonad to mount an attack, but the planet-wide peace would dissolve when the Names left the City.

At that time, everyone would know Rukan came from Far Island, and more clans than just Tenthonad might be tempted to send a boat to check it out.

Joshua was glad Rukan's ingrained desire to be a respected Name at the Faces overrode his nomad's desire to stay hidden. It was a giant risk for the new Name.

It's a risky few days for us all.

Tenthonad had been staying silent about its loss of power from space. The clan had been delivering stored power as usual, although there were many complaints that deliveries had been slower in coming. The Faces gave every clan its moment in the sun, and Tenthonad might use its High Perch to call for a planet-wide counterattack against its usurpers. At the moment, Rukan was the suspect.

Kakil's Elehadi had kept his plans for a world-wide slaughter of the U'tanse quiet, except for secret meetings with select neighboring Names. The battles just recently canceled for the Faces might have upset those plans, but until Elehadi had the attention of all eyes as he sat on his High Perch, Joshua wasn't sure he *wouldn't* call for the simultaneous *flicking* of all Homes by all the clans.

Those neighboring clans, Graddik, Dallah, Sanassan and the minor clans also affected, would all be on their High Perches calling for more severe penalties for Kakil. Elehadi was already under restricted power deliveries from his last debacle—the mass attachment that had broken out in Rikna Home.

And everyone knew of the possibility of organized, rogue U'tanse. Jinger's slip and the subsequent probes of her thoughts had convinced many that there was some substance to the idea. Any Name might call for an organized hunt to wipe out the Free U'tanse. The Faces was certainly the time for such an action.

And now was the day.

Joshua brought his focus on the City of the Face, half the continent away.

There were more Cerik walking around together than he'd ever seen. And they weren't fighting. Such a strange sight.

They were gathering around the Tenthonad High Perch. Although every clan was to have its moment, in practice, the most important clans had their feasts first. Indeed, many left the multi-day event early, once they had their say, leaving the minor Names to preside over much smaller crowds.

Tenthonad had been first for many years. Its lands were vast, the largest clan on the east coast. It had been the first clan with U'tanse, and for a long time, the holder of the power monopoly. Its wealth was the greatest, and its feast had runners for all.

The pens were large, and when they opened and the runners came spilling out, it was every Name for himself, catching, slaughtering, and devouring all they wished. Tenthonad's feast was so large that it often took many hours. Sometimes with large feasts like this one, there was so much meat that although only Names were allowed to hunt, the favored attendants shared in the excess. There was blood everywhere. Spirits were high.

Joshua tried to watch what he could. But there were so many Names and he only recognized a few of them. Claws were flashing, and bitter enemies hunted side by side, reserving their killing instincts for the prey.

Eventually, the feast ground was covered with *ska*, picking apart the remnants of the unlucky prey.

Beneath the ornate carved logs of the High Perch, where the Name of Tenthonad rested, the other Names collected to deliver their grievances.

Joshua reported to the others in the undersea throne room what was going on.

"Tenthonad is taking a border dispute from its friendly neighbor to the north, Ghader. I can see a number of Names anxious to get their say."

Sally asked, "If every Name gets to question every other Name, this could take forever."

Cyclops chuckled, "I've monitored every Festival for the past twenty years, and it does get tedious. The same complaints come up time after time. So-and-so hunts on my side of the border. This other Name should be penalized for keeping me from the seacoast. A lot of the complaints are just noise—a Name getting the opportunity to vent his frustrations among his peers. Only rarely does a clan get penalized. They all bend the rules and sneak across borders."

Joshua raised his hand. "It's starting. Ruthenah complained that the power that runs its aluminum mine was supposed to be recharged before the Faces, and the boat never showed up. Tenthonad claimed the deadline was never certain and that the charge is coming. Several other Names are agitating to be heard next."

Sally asked, "Is your guy in the group?"

"He's waiting his turn. The Tenthonad Name knows who he is, though. I can tell that he looks at Rukan from time to time."

The next complaint was about a missed delivery of power cells. The one after that was an angry claim that Tenthonad failed to charge his boat, making him almost miss the Faces. Two more complaints of delayed deliveries came after that. Tenthonad underplayed them all, blaming the demands for power due to the war on the west coast.

"Rukan speaks: Why don't you just admit the truth? Tell the Names that you can no longer deliver power!"

Joshua watched the reaction in the crowd. The previous complaints had set the stage, and Rukan's confidence added to his believability. Noise from the crowd increased.

Tenthonad broke tradition. The Name on the High Perch was supposed to answer the challenges, not deliver them, but he growled, <So you are the one who has attacked my boats and interrupted the delivery of power!>

Rukan hissed. <Not me. I've never ridden in a boat until I came here. I just buy my power from the Free U'tanse.>

The crowd was so loud it was barely possible to hear the speakers. The unusual term "Free U'tanse" was spoken several times. It translated like "Wild U'tanse" or "Rogue U'tanse". Only the dozens of U'tanse across the planet telepathically listening into the Faces heard the term for what it was.

Tenthonad shouted. <You speak nonsense!>

Rukan said, <Listen for yourself!>

Joshua raised his hand to signal his blind father.

Cyclops cleared his throat. The device in his hand fed his voice up the cable to the T-boat on the surface. Hovering in the distance from the City of the Faces, another boat had engines modified by Betty. Instead of the buzz of engines evenly grabbing the air, his voice modulated those same engines, blasting his words at earsplitting volume across the open distance to the Cerik below.

The Words of Cyclops

<This is Cyclops of the Free U'tanse. My respect to the gathered Names of Ko.>

On the ground, the voice was still loud enough to overpower the shouts of the Names.

Stakka, Elehadi's telepath, signaled to him. <I recognize that voice! It's from the U'tanse girl's dreams.>

Joshua positioned himself carefully in his chair, opened his eyes wide and called out telepathically to selected Cerik telepaths, leaving his mind wide open.

<Stakka, Kittok, Gotak—look through my eyes!>

Cyclops was an imposing figure, sitting in his throne. His costume was more ornate than even Aarison had dared. And his vacant eyes stared down at him, and through him, to the audience around the world, Cerik and U'tanse telepaths alike.

The shiny metal throne had a barbaric magnificence to it as well, the armrests formed from jandaka teeth and the cushions a dark, tinted fabric that might be mistaken for an unknown leather. To the side was a Delense skeleton. Cyclops looked totally at ease, gesturing with his hands as he spoke.

<In honor of your laws and painful history, the Free U'tanse would never think of setting foot in the City of the Face. So please pardon this loud-shouter I must use to speak to you all.

<Rukan of Far Island speaks the truth. His clan has not gone into space to take the making of power away from Tenthonad—the Free U'tanse have. We own all the starships and have blocked the way for any Cerik to ever use

them again. Any attempt to fly up there to retake them will just mean the loss of your boats and the warriors who fly in them. Ask Tenthonad how successful he was, if you doubt my words!>

His Cerik was obviously spoken with the U'tanse accent, but the challenging hiss he added for emphasis was all Cerik.

Cyclops continued, <Nor can you ever destroy us, as you did the Delense.>

He stroked the skull of the skeleton beside him.

<We have learned the lessons they left. We have all of their technology; we are secure in many secret bases scattered across the planet. Here, where I sit on my Perch, I am hundreds of feet below the surface of the ocean, beneath a mountain of rock. You could *flick* this spot all you want and I would barely hear a thud.

<Free U'tanse live in protected burrows and now, also in the unreachable starships left by the your ancestors and the Delense. You cannot claw down the moon from the sky and you cannot reach us, either. And now, we have the power to fly boats and you do not. The surest way to lose what you have is to attack us.>

Joshua was doing his best to be a pure channel through which telepaths could listen and observe, but his own confidence was leaking through, as well. He had memories of this base and the ocean above it. Any telepath listening through him couldn't help but believe what Cyclops was saying.

<We have the power, and enough to share. If a Name desires power for his boats, or to keep his U'tanse breathing, or to keep his factories running, we will trade for it. Just as Tenthonad traded power cells for lands and herds and goods, we will trade power cells for what we want as well.

<Listen carefully, for this is the new deal, and decide yourself whether it is *soso*.

<The most valuable thing on Ko is a U'tanse. Trade me a U'tanse, any U'tanse—a worker, a female, a cub, an old one too weak to work—they are all valuable as trade items for power cells and for charges to your boats and factories. Respect the original pledges Tenthonad made with the ancestors of the U'tanse and work with the elders to see which U'tanse could be traded.

<But remember that Free U'tanse are like the Delense from before the time of Ghader. We answer to no Name. Just like the ancient Delense, we can trade and work with the Cerik, but we sit under no one's Perch.>

Cyclops tapped his fingers on the *jandaka* tooth.

<Some Names cannot change. Some will not trade with any U'tanse. Unlike their ancestors, they cannot be open to new ideas and new realities. For them, I have made a deal with Rukan of Far Island. He will trade power cells supplied to him through us.>

Cyclops did a creditable job of the hissing laugh. <But I cannot guarantee that he will trade you power as cheaply as I will, nor even as cheaply as Tenthonad used to.

<And to protect Rukan of Far Islands for this service, the Free U'tanse will use advanced Delense and U'tanse technology to see that his lands, his warriors and his holdings won't be taken from him.>

Cyclops made a slash with his hand. <That is all I have to say. If you want power, talk to Rukan.>

Joshua clamped down his *ineda*, shutting off the view. The boat with the loud-shouter turned and raced away from the scene.

He sighed. "Now we just have to see if we've triggered a bloodbath or not."

...

Kakil Home was high on Joshua's list, and by the time he began monitoring, there was already a Cerik at the door.

<Please! It's not us. We are loyal to the Name!> Aarison said, as two of his Smileys, Porter and Ned, stood in the corridor, trying not to look like they were blocking the Cerik's way.

The Cerik hissed. From Porter's thoughts, Joshua realized that this one had been the guard who had chased down and killed the two attached girls. He took a step back.

The Cerik hissed again. <Elehadi won't ignore this challenge! He will give the order, and I will be first in line to take your heads!>

Aarison moved closer. <But we are the Name's chosen! He won't want to kill us.>

<Be silent!> The Cerik slashed his claw, not deep enough, this time, to take the head, but Aarison collapsed, his hand to his throat, and blood dribbled out through his fingers.

Another Cerik arrived. The first asked, <Has the order come?>

The other glanced at the bleeding U'tanse on the ground. <Stakka has orderd that the U'tanse should be kept alive.>

<What! Why?>

<Elehadi needs our idle boats back into the air. Save your 'eeh for the Graddik.>

The messenger said to Porter, <Get that one to your healers!>

Porter nodded, <It will be done.>

When both Cerik left, Porter sealed the door with a shaky hand and sighed. He looked down at Aarison, still struggling to breathe through the blood in his windpipe. Porter looked over at Ned. "Somehow I don't think the healers will arrive in time. Go find one, but don't rush." Ned glanced at Aarison in the growing pool of blood, and then stolled away.

Porter sat on a bench. "I suppose it's a good time to think about new elders."

. . .

It was chaos across the planet as well. The Names were all at the City, and close to a dozen U'tanse workers were slaughtered by frightened Cerik overseers. For a collection of the most powerful and bloodthirsty Cerik on the planet, the Faces itself was bound by too many traditions to devolve into face to face battle. Even Rukan, with all faces turned to him, walked about freely. He had already started reporting power cell requests from other Names over the shouter. A group led by Ruth, one of the elders at New Home, was logging each request. Tracking and delivery were going to be a major operation.

Cyclops was resting, aided by more sleepy juice. He had done well, and his mind seemed stronger by the day, but he had insisted on writing a personal message to Ford and Otto explaining his role as spokesperson and assuring them that the trappings of power were just there to impress the Cerik. *"At no time will I ever return to the administrative duties I lost when I was injured."*

Sally looked through the seemingly endless crates they'd found behind the welded-shut access hatch. The metal scrolls were all in Delense script, but there were many thousands of them. Whether they explained their technology, or the great mysteries of their history and their cultural identity, these were the records they'd deemed so valuable that they'd died to protect them. U'tanse scholars would be working through this library for a very long time.

She smiled at the man sitting on one of the crates, writing on a pad of paper.

"So, Prometheus, are you translating all these scrolls?"

He looked around him and sighed. "It looks overwhelming, doesn't it? Especially since we know so little of their language."

"But you've started?" she asked, pointing to his pages.

He shook his head. "No. This is something different.

"You know, when I saw the starship with my own eyes, I thought, 'This is it. This is what I've lived for. I can die happy.'

"But then, I looked out the window and saw all the thousands of stars. I realized then that my job wasn't done. I have to map all those stars. I have to find every star map made by Abe the Father, by James bar Bill, and every other U'tanse that looked at the sky and wondered which one is our true home.

"That will take all my life, and longer, I suspect."

He looked down at his papers. "But you know, my highest priority right now is being a historian. I've transcribed the speech Cyclops gave, and I think I need to write a whole book, telling future generations how we reached this point, where U'tanse are free and the Cerik will just have to adapt to the fact."

Joshua smiled. "The book of Prometheus. I would like to read that one. It's surprising that we've come so far, so fast."

Prom folded the page and held his pen. "Um. Could you tell me a few things?"

"If I can."

"What'll you do if Elehadi offers you one of Aarison's Smileys in trade for a power cell?"

Joshua winced. "Take him, of course. The whole purpose of this trading business is to put a hard floor under the value of an individual human life. No longer will any Name get to think that people are too much trouble to rescue, or to provide for in their old age. We'd never get a Cerik to respect human life, but even the worst of the Names will care for their herd animals, because at worst, they can be traded off.

"Those Smileys—it's a tough call, but certainly break them up and send them to different communities. I'd put the first on Larson's crew at Factory's docks. No girls to abuse and co-workers with a lot more muscle than any of them."

Prom nodded and began writing.

Sally linked her arm with her husband. "We're going to need more communities soon."

Joshua looked off into the distance. "I know. It'll be tough, with most of the people traded first being the ones Cerik value the least. I'm hoping for more elder candidates among them."

She chuckled, "I suspect a lot of old grandparents are hoping to be traded first."

"That's what I wanted to accomplish the most. I wanted there to be *hope* among the U'tanse. The Cerik aren't the biggest danger, it's our own danger of attachment. Hope is the real power of the U'tanse. If we have hope—hope for our future and hope for our children—then we can keep despair and attachment at bay."

Then he sighed and shook his head. "But there's so much work to be done!"

Prom, his head down, writing, chuckled and said, "I'm never going to be bored again."

Sally gave Joshua's arm a squeeze. "Hope for our children. That's something I can really believe in."

The End

Cerik Terms

Cerik Term	Definition
'eeh	The bloodlust, a heightened sensual awareness.
Cerik	Literally, 'Hunter', the name of a race of predators
chitchit	A small predator from the Cerik home world that were used to root out burrowing prey. They were also used as pets.
conek	Tall slender trees, often used for construction of lightweight structures such as huts and decorative walls. Conek trees only grow at high altitudes.
dak	A substitute kill. Used when an honored soldier is killed. An enemy is killed, the blood drunk, and the kill attributed to the honored soldier.
dakka	A swamp-living prey, wide and flat in front with a long snake-like tail behind. Cerik like the taste, but since they live in the water, the Cerik hate to chase them.

Cerik Term	Definition
dan	Cerik biology alternates between periods of intense activity and deep rest. In dan there is limited awareness, but no real thought. Many of these rest states have their own names in the language, such as erdan, or fenke dan.
Delense	Literally, "Builder," the name of a semi-aquatic race of tool users. The Delense were enslaved by the Cerik in prehistory, and existed in a symbiotic relationship for thousands of years before they were exterminated by the Cerik.
dlathe	A broad shade tree, with many low-hanging branches. It was a favorite hunting Perch for Cerik.
doonag	A swamp-delling prey animal like a smaller version of the Delense. Mentioned in the Tales, but extinct on the mainland.
dul	A traditional net used to hold a captured prey
erdan	The long wait. A semiconscious trance state when no prey were expected, but instant alertness might be required.
fenke dan	The meal, and the following period of torpor. In good times, a Cerik would eat once a day. Digestion has its own heavy demands and causes a deep lethargy that is not easily overridden.
Ferreer	A telepathic, hive-mind alien species that had inhabited several planets. Some Cerik refer to attached U'tanse as Ferreer as well.

Cerik Term	Definition
flick	To bomb an enemy with an overloaded TP core. Invented by the Delense to attack the Ferreer, the only race the Cerik could not attack directly face to face, it was also used in the fatal rebellion against the Cerik. It has the blast effects, but not the radiation, of a small tactical nuclear bomb.
Ha	The Ko Moon. Large with an elliptical orbit that brings tides and triggers quakes and volcano eruptions.
Hae	Cerik mythology—the male spirit of the moon.
haeka	Larger predator, sometimes known to capture Cerik cubs or nomadic females. Generally preys on runners in the foothills
hatsen	Mid-sized predator that feeds on small prey like *chitchits.*
hork	Large burrowing herbivore. In desert regions, horks dig down to the water table and the resulting spring provides water for the local ecosystem.
hurru	A Perch. The rear talons of a Cerik efficiently grip any branch large enough to hold them. The Perch of a Name was a ceremonial throne from which the Name ruled as he rested above all the others. It also came to refer to the buildings around it.
ineda	A telepathic block. This skill can be learned by any Cerik who needs to be a leader over telepaths. Before the arrival of the telepathic U'tanse, an ordinary Cerik who practicesd ineda was, by definition, a suspected thief.

Cerik Term	Definition
jandaka	A deep-sea predator with snake-like body and large teeth that preys on a variety of other marine animals.
janji	A freshwater fish that is edible by humans. The meat is chewy. More common in the north.
jenna	Common saltwater fish that can be digested by humans.
kadan	The anticipated kill wait. Like erdan, but with heightened anticipation that prey would appear any second.
katche	The "peace." During the Face, all clans are bound to refrain from clan-on-clan attacks, with the threat that all other clans would turn on the aggressor.
Katranel	A sky demon in Cerik mythology, blamed in some of the Tales for a clan's bad luck.
kede	A Broken Hunter. Any Cerik who is valuable even though severely injured. Surgery is unknown among the Cerik and it is up to the clan leader whether to support anyone crippled by injuries.
kel	A common tree that is found near streams.
klakr	The Cerik world's version of a triceratops. Twice the size of a Cerik. Large massive head with spikes and tusks. A spiked tail. Vegetarian, with easily offended sense of territory. Nearly extinct.

Cerik Term	Definition
Ko	Literally, "all lands." This became the name of the Cerik home planet when they discovered that other planets existed.
Koee	Cerik mythology—the female spirit of the land.
koodak	A ceremonial way to resolve descisions where all parties bring competing gifts to the leader.
La	Literally, "First," also referred to as "Named." The title of the leader of a clan, family or guild. A First was the only individual Cerik with a name. The First names himself when elevated to rank. All other adult males are addressed by their rank, and known unambiguously by their scent. Females and cubs are known by their scent and genealogy.
Larek	Literally, "Second," the second in command, and prime assistant to the First. Second is also heir to the First and can usurp his position with a physical challenge. In addition to the possibility of death in such a challenge, there are numerous social- and clan-level sanctions against a Second who endangers the clan by a challenge at the wrong time.
lulur	Large centipede-like creature with tubular body and a pair of legs per segment. Carrion eaters, for the most part. Cerik disdain them and eradicate them only for sport.
ooro	Coastal lizards that are a food delicacy, traded to interior clans

Cerik Term	Definition
po	Flying reptile that nest in dlathe trees.
pree	To register personal satisfaction. Physically there can be a purring component, a salivating component, and/or a relaxing of the subdermal plates.
Roostata	Cerik mythology—the demonic embodiment of the tsunami that regularly swamped the shores of the planet Ko.
Rakladel	Cerik mythology—telepathic demon who could make a Cerik mindlessly crazy and who could not be killed.
ralak	Speaker. A clan-to-clan personal ambassador, with various levels of importance.
rettik	Literally "right eye," a close assistant, with status over other assistants. Often personal soldiers or bodyguards.
Rotaak	Literally "Face to face" or commonly Face. A traditional meeting of clan Names on neutral ground. Historically, there were a number of regional Faces, but since the Delense gave them flying boats, there has been one central Face. The orignal grounds were destroyed when the Delense made their failed attempt to escape the Cerik.
ruff	A territorial noise and posture, a threatening purr.
sendt	Literally, "Runner," a grazing herbivore that make up a dominant prey for the Cerik. There are dozens of native varieties and several off-world species, prized for taste or for being skillful prey.
shash	A reed-like plant that grows along stream beds.

Cerik Term	Definition
shillee	Long mid-sized lizards know for their erratic running path.
soso	A trade that both parties were happy with. "Fairness"
ska	Flying predators that prey on coastal fish.
ssitt	Literally, "Take the eyes." In battle among Cerik, the ritual death stroke was to take out the eyes of an enemy and eat them. Due to the tough skin of the Cerik, the most common death stroke in duels was a blow at the weakest part of the head, at the eyes.
tetca	Literally, "dance." A guild, an organized collection of Cerik workers with their own First, Second, and lower workers. A clan First will have many tetca First's under his direct command. Some common tetca: Rear Talon - Boat and spaceship pilots Telepaths; Scientists—nearly obsolete. This tetca came into being after the extermination of the Delense. U'tanse were better scientists than the Cerik by far and took over that task; Herders; Tale tellers; Ralak—messengers.
uuka	The ritual of submission where a Cerik lays face down, defenseless and awaits either a killing blow or the opportunity to swear allegiance to the new master.

U'tanse Terms

Over time, the original language of the U'tanse, English, has acquired a number of loan words from the Cerik, but has also added new terms of their own, or redefined old ones.

U'tanse Term	Definition
attachment	A disorder of telepaths when their thoughts become so tightly linked that individuality is lost and they become a hive mind.
creeper	A bug, but the Ko varieties range from tiny crab-like species, to legless worms. Multi-legged varieties do grow larger, but many of those have their own Cerik names.
cutie	A U'tanse child old enough to walk, but too young to have come of age.
Festival	A trade and exchange of females between U'tanse Homes designed to reduce inbreeding. Over time, selected goods were exchanged also.

U'tanse Term	Definition
Home	A colony of U'tanse inhabiting a Delense burrow.
random	A person whose genetics was dictated by the random combination of the parents sperm and ovum, rather than having been controlled by the mother. A term of abhorrence, due to the history of birth defects whenever it was tried.
slurk	Monitoring thoughts or activities with salacious intent.
tenner	By policy, one in ten males is bred with no psychic abilities, in order to keep the U'tanse from drifting too far from the old human stock. In practice, tenners have proved superior in science, engineering and math.

Slave Races

A variety of species were conquered by the Cerik as they scavenged Star damaged planets. Most stayed on their home worlds. Only a few could survive the Cerik atmosphere and were valuable enough for the Cerik to make the effort to bring them to Ko.

Species	Type	Value
U'tanse (Human)	Erect bipeds	Technically talented, and could design and repair tools.
Dadada (BaBaBa)	Radial symmetric turtles, triangles at birth, add legs as they age.	Young ones used as pets, older ones as slow transport. Can carry heavy weights and understand spoken directions.
Uuaa (Wob)	Quadruped with long, multi-jointed arms and thicker hind legs for jumping.	Favorite pet of the Cerik because they jump the same way as their masters. Used to quickly climb trees and harvest fruits and nuts that the Cerik can't reach. Not vocal, but they can be trained.

The Ko Calendar

The Cerik have always lived by the moon. There are two types of cycles. One cycles through the phases, just like on the moon of Earth, but there is a more important cycle as well. Their moon, Ha, is in a highly elliptical orbit that brings it close enough to regularly trigger quakes across the globe. The Large Moon dominates the sky much more than Earth's full moon, regardless of which phase it is in. While the Cerik have noted that certain stars are in the sky following a "yearly" pattern, it makes no difference in their lives. With no noticeable yearly weather pattern, months, marked by the Large Moon, are the dominant measure of calendar time. On a day to day basis, the Large, Small, Full, and New moons make convenient markers even though these "weeks" can vary from 1 to 12 days in length.

The phases of the moon are slightly less than half of this month, with a Full Moon taking place every 24.4 Cerik days. Important days such as the Face are often marked by the conjunction of these 2 cycles, i.e., a Large Full Moon.

When the U'tanse arrived, Father began documenting what he could. There was a wristwatch, by which he determined that a Cerik day was slightly more than 20 Earth hours. A Cerik month was a little over 58 Cerik days.

The U'tanse set up their own calendar system, one that more closely matched the human norms. A Normal week was seven Cerik Days, with the same names Father and Mother were used to. Each Normal month was 5 weeks. There were 10 Normal months, which didn't quite match the Cerik year, but it was close enough. The month names were: January, March, April, May, July, August, September, October, November, and December.

Power of the U'tanse

U'tanse count birthdays and ages by the Normal year, which is only 80% as long as the Earth year. A 20 (Earth) year old would be deemed aged 25 on Cerik.

	Hours	Earth Days	Cerik Days
Earth Day	24	1.000	1.198
Cerik Month	1162.4	48.433	58.033
Normal Month	701.05	29.210	35.000
Normal Week	140.21	5.842	7.000
Cerik Year	6867.3	286.138	342.851
Normal Year	7010.5	292.104	350.000

Check out all books of the **Project Saga**:

The **Earth Branch** consists of:
Star Time
Kingdom of the Hill Country
In the Time of Green Blimps
Captain's Memories
Humanicide

The **U'tanse Branch** follows **Star Time**, as well, consisting of:
Tales of the U'tanse
Free U'tanse
Secrets of the U'tanse
Power of the U'tanse

Other Novels by Henry Melton

Emperor Dad
Roswell or Bust
Extreme Makeover
Lighter Than Air
Falling Bakward
Golden Girl
Follow That Mouse
Pixie Dust
Bearing Northeast
The Copper Room
Breaking Anchor
Beneath the Amarillo Plains

Short Story Anthologies by Henry Melton

Henry's Stories: Volume 1
Henry's Stories: Volume 2

Childrens' Book by Henry Melton

Chipper Flies High

If you want more stories by Henry Melton, the best way you can help is to spread the word, and leave a review at the high traffic sites like Amazon and Goodreads.

To follow Henry Melton:

On Facebook, like the page HenryMeltonFan

His twitter handle is @HenryMelton

Check out www.HenryMelton.com